MAGIC WATERS

MAGIC WATERS

CALL OF THE OCEAN, BOOK THREE

by

GINNA MORAN

For those who care about the land and the sea. This is for you.

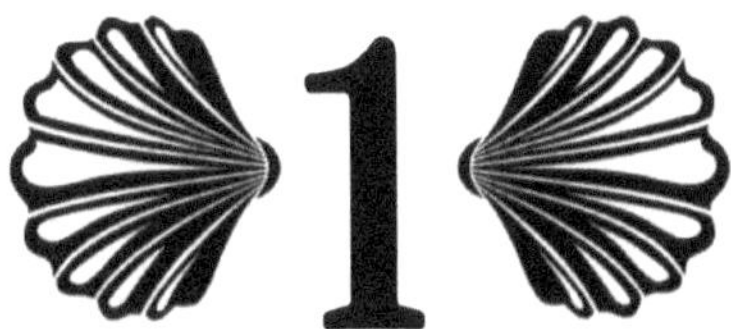

TREACHEROUS LIFE

"LUNA? LUNA, LOOK AT me." Cool fingers touch my cheek, bringing my focus away from the pain burning through my chest. I meet Ryan's eyes, his dark brows low on his forehead. My fear reflects back to me in their glassiness, but he blinks, clearing his vision. "I'm getting you out of here, okay? I will not let you die. I promise."

I open and close my mouth, forcing the stale air in and out of my lungs. I don't respond to him though. I don't even know what to say. It's not my escape I'm worried about. It's his. It's Giselle and Talia's.

Because I crave the cool, saltiness of the sea—more than

crave it—I need it. The call of the ocean beckons to my soul the longer I resist my mermaid transformation. I've never needed to so badly before.

But I have to.

If I transform now, the sea will sink the boat. I know it will with every swell that sends my heart into my throat and then into my stomach. The rolling water does nothing to suppress the agony and panic shadowing the edges of my vision. My pearlescent skin shimmers in the dim lighting, and thankfully, that's all that is morphing right now. Because this is different than a triggered transformation, caused by the longing in my soul. This transformation is not my doing. It's the moon's. The sea's. I'll fight for control of my body and not give in as long as I can.

"Deep breaths," Ryan says. "You're doing great. Concentrate on the land."

"Think about Ryan's strong legs," Giselle muses.

I groan. Any other time I would have laughed, but my body refuses to do anything other than make me miserable.

Reaching up, I run my fingers across Ryan's scruffy cheek, finally forcing myself to talk. I don't have time to waste, even if cuddling in Ryan's arms is the only thing I want to do as the seconds tick by, counting down to the moment I feel like I'm not just going to transform but explode into a mermaid and kill everyone around me. "Help me closer to Talia. I have to finish getting the cuffs off."

If the ocean swallows the boat and Giselle and Talia remain

trapped, we'll all be worse off. I don't say the thoughts running through my mind because everyone's freaking out enough at my safety. If they knew what I know, that the sea would rather sink the boat and drown everyone rather than let me die, they might lose it completely. And I need them. I need everyone to stay clear-headed so their panic doesn't leave me incapacitated. I rely on their hope to get us all through.

"Save your energy, Luna. We'll be fine." Giselle's soft voice wraps around me, drawing my attention away from Ryan and to her. She leans back on the bar she's bound to with her knees curled to her chest. "Sun will find us, and all these dang pirates will get what's coming. I know it. You guys are freaking fierce, especially on the full moon."

She's always been hopeful even in the darkest situations. I can almost imagine the day she agrees to officially couple with Sun, her merman boyfriend who's part of the royal guard of Reefaria and a loyal warrior to me. The mermaid essence will shine through all the seas with her. I know it. Because of this, I will beg the ocean not to sink the boat to save me. The sea would fare better with a beautiful soul like Giselle, unlike me, the daughter of a shunned merman king and a lost mermaid queen. I'm nothing but a failure, lost to the dangerous surface.

If the ocean saw more potential in me, I'd have been gifted with skills better than navigation and creation of goods for the merpeople colonies. I wouldn't have been led to this ship of lost pirates to brave the perilous seas they've created to be tested. I'm about to prove my dad's assessment of me right. I do have to be a warrior to change the pirate way, and even then, they'll never revert back to their heritage of protecting the sea.

"I know," I whisper, finally responding to Giselle. "He'll be an incredible mate to you, Gi. Just knowing that brings me happiness even if things—"

"Stop talking like this is the end," she snaps.

But it very well might be.

Another swell lifts and drops the boat. Both Giselle and Talia slide with the sudden shift of the vessel. Ryan grabs Giselle's legs to stop her body from yanking on the cuffs, but Talia doesn't resist the motion and hits the wall. The boat rocks again, the waves shifting the yacht on the rough sea, and the force dragging Talia is enough to snap her weakened cuffs. She skids across the floor and bangs her feet into the door.

"Yes!" she yells, scrambling to her feet. "You did it, Luna."

Relief washes over me, pushing away my despair. "Giselle, it's your turn. I don't have long." If I can break Giselle free, we'll be okay in the end. Even if the ship capsizes, I'll figure out how to get us all out. It gives us more time if I only have to concentrate on cutting through the door.

"Stop saying that. Everything's going to be fine." No matter how much Giselle says it, I have trouble believing her words. Even with Talia free, nothing feels fine. My stomach twists and turns, making me curl in on myself. My dry tongue sticks to the roof of my mouth, and it feels like I'm drowning and dying for a drink of the sea as the air presses in on me.

I crawl forward toward Giselle. Ryan scoops me up before I

can get far and carries me the rest of the way. He trails his gaze from my eyes and down the rest of my body, his frown deepening to where his eyebrows nearly hide his beautiful, sea glass green eyes.

"Please, don't look at me like that," I whisper to him. "My heart hurts enough as it is."

A tear trickles from his lashes to splash on his cheek, and he swipes it away, leaving a shiny streak on his face. His nostrils flare as he takes a deep breath, tensing his muscles. Shaking his head, he forces his features to relax and offers me a ghost of a smile.

He leans in and kisses me softly. "Work on Giselle's handcuffs, and we'll work on the door. It'll help keep your mind off things." Even concentrating solely on Giselle won't pull my mind from my changing body, especially now that the webbed skin tightens my fingers.

I nod anyway. "We'll be out of here in no time."

Ryan meets Talia at the door, and they lean into each other and whisper words I can't hear. I expect them to try to break the door down, but a metal plate reinforces the wood. This isn't some ordinary cabin we've been locked in. It's a jail cell made to imprison even the strongest person. But the crew of Wren Reyes, self-proclaimed pirate king, has never met a mermaid like me. I might have failed the ocean, but I will not fail my friends. They're more important to me than my life.

"What can I do to help you?" Giselle asks. "Your skin's changing. There has to be something to slow it down. Do you remember two months ago? You, Ava, and Carter made bets on who could resist the longest?"

"I lost to Carter," I whisper.

"But Carter managed until almost midnight. And you're a badass warrior princess. The stakes are higher. I believe in you, Luna. You can beat Carter."

Except I already have. I don't have to look at a clock to know it. But it doesn't matter. I'm changing. It'll be minutes at most.

I glance at the pearlescent sheen turning my tan skin shiny enough to sparkle in the soft light like a pearl. A few gold scales sprout across my thigh, crawling toward my knee. "Distract me. The pain—" Blinking, I clear my oncoming tears away. "The call of the ocean, Gi. It's—I can't slow it down much more."

Spasms ripple through my muscles, stealing my words. I squeeze my eyes shut and concentrate on my fingers against Giselle's handcuffs. If I transform now, I'll be able to cut through the metal in minutes, but that doesn't give me much time. I'm afraid I'd be in so much agony that I couldn't concentrate. And even though my human form isn't as powerful, it'll do. As long as I can keep resisting.

Giselle pushes my hair away and rubs her hand over my back. She softly sings one of my favorite songs, about being madly in love, reminding me of all the times we spent together in our condo back in La Tortuga Point. Her voice forces away the panic and pain tensing my muscles with spasms, and I rest on my knees and elbows, working my sharp nail back and forth over the metal of her handcuffs.

"I can do this," I whisper to myself. "Just a few more minutes."

"Oh, my God." Giselle's soft song cuts off. "Ryan! Talia! Get that damn door open. I see her pectoral fins."

I squeeze my eyes shut, ignoring the commotion of Talia and Ryan the best I can. Every breath I take doesn't come. I can't breathe at all. Sweat beads down my face, and I rub my arm across my forehead, feeling the fin jutting from my arm. Pain rushes over me unlike anything I've ever felt. Even the times I triggered my transformation doesn't compare to the imaginary fire licking over my skin. But I'm afraid to look at myself.

Falling over from the sudden change of my body, I land hard on my side. My eyelids flutter, and I stare up at Giselle through the shadows crowding my vision. She releases a sob, screaming at Ryan and Talia, and the world rocks around me. I roll across the floor and hit my back into the wall. The lights blink off, leaving us in the dark, and everyone yells again.

Talia fumbles from Ryan, who continues to beat on the door, leaving blood from his bleeding hands on the metal plate. She kneels by my side, brushing her fingers over my face to pull the hair from my mouth. "Luna? Please, you have to hold on. Please. I can't lose you. You need to hold on."

I bring my hands to my neck, feeling my gills open and close with my mouth that can't suck in what I need into my lungs. I have minutes, if that.

My head spins, sending dizziness over me. I can't stop the trembles rolling through my body. I thrash, bucking, grabbing my throat, willing the oxygen to give me what I need. The pounding in my head cuts out the sound of Talia's screams.

I black out, the world fading.

"Luna," Ryan says, cutting through the darkness. "Luna, don't leave me. You said you'd never leave me. Just breathe."

I blink, fighting to stay conscious. Opening and closing my mouth again, I fight to say his name, reaching out for him. A silhouette hovers over me, and warm lips touch mine, sending a breath of air into my lungs, burning my insides.

"She needs water," Talia says.

The world shifts again, and Talia topples over me. Ryan yells out from somewhere beside me, but I can't see him through my hazy vision. The three of us tumble into the side wall, and I land with a thud. Giselle cries out, and I stare in shock at her blurry form dangling from her handcuffs above me, the vessel no longer in an upright position.

"Help!" she yells, swinging herself back and forth, trying to break free from the cuffs I only managed to saw halfway through. But her movement isn't enough to do anything.

Talia scrambles to her feet and spins around. It's too dark for her to see anything in the now lightless room. She stumbles around, trying to reach Giselle, but there's no way. I don't think she even realizes she's above her and the boat is on its side.

"To your right. We're capsized." I somehow manage to

push the words from my lips using the breath Ryan gave me. "She's hanging by her arms."

Talia extends her arms up to reach for Giselle, but she's not tall enough. There's no possible way for her to help Giselle from her position. "Am I close, Luna?"

"You're too short," Ryan says. "I'm coming. Hold on."

The world sways again, rolling me across the wall, which is now the floor. I hit something soft, and Ryan releases a gasp. He wraps me in his arms, shifting me on his lap. My spark blinks in quick successions, lighting the world between us. He touches my face, his brows pinched together, and then he kisses me softly on the lips.

I send him a dozen images, unable to form words. He stiffens at my thoughts of the sea sinking the vessel and the fear I carry about it taking everyone with it to save me. Slowly pulling back, he stares at me with wide eyes, now silver in the light from my spark.

A mixture of fear and relief crosses his face, his eyes darting from mine to glance at my chest. He turns and peers at the others from over his shoulder. Cool liquid trickles across my hand, surprising me.

"Ryan?" Giselle asks from above. "What's going on? Is Luna...?" She's afraid to finish her thoughts.

I shimmy in my spot, failing to flip over to land face first in the ocean water spilling in, never so thankful for anything in my life yet hating every ounce that floods the room. Because it doesn't stop. And it won't. If water pours in through the crack under the door, it means the rest of the vessel fills with the sea, and we might already be sinking toward the ocean's depths.

He clears his throat, running his hand across my tail until he shoves his fingers under my body to turn me over. His heavy panting sounds over the water turning from a stream to a gush. "Give me a second," he manages to say. "There's a leak."

Ocean water splashes on the side of my face. Ryan cups more water in his hand, doing his best to wet me with the sea-water to ease the burning in my lungs until it's high enough to submerge in.

Ryan rolls me more, the pooling water deep enough to give me the breath of the sea I was dying for. He rubs his hand into my back, keeping my hair out of the way, continuing to gasp small breaths before he releases one as long as the gulp of water I take into my lungs.

"A leak? Luna. Are you okay? Is it enough?"

I don't respond, just breathing in and out into the few inches of water spilling inside.

Ryan shifts away from me, splashing his hands across the area around us. "She's going to be okay. Just let her breathe a minute. More water is coming in through—shit. It's rising fast."

"Oh, God," Giselle says. "Someone get me down!"

"Talia, feel around for anything we can stack to stand on," Ryan says to my cousin. He slides his arms under me, pulling my face from the water to carry me toward where he found the leak gushing in the sea.

"We're not going to need anything," Talia responds.

Giselle whimpers from above us. "What? Why?"

"Don't freak out, Gi, but we're sinking," Ryan says to her. "And fast."

"I'm not freaking out," Giselle says, releasing a strange noise from her throat. "I'm not freaking out. We are with a mermaid. Mermaids are superheroes. Luna is a badass warrior princess. She will demolish this ship and get us to air. I'll be home in time for school." The words spill from her mouth as she says them to herself. "It's going to be okay. There's nothing to freak out about."

I lift my head from the stream of water, clearing my lungs to talk. "Yup, Gi. That's right. I promise you I'll get you out."

She releases a breath without saying anything else.

"Luna, can you break through the door?" Talia asks from her spot under Giselle, stretching up as high as she can, alleviating Giselle's weight the best she can with the tips of her fingers.

Ryan shifts next to me, pressing his fingers to the busted seal in the door. "Not yet. If we open the door now, it'll come in too fast. We could drown."

"Someone hurry up and get me down," Giselle says.

Ryan touches my shoulders. "Just a few more minutes and Luna can reach you. Hang on. Leaning into me, he scoops me onto his lap and pulls me up to whisper into my ear. "Save them first, okay?"

I blink the tears from my eyes. He wants me to put Giselle and Talia before him if it comes down to it. As much as it goes against my instincts as a mate, I know the reason for his decision, and I accept it.

"This is my fault, and I won't allow you to risk their lives for me, not when..."

His voice trails off, his gaze drifting to stare at my mermaid essence, glowing for him under the full moon we can't see. The fact that he can see it still, use it to light his vision in the room, gives me the strength I need in a moment I feel so weak. Because it reminds me that even if his human life ends, I can still save him. I can give him my spark, and we can manage.

And maybe—maybe this is how our lives were always supposed to be. The ocean didn't put me and Ryan together just to rip us apart. The ocean isn't as cruel as Ryan always says when he doubts his worth in our relationship. The ocean knows what it's doing, and I will listen to the call and follow my heart that will soon beat for him. I know with everything in me that he's my intended mate despite his heritage or where he came from. Despite anything he's done wrong. We all make mistakes—this one, putting my friends in danger, is mine. Regardless of our faults, I know we're meant for each other, no matter the land or sea, because we better each other. Ryan will assure I'll never fall blind to the world around us, and I'll assure he can rise above his treacherous life.

"We're all getting out of here," I whisper, refusing to let him give up an ounce of hope even when things seem hopeless with the rising water. "As we are."

The sea continues to spill through the room, and I finally

manage to sink deep enough to submerge myself completely. The noise mutes, helping me clear my mind, making it so I can think beyond the gasping breaths and panic filling the room as fast as the ocean. Ryan waits for me to sit back up on my own before touching my cheeks again.

"How are you two doing?" Ryan says to Giselle and Talia, taking his attention from me.

"Oh, just great. I'll have to go shopping for new long sleeved shirts after this, so at least there's a plus side to all this crap," Giselle says, dodging her nerves as she thinks about something trivial.

I flick my tail, splashing water. "I'm sorry. We will all go together. I'll hold all your bags and everything."

She releases a small laugh. "I'm holding you to it."

I wish with everything in me that Ryan could lift me over his head, so I could at least hug her legs. "I promise I'm getting us all out of here. I just need a little more water."

The boat creaks, and the world shifts again. Giselle screams out. The world drops out so fast from me I don't even have a chance to gulp in a breath. I fall through the air with Talia and Ryan and land with my stomach on the other wall. The ocean rocks us back and forth, demolishing the ship as it drags us under. If it doesn't stop, someone's going to get hurt before the water has a chance to flood the room.

A loud crack sounds through the air, piercing my ears. Water sprays from the wall, coming in through a gaping hole in the side of the boat. We must've hit something like a rock or a reef.

I can't be sure.

"Give us a break, Ocean!" Giselle yells, now lying on top of the pole instead of dangling from it.

I splash my hands into the water, trying to drag myself forward to her. I just need a few minutes, and I can break her free. I made Sun a promise, and even if I hadn't, I will not let anything happen to her. She's one of my best friends in the universe.

A groan sounds out from my right, and I glance over and see Ryan getting onto his hands and knees. My heart sinks into my stomach, noticing the body next to him. Talia lies on her back unmoving. Blood trickles from her forehead from a gash caused by the shift of the vessel.

"Ryan, get Talia," I say. "She's next to you. Keep her head up."

I've never been more grateful that he can see my spark lighting the dark room than in this moment. I'll never understand the extent of our bond as a mermaid and human, but I don't even care. It's there, and it's all that matters.

"She's breathing. Knocked out," Ryan says.

I groan. "Oh, Ocean. Please. Please, stop trying to help me."

The world rocks again, sending panic into my heart. Everything happens so fast. I don't have time to process that the crack splits wider, sending ocean water gushing in. Giselle dangles above me again, out of reach. Ryan jumps up with Talia on his shoulder, keeping her head above water. It won't be long until we're all submerged completely.

"Help!" Giselle screams.

Sinking under, I flick my tail, hitting the floor. I try to breach out of the water to get to her, but it's no use. I can't reach her. The water isn't high enough even though it flows to Ryan's chest. Circling the room and Ryan a few times, I push my stress and anxiety away. I pop up next to Ryan, giving him a once over to make sure he's okay.

"Luna, I know you're scared, but you're making it hard to stay afloat with your swimming." He reaches out and clutches my shoulder. "I think it's best to put your energy into breaking through the crack. We can get out if it's wide enough."

"I need to get to Giselle first."

"Luna—"

"I have to get her!"

He shifts Talia's unconscious body, staring up at Giselle swinging back and forth, trying to break the metal cuffs. She groans through her quick breathing, and I dip under to try to reach her again.

I swim a quick circle in the water. I can't help it. I need the speed to breach. The boat rocks again, the crack widening, sending me flying back through the water. Muffled screams sound from the surface, and I dart up to pop through. The water's risen so much that Giselle's feet touch the surface.

The boat quivers, thrown by the swaying sea, and the crack opens more, sending a wave of water through the room. It knocks me, Ryan, and Talia back into the wall. The strong current locks me in place, making it difficult to break free. I shove Ryan up, bending my tail to catapult him and Talia to the pocket of remaining air.

Using the wall, I drag myself up, digging my nails into the wood to do so. Ryan's fear floods through me, and I gasp a breath. Water blurs my eyes, the room nearly submerged. My heartbeats count down the seconds, pounding hard enough that it feels like it might break my ribcage to give into the sea forever at any moment.

"Luna, hurry!" Giselle yells, kicking in the water.

I swim closer to her, fighting through the rocky waves to keep my head above water. "Ryan, give me Talia. I'll take her with me to get her out first."

Ryan swims closer, handing Talia to me. "Hold her mouth and nose so she doesn't breathe in the sea."

I nod. "On the count of three, everyone take a huge breath, okay?"

"Okay," Giselle whispers, her voice barely audible through the hum of the sea.

"One," I say, positioning Talia. "Two. Three!"

DAUGHTER OF THE SEA

I DIVE UNDER, PINCHING Talia's nose while covering her mouth. Swimming against the water now pouring into the room, I force my way to the crack. I silently count the seconds in my mind. The current dissipates as the ocean fills the room completely.

With one hand, I use my nails to scratch the wood surface to cut pieces away. It'd be faster with two hands, but I need to get Talia out. The boat rocks again, sending fear to my spark. I'm taking too long. A minute ticks by in my head, and I resort to swimming back and hurtling forward, ramming my shoulder into the wood to crack it more.

"Princess Luna? Can you hear me?"

I never knew how amazing Sun's voice was until this moment. "Help Sun! We're on the Storm sinking. I can't get us out, and we've submerged."

"You're on the sinking ship?" he asks.

"Hurry. I can't break through alone."

"Tide's closest. He's coming. I'm following. We won't let you down."

I continue to rip out the wall, cutting small pieces with my nail.

"I'm here, Princess Luna. I can't get inside. The entrance is blocked. The vessel is caught on a rock." Tide's voice hums through my mind, his words stealing away the hope Sun had given me.

Talia has seconds.

"Do you see a crack? Water was flowing in, but we're all under. The others will drown."

"I'm here, Princess Luna. Brace yourself."

I dig my nails into the wall next to the crack to hold on. Tide smashes into the side of the boat, sending silver moonlight into the glowing room. He reaches his hand through, pulling at the metal frame with his warrior strength while I rip the hole wider.

The vessel suddenly shifts, rocking forward. Tide presses his hand to the frame, flicking his powerful tail, trying his best to stop the boat from dropping to the ocean floor. My spark blinks like a strobe, and I glance up at Ryan, tugging at Giselle's cuffs. She thrashes in the water, desperate to break free for air.

"Take Talia, Tide," I say. "She'll drown if you don't."

"But, Princess Luna—"

I shove Talia toward him, forcing him to release the boat. His voice echoes through the air as he commands the other warriors to hurry to stop the boat from hitting the floor. I swim as fast as I can to Giselle. Ryan holds the chain of the cuff up for me, and I dig my sharp nail into it, sawing so hard that my nail breaks in the process. I switch hands and continue to work the handcuffs. Locking my fingers to them, I rip back, flicking my tail as hard as I can, and finally, they snap free.

Hooking my arm around Giselle, I pull her with me, taking Ryan's hand in my other, and I swim us toward the opening. The ocean floor rises toward us, and I freeze. If I try to swim us out, I'm afraid the boat will crush us.

"Sun!" I scream. "Anyone! Push the vessel."

But it's too late. Sand clouds the ocean around me, hazing the sea, and we're cut off once more, trapped in a room. Giselle squeezes my shoulder, digging her fingers into my skin. She covers her mouth and nose with her hand, her eyes wide with panic.

"Hold on, Princess Luna!" Sun calls. "We're coming. Brace yourselves."

We sway in the sudden shift of the boat as the warriors push at it to flip it to open the hole. But it's no use. There's no time. Jetting up, I ram into the door, hitting it with my shoulder to try to break the frame.

"Giselle has seconds. Go through the boat and to the door," I say. "I'm not strong enough."

"I'm coming!" Sun yells to me.

Giselle slackens in my arms, and fear flows through me. I turn to meet her still wide eyes, no longer lit with life. Pain and anger rush through me, seeing my best friend in the entire world release her very last breath.

I can't believe this is happening. I can't believe I failed her.

Ryan squeezes my hand, and I draw my attention from Giselle and to him. He reaches out and presses his hand to my chest, his fingers shadowing in the light of my spark. His gesture touches my very soul, sending warmth rushing from my chest and up my throat. Something strange slides through me as my whole body lights from my mermaid essence, and Ryan touches my cheek.

He knows what I'm going to do, and he's reminding me that no matter what, we'll be okay.

I turn to Giselle, cupping her face in my hands. "Giselle, please. Please, you can't leave me."

Leaning closer, I press my lips to hers, feeling my mermaid essence rush from my chest and to her mouth. My skin buzzes with life and love and everything Giselle means to me as my best friend, as the soul who has stood by me and has taken care of me as I transitioned to a life on land. My love for Giselle encompasses her in a glowing light, stirring her dark hair while lighting her skin.

And she accepts my bond as a mermaid. Bright light flows

from her lips and down her throat, lighting her dark chest in quick beats that mirror my own. My mermaid essence flows through her veins, stealing her human life completely while giving her a piece of my soul. Nothing has ever felt so utterly right in this treacherous world than taking Giselle's breath as a human only to give her mine as a mermaid.

Giselle thrashes in the water, kicking her legs, and then she wraps her arms around me. Her mind opens to mine, her feelings, her soul engulfs me in a wave of fear and love and every piece of her as she hovers in a state between giving her human life and accepting her eternity as a daughter of the sea.

"Giselle, I'm so sorry," I whisper into her mind, our souls closer than ever before.

"What have you done? You gave me your spark," she says, leaning back to touch my cheeks. "It didn't belong to me. I don't understand."

I press my lips together. "But it did. I can feel it with every beat of my own heart. Of yours."

"But Ryan," she says.

My eyes burn though I can't cry in the sea. "I don't know. I don't understand any of this, either."

"Princess Luna, I'm here. Please, hold on. Tell my beautiful Giselle to hold on," Sun says through the door.

Giselle and I look at each other in the water, and then Ryan squeezes my hand. He covers his own mouth and nose with his hand, and panic rises in my throat. He might be capable of holding his breath longer than Giselle, but it's already been too long. He thrashes in the water, wrapping his arms around me, his heart slowing as it thunks against mine racing at the same speed as Giselle's.

"Hurry, Sun! Ryan, he—I can't lose him." My voice falls flat in my mind, and Sun doesn't respond to me. He didn't hear my voice. The glowing world darkens the longer I embrace Ryan.

Pain rushes over me, starting in my toes and tingling through the rest of me. Giselle touches my shoulder, getting me to look away from Ryan, and she points down at my fin. I realize I can't hear her either. My mind closes off as my humanity takes over. I have no idea how much time has passed, but the pull of the moon releases me, and my panic caused my body to trigger the transformation back to a human to take the form of Ryan—maybe Giselle. This is all so confusing as I see my spark blink in Giselle's chest.

My lungs burn from needing to breathe air as a human, and Ryan shakes me, motioning for me to transform back into a mermaid. But I can't. Something's wrong. The ocean went through so much trouble to save me, but now it's turned against me, not letting me change.

Or maybe it's my love for Ryan. Because I can't lose him. I can't allow the sea to take him. I gave my one chance to transform someone on Giselle, but I'm not angry. I'd do it again. It feels right. My bond to her feels like this was meant to be, following in my great-grandmer's current like when she saved her best friend.

But where does that leave me?

"Luna," a whisper of a voice says, trickling into my mind. "Don't resist."

I blink my burning eyes, my vision darker now that my tail splits apart and leaves me in human form.

"Luna, my daughter. I've been waiting so very long for this moment. Please, don't resist."

My heart picks up pace, and I watch Giselle's glowing heart speed up to match mine. She swims away from me, ramming her shoulder into the door. The boat rocks again, and I sway in Ryan's arms. We meet each other's gazes, and he runs his hand across my cheek, pushing the hair from my face.

Leaning in, he kisses me, sharing a dozen images of me throughout the last few weeks—moments that I had forgotten, moments important to him—snapshots of his love of me flickering through my mind to end in this moment.

He sends me image after image, and I return just as many, hugging him to me, savoring the love we share, the bond we never got the chance to make official, the part of me I'll never be able to give him. But none of that matters. Because I love him, and even if my essence chose Giselle, even if I'll never have the life in the ocean with Ryan I imagined. I don't regret it.

Because the ocean is clear.

It no longer wants me.

It's giving me to the land. It's still allowing me to share my life with Ryan no matter how short it may be.

"Luna, don't resist," the feminine voice says again in my

mind.

"Don't resist!" Ryan repeats, holding my face in his hands.
And with his words, he releases all his breath.
Everything turns dark.

SAVE THE SURFACE

A COOL HAND BRUSHES along my forehead, combing my sopping hair from my face. My eyelids turn from black to red, and I roll on my side. My stomach heaves, making me throw up saltwater. I curl in on myself, sobbing through my pulsing muscles. I have no idea how I managed to free myself from the sunken ship, but I have, and now I sink into the soft, warm sand of a beach.

Someone gently rubs their hand along my back until I stop heaving and crying. My knees dig into my stomach. I'm human. *Human.* The thought flits through my mind, my heart hurting at the possibility that this might be my life now. The ocean gave me what I wanted still in the light of the full moon by allowing me to be with Ryan in the form he'll remain forever. One I can't even wrap my mind around. It wasn't supposed to be this way. It was always supposed to be me and him and the sea—not the land.

"Ryan?" My voice cuts through the quiet air, hoarse and barely audible over the beating of my heart and the sound of the surf as it sneaks up to wash over my legs. "Ryan? Are you okay? Can you say something?"

I flip over to reach for him and stare at his silhouette haloed in beautiful sunlight. But who I thought was Ryan wasn't him after all, and fear swells in me like the crest of another wave that washes over my body. Fractals of light bounce off my skin, still pearlescent and shimmery even without my tail. My vision burns in the magical light, and I blink through the haze at the figure, who reaches out to touch my cheek.

I freeze, recognition washing over me in waves of love and uncertainty—a small blip of fear. A groan sounds from beside me, stealing all my attention away from the sparkles of light forming the familiar presence I'm afraid to confront, one that shouldn't be here if I am.

I shift to glance at Ryan lying in the sand next to me. His sea glass green eyes flutter open, brighter than I've ever seen them, and I roll closer. I climb on top of him, pressing my sandy body to his and frame his head in my arms. His warm fingers slide around my waist. He maps my body with his fingers, inspecting every inch of my skin.

"Oh, Ocean. You're okay. I was so scared." I lean down to shower him with a dozen kisses, starting with his scruffy cheeks until I meet his mouth. His lips lightly brush against mine for a second before he devours every kiss I offer, sucking my lips into his mouth, still tasting of the sea that fissures my heart at the memory of him inhaling the ocean. "I thought I lost you to the sea. I thought I lost—"

My tears splash his face, and I kiss the salty drops away. I can't bear to say the words out loud, to think how close we were to facing an uncertain eternity without the vows and the official bond mates create through a traditional coupling ceremony— one where Ryan was supposed to give his last breath to me, something that can't happen now.

I shake my head, pushing the thoughts away. "It doesn't matter. What matters is that we're here and safe."

"But how?" he whispers, his voice gruff. "The last thing I remember was...a voice? You told me not to resist." He searches my face like I can give him the answers I'm not even sure of. I have no idea how we ended up on this beach. And what he's saying? Impossible.

I blink a few times. "I can't speak to you telepathically."

Someone clears their throat. "But I can. And I've been waiting so very long for this moment, my daughter. And to meet your handsome chosen, it brings me such joy."

Ryan's gaze darts to look behind me. He stiffens, clutching me tight enough that his reaction startles me, but he doesn't let me get far. "Oh, shi—oot. Are we dead?" His eyes return to mine, his brows pinched, wrinkling his forehead with a frown. "We're dead," he breathes into my ear. "God, no. Not you, Luna. I never wanted this for you or anyone."

Sadness washes over me in a wave, stealing my breath away.

"Ryan, I—" I don't know what to say. I never for a second thought we were dead. He has to be wrong.

I pull myself away and help Ryan sit up. Swiveling in the sand, I meet the familiar gaze of the woman I mostly only remember through other people's memories. Her long, black hair rests in an intricate braid down her back, and her ocean blue eyes, a few shades lighter than mine, sparkle in the sun. She slaps her glittering silver tail in the surf and reaches out to touch my cheek. Rainbow prisms of light scatter across the beach with her movement like the familiar magic I sense in the cove.

"Oh, Ocean." I'm afraid he's right. There's no other explanation for seeing my mom. She's long since given herself back to the sea. I close my eyes, searching my memory for the last thing I remember on the sunken Storm, which is the voice Ryan described. I heard what he heard after my body transformed against my will to be in the same form as Ryan after I gave my essence to Giselle to save her life.

I squeeze my eyes shut and push the thought away, tightening my hold on Ryan's hand.

"I'm sorry," Ryan whispers.

"You do not need to apologize. You're very much alive, my son," my mom says, cupping both mine and Ryan's hands in hers. "This is the magic of the sea allowing us to meet. I've hoped for this moment, but I'm so sorry it had to be this way."

I release a breath. "Was this your doing—with the Ocean's King and the Storm? Why are we even here? And Giselle? How could that happen? She wasn't my intended. She was Sun's. And now—" So many questions fly from my mouth. I can't stop to allow my mom to answer any of them. I'm not so sure I want her to. Instead, I scramble to my feet and run into the lapping surf up to my navel and smack my hands against the surface. "Why? Why do this to me? Why do this to Ryan? I need to understand my fate if it's not the one I imagined."

A wave knocks me off my feet and washes me back to shore in the spot Ryan sits with his knees bent to his chest. He leans over and pulls me from the surf and onto his lap, stretching out his legs to touch the water. Confusion darkens his eyes, but he doesn't shout his questions to the sea. He does nothing but embraces me, breathing into my hair, telling me how much he loves me and that everything will be okay. Because we're alive.

The pain clenching my chest proves as much, and I sob, bawling into his chest, feeling like the ocean betrayed me. But maybe this is what I deserve for failing. Maybe I deserve such a life with my heart split between the land and sea.

I sniffle into his shoulder, wishing I was breathing the sea, that we were breathing the sea together. "I've ruined everything. I should've listened to you about your dad. I just thought I knew what the ocean's plan was for me. It felt so right until..."

It still feels right. I can't help it. I know things turned disastrous, and I know I failed to change things immediately, but deep in my essence, I still believe I was meant to board the Ocean's King. I was meant to share my essence with my best friend, no matter how unfair it feels for Ryan's sake, because he already has the rest of it.

I've known from the moment I met Giselle that she would make an amazing mermaid—and who knew it'd occur because of me. She's so deserving of a life so full of love with her mate. And I'm grateful to have been able to fulfill my promise to keep her safe.

But my heart doesn't hurt any less.

My dreams still feel shattered.

My future with Ryan still feels out of my reach.

"Luna, please don't cry. Don't feel bad for me or worry about what this means for us. Because I love you, and what matters is we're all alive," Ryan says, resting his head to my cheek. "I don't care if I never transform into a merman or if I have to experience a thousand dark oceans to swim with you. None of that matters to me as much as you do. I just want to be with you. I want to make the world better for you. With you."

"But I—" More tears burst from my eyes as guilt squeezes my breath away. It's so selfish of me to be angry when I know I did the right thing. My best friend would be gone otherwise— and Sun? I made him a promise. Ryan's right. What matters is we're all alive. My love for him hasn't changed. If anything, I love him more if such a thing were possible.

"This was my fault." Ryan runs his fingers across my cheeks, drying my tears. "You should have never been in this position. Right now, I don't deserve anything the ocean has to offer. I haven't proven myself."

More tears escape my eyes. I'll surely be responsible for the rising sea levels if I can't get myself under control. "Don't say that." Because I don't need him to prove himself to me. It's not about earning a piece of my heart. My love doesn't come at a price. I give it freely. I wish he could see that. I wish—there's no point to wishing. I can't change our circumstances, but I can show him that I want to make this work. Now more than ever.

"Luna's right, my son. You should never speak so lowly of yourself when the ocean chose you for a life of magic and love with my daughter. A prince fit for my princess, who still has a long journey ahead to find the answers she seeks."

"The ocean seems pretty obvious." Ryan's voice barely sounds over the waves. "But I can only hope to show Luna how much she means to me. I'll do anything for her."

"I know," Mom says. "She'll need your guidance to navigate the surface. She'll need your bravery. Your knowledge of a world far more dangerous than it should have ever become."

I frown at her words. "What does any of that mean? You need to tell me everything. Don't you think I deserve it?"

"There's no time, my daughter. All the answers you seek are scattered throughout the seas."

I clench my hands into fists. "No, they're not. Wren took everything. My answers might be lost to the waves forever. The boat—" A cry wracks through my chest as everything starts catching up to me. The Storm sunk. Who knows what happened to the Ocean's King. The royal guard was with Sun. It could very well be at the bottom of the sea, too. And Ryan's family? I can't even think about it. I'm so incredibly angry at Wren, but it doesn't mean I wanted the ocean to take him. Or Dara. Hawk. They were coming around.

Mom slaps her silver tail over the surf. "You've lost nothing, Luna."

"Are you kidding me?" I ask, my voice rising. "I don't even know who I am anymore. The sea is so quick to wash things from me and rise up when I'm not strong enough. It hasn't even given me a chance."

My mom reaches out and wraps her arms around me and Ryan, hugging us both. "That is you. The sea has been freed from Attilonious's reign. It's reacting to the shadow of magic still coursing through you. The sea is not against you, but it seems you are against yourself. You must have faith in who you are. You are my daughter, a being of magic with the ocean in your essence."

I touch my hand to my chest. "What? I don't understand. I have no magic."

I can't control the sea. I can't change the currents or ask the seas to rise in my defense. I can't do anything except bend to the ocean's will, and now it shapes me into someone unfamiliar and lost. Even knowing every inch of the sea and how to travel the currents seems to leave me in a state of confusion because I no longer know what I'm truly looking for. All I can see is the mess I've left behind like the human artifacts across the sea floor out of place and no longer where they belong.

I open my mouth to tell her all my thoughts, to argue with her over her assessment of me. She might be my mom, and she might also be the sea that breathes life into my soul, but she knows nothing of me. How could she? I've been in my dad's care for all these years.

She purses her lips. "I know you more than you think," she says, responding to the thoughts I never said out loud. "And you're my daughter, Luna. Magic runs in our essences. Magic powerful enough to change the tides. A queen's liaison. The colonies' advisor. You, my daughter of the sea, can tame the treacherous surface as your fierce mate, a warrior in his own right, stands beside you."

I release a huff of air, not believing anything she says. My inability to even survive a few weeks on the Ocean's King proves I'm anything other than a powerful daughter, instilled with magic. I can't tame the violent surface. I can't do anything except beg the sea to hear my cries. "You're wrong. I've never done anything remotely magical," I argue. "Whatever you think I carry inside me was lost to the land, Mom. You have ocean magic, but I'm starting to think I'm more human than anything, cursed with a tail to live in a world where I never belonged."

Her serious face softens, a look of sorrow puckering her features, making my grief worse.

"How can you say that?" Ryan says, speaking up.

"You're on her side?"

Ryan narrows his eyes, surprising me. "I'm on your side, and you're the most magical, incredible, fierce, badass mermaid princess I'm lucky to have had fallen in love with me. The fact that you have shared such a life with me feels like magic."

Mom reaches out and touches Ryan's hand, her sadness disappearing with a blink of her eyes. "It's okay, my son. Luna has every right to question herself and me. I've had to make tough decisions in my life, ones I didn't want to."

"We all have," I whisper, wrapping my arms around my knees while staring off into the blue horizon.

Ryan shifts in the sand to sit behind me, hugging his arms around my knees, his warm chest resting on my back. His lips brush my shoulder like he knows I need his strength to hold me together because I'm so tired. I'm tired of the world feeling like it's against all of us.

"And I'm sorry for that," Mom says, staring into the same horizon. "I've deprived you of part of your essence for far too long. But I felt like I had no choice. When you were born, the sea was imprisoned under Attilonious's reign. I tried all that I could to shift his tides, to show him the damage he was inflicting on the colonies and the ocean. I warned him that his need to protect us would only hinder our ability to grow and adapt. But he could not see past the surface."

"I know all this," I say. "That's why the ocean stripped him of his magic."

"But it's also why your magic was stripped from you. Taken and locked away from you as a merbabe, but the sea still calls to you. It reacts to you now that it's free. But until you find your lost stone, it's how it'll remain."

I laugh in shock, trying to wrap my head around her words. "You're joking."

Ryan laces his fingers through mine, bringing my attention to him. "I don't think she is. Every time you're scared or nervous, the water gets rough. I've always noticed it. Remember our first kiss?"

I scrunch my nose, remembering how the ocean nearly drowned me, trying to force me to transform. "That was definitely the ocean."

He brushes his fingers across my chest. "I know you think it is, and you've always told me that the ocean would protect you, but it was always you protecting yourself, calling the sea to rise up to help you through something. Like helping you decide if I was your mate."

"I knew that."

"But I'm your hero, remember?" He smiles as he says it, for the first time embracing a moment where he felt he proved his worth to me, even if I wouldn't have drowned.

"Always." A cool sensation drips down my back, making me shiver. The more I think about it, the more I realize the truth. The sudden swells, the rough water, even the moment where the tide rose to stop Talia from running from me—it was me all along.

Surprise and awe wash through my mind before fizzling into pure hot anger. My mom holds her hand out, freezing the sudden swell forming in front of us. It falls short of us and sprays our legs and her tail with sea mist, sending my heart racing.

I tilt my head to the sky. "You said I was stripped of my ocean magic, and it was stolen from me. I knew Dad was ruthless and cruel, but I never imagined he could do something so horrible as to take part of my essence away."

Mom's frown deepens. "Luna—"

"Why am I so surprised that Dad would do such a thing? I know he changed my appearance. He stole my identity. Of course he stole my ocean affinity. He stole every chance I had to rise to the surface to guarantee I never left the sea. And now this? I bet he'll tell me this is a sign from the ocean about Ryan being the son of a pirate."

"Please, you can't blame him, my daughter. I'm so sorry for what I felt I had to do so long ago. But I was left no choice. I couldn't leave the sea with you, and I knew when Attilonious discovered your talent, he'd have taken it for himself as he did your identity. So I took it first. It was the only way to assure you'd have the chance to emerge from the sea."

"So *you* stole my magic?" I ask. All this time—all my life—I had assumed I was gifted with knowing how to navigate the seas. I had never suspected having anything more. And now, I don't know how I feel. "You couldn't have known he would have done that to me."

"I'm sorry. The risk was too great," she says, like those words make a difference. "It had to be done."

Tears burn my eyes, and I shift away from Ryan to get to my feet. I stand tall and stare down at my mom, my shadow dimming the rainbow fractals of light bouncing from her tail and onto the cream-colored sand around her. "None of this would have happened if I had magic. I could've controlled the seas. I could've controlled the pirates. Giselle would still be human, and Ryan would still have the chance to transform into a merman."

My breath quickens, the air seemingly harder to breathe. Hurt flows through me, stiffening my muscles while heating into anger—fury even. Because this situation could've been prevented if she had even an ounce of faith in the ocean she gave her life back into.

"You ruined my life," I whisper. "You let your fear cheat me out of what the ocean had given me. And now I'm as lost as you are, Mom."

Mom straightens her shoulders and meets my gaze. "I have never been lost, my daughter. And you're most certainly not lost. You know the oceans, and your mate knows the land. You make an exceptional force that'll save the surface."

"Without my magic, I—"

"You're still my powerful daughter. Now be brave and follow your current. It will lead you to your magic. It's the only way to save the surface."

"Save the surface? But it's the sea that needs help." It's so hard to wrap my head around her words, especially with how painful the knowledge cuts into me. Me with magic? Do I even want it anymore? It'll pull me deeper into the ocean and away from Ryan. It'll lure me into a form he'll never be able to take. What if it drags me so deep that I can never surface, leaving him on the shores like my mom left Darren? I can't imagine a life with magic could be worth my heart stranded on the land.

"Saving the sea starts at the surface." Mom curls her fingers, raising the tide behind me. Its glittering shadow reflects across her and makes Ryan get to his feet to take my hand. She looks between us, a smile playing on her face despite the sorrow clouding my vision.

"And Ava is—"

"Ava is so worthy and a great leader for our colonies, but a human-born queen needs a talented ally, and you're her advisor. The sea is a vast kingdom and needs the care you can help provide with your intended. It must be you, my daughter. You and Ryan."

I glance at Ryan, silently taking in my mom's words. His doubt shines as brightly as mine, but I know he doesn't doubt me. We both doubt ourselves. Possibly the world.

"Because you, my son," she continues, drawing Ryan's attention back to her, "made a promise to the ocean, and I know you'll stay true to your word. You care for the sea despite your circumstances."

The doubt in Ryan's eyes dissipates, and he swivels on his feet, reaching out to run his fingers across the frozen wave behind us.

"I made a promise to your daughter that I intend to keep,"

Ryan says, his frown pulling into a whisper of a smile, lightening the weight of the imaginary anchor tied to my heart.

I bring his hand to my chest. "And I made a promise to you."

"So, a new adventure, huh?" he asks.

I want everything in me to agree, to lighten the darkness stealing the glow from my chest. But it's hard to still process anything. I've been waiting for weeks for the ocean to give me a sign, to point me in the right direction, to speak to me so I wasn't left having to interpret every wave or current. And having my mom be the one to finally fill in the hole in my life left behind by her disappearance is overwhelming. To have her tell me she hindered my ability while still expecting me to do great things I never thought myself capable of doing leaves me scared and unsure.

"Ryan, I—are you sure? Look at what I've cost you on the last adventure I dragged you on."

He hugs me, pulling me into his chest and breathes into my hair. I listen to his heartbeat thrumming in my ear as he holds me together. I don't think I could even fall apart if I wanted to. "You dragged me nowhere I wasn't willing to go, and if I have to fight a million pirates and face the deepest trenches in the ocean to help you, I will."

Mom nods at Ryan. "Listen to your mate, Luna. Use his strength. Give him yours. He will be there for you when I can't."

I exhale a breath. "Oh, Mom. Why can't you? You should

be. You should have to help me through all this." The words fly from my mouth with another breath of uncontrollable tears. I hadn't felt my mom's absence so deeply until this moment. I don't even want to think about the world outside this beach in this paradise I can't be certain is real. "I'm lost without you, you know. I feel betrayed. How could you leave me with Dad? How can I still love him after everything?"

"Oh, Luna. I want you to hold onto that love. Love is a beautiful thing that gives you the strength you need. And Attilonious wasn't always lost. He cares deeply about our colonies. Even now. I've forgiven him, and so should you. We have made amends, and I know you will to. But you must return first."

I reach out and take her hand. "I'm not ready. You still have so much to teach me. I have so many questions. I don't want to leave you."

"You won't. I am with you. Always. The sea is me, and I'm the sea. We are one," she says. "And we listen."

I sniffle. "So, what now? Where do I go from here? How can I face the mess I made? And Giselle? Oh, I still—what if she can't forgive me?"

"We're going to figure this out," Ryan says from next to me, speaking up. He shares a silent conversation with my mom, stirring something warm in my heart. "You, me, and the sea, Luna. No matter what. No matter if I'm stuck breathing air."

"Then I'll breathe air with you," I whisper.

"I'll work on holding my breath, too."

His words bring a smile to my face, and I turn to meet my mom's beautiful ocean blue eyes. She motions for the both of us to return to her side in the sand and touches her hand to my heart, the glow of my spark flickering through her fingers. "I know this is overwhelming, but the ocean taught you how to endure the stormy waters. Let it guide you into following my trail, and you'll find what's been lost."

"Mom—"

She shakes her head. "You have to wake up now."

"Wait, I—"

"Luna, wake up. Oh, God. Luna, you have to wake your damn ass up before I—"

Water splashes my face, and I jerk upright, gasping. The hot sun beats down on my legs, and Giselle hovers over me. She bares her teeth, searching my face for a moment, and then digs her arms under me, pulling me from the sand and into her lap to hug me against her.

"Thank God—the Ocean, whatever the hell magic that you're awake. I thought you weren't ever coming back to me, and you know how much that'd piss me off. You can't just give me your damn mermaid essence and abandon me."

My chest heaves, and I cover my mouth, suppressing my oncoming sob. The reality of the world crashes around me with a rising swell that makes Giselle yelp and grip onto me while water splashes our faces. "I'm so sorry."

"Sorry for saving my life? No way. You gave me part of yourself. I'm just sorry I suck at holding my breath, and you felt that you had to."

I frown. "You're my best friend. You think you'd be angry if I abandoned you? There was no way in the ocean I was letting it take you from me. It was my fault—"

Giselle cuts off my words with her hands. "It was that dang pirate's fault. I don't want to hear you blame yourself again. As your...best mate? Second mate?" She laughs. "Soul sharer? Soul...sister?" The lightness of her voice lifts the heaviness of the land weighing me down. "Yeah, soul sister. As your soul sister, I will not allow such talk about our accidental coupl—bonding."

I nod my head, letting her hug me again. "I love you, Gi. You can call me whatever your spark wants as long as you know how important you are to me as my best friend."

Her face softens, and she touches her fingers to her chest. "You know, I thought Ava was joking about the blinking. I'm like a flashlight in the dark." Releasing a small laugh, she hugs me again.

"You have no idea how happy I am you're okay," I say into her hair. "Is Talia?"

"Whoa. That's crazy weird," she says without answering my question.

I tilt my head. It takes me a moment to realize she's reacting to the sudden wave of emotions washing from me to her. I know this, because I can feel her surprise.

"Oh, I'm—"

"Luna." Ryan groans from next to me, and I wiggle in Giselle's arms until she lets me go. I turn toward my mate, trailing my eyes up and down his body as I inspect every inch of him. Our gazes meet, and everything comes crashing back to me. He doesn't have to say anything for me to know that the moment I experienced with my mom was utterly and completely real. It wasn't a dream.

"Oh, Ryan." More tears burst from my eyes, and Giselle starts crying next to me. We both turn to each other, and then she starts laughing, which makes me laugh.

"Oh, my God. There's gotta be something we can do. Ava never mentioned her bond with Carter being this intense. How are we—"

"Princess Luna! Ryan." Sun's voice cuts through the air, and a rush of love and desire crashes from Giselle to me, making my cheeks warm. "Thank the Ocean."

"Thank the Ocean is right," Giselle whispers from next to me. "You should've seen him last night, Luna. He and the guard dragged the Ocean's King here and managed to rescue everyone on the Storm."

I was prepared to experience such a bond with Ryan since I can already feel some of his emotions, but feeling Giselle's too? She's right. It's the strangest experience ever, and I'm not sure how much more I can endure.

Releasing a deep breath, I focus on suppressing Giselle's emotions. If Sun wasn't rushing us with such love lighting his face, I'd elbow Giselle and ask her to take a breath. But feeling the foreign love not meant for me fills me with such relief and assurance. It confirms that I did the right thing for Giselle no matter the consequence for me. She and Sun deserve such a life together. The ocean will thrive because of them.

"They're here?" Ryan's question pulls me out of the haze of love stretching my mouth into a smile.

"Yup." Giselle shades her eyes from the sun, pointing at the boat not far in the distance. "They can't go anywhere either. Serves them right for locking up a mermaid princess on a full moon."

Ryan swears and gets to his feet the same moment Sun's shadow crosses over me. I don't have a chance to react before I'm lifted into the air and set on my feet. Sun stands in front of me and Ryan, his arms opening for Giselle to fall into. They kiss each other, making me shake my head to focus back on the Ocean's King floating on the surface.

Something dark crashes over me, and I grab Ryan's hand, pulling him into the surf. My body trembles with muscle spasms, and I transform before I'm even deep enough to swim.

"Princess, wait," Sun calls. "You shouldn't go out there."

A wave rises, lifting me from the shallows, pulling me into deeper water with Ryan. "I'll be right back. Gather the others. It's time everyone finally meets."

MAGIC WATERS

SEVERAL OF THE ROYAL guard from both Pearlestria and Reefaria circle the Ocean's King. This is one of the few times I've seen so many together apart from celebrations and holidays. I almost forgot how intimidating those gifted as warriors are. Tide greets me first, pulling me into his arms. He jets us to the surface, and we both spit out water while Ryan gasps a breath of air.

A whistle cuts through the sound of the ocean, and I spin in the water and peer at a few of the crew members standing along the deck, pointing at us. Voices hum through the air, and someone yells for Captain Reyes. Hearing his name elicits anger worse than knowing my mom stole my magic from me for safe-keeping as a merbabe. My whole body trembles in the water, I'm surprised a swell doesn't lift me up to spit me out on the deck to confront the man who deserves an existence bound to the land like my dad.

Ignoring the commotion, I turn back to Tide. "I'm boarding the vessel to talk to my mate's dad."

Tide reaches out and grips my shoulder, bowing his head closer. "Allow me to escort you. The humans are quite angry. They've sent three men with spear guns into the water. Some have even attempted to fire weapons from the surface. It's too dangerous for you alone."

"Is anyone hurt?" I ask, fear gripping me worse than before. I shouldn't have put it past the crew to surrender so easily.

He shakes his head. "They're no warriors, princess, only scared people. Those who enter the water are immediately relocated to the far end of the island away from the cove. We've managed to get two others off the boat as well, but many resist."

Lifting my hand, I squeeze Ryan's fingers holding onto my shoulder. "I think I need to board with only my mate, Tide. They probably assume the worst of their friends."

"You're right about that, Princess Luna, and that's what worries me."

I straighten my shoulders. "I'll be fine." I don't need to be a warrior to face the pirates. Not now. It's time I do what I had planned to since the moment I realized I was getting nowhere. I need to take the Ocean's King and kick everyone off. Giselle was right the first time she suggested we bring Wren to an island. But I don't plan on leaving him here. I only need him to see what happens to those who lose sight of who they are—like my dad, the shunned merman king now without his ocean magic.

"Princess, they tried to keep you from the water on the night of the full moon." Tide's dark eyes turn serious as he tries to shoot down my idea. "You could've died."

I hate to think of the thought, because he's right. Had it been a time when my dad ruled, I might have. Now with my mom's revelation about my ocean affinity, I'm starting to piece together the last few months. I spent too much time ignoring the ocean and exploring the land to realize that I wasn't the only one to change.

Before, I think the ocean wouldn't have reacted to my needs. I've only been out of the water for a few months, and I lack the experience of knowing more than my instincts, but I'm pretty sure I felt more connected, even at a distance, living on the beach. I can't control the waves like Ava, but the sea shifts with me. Maybe it was my spark all along, taking me to shore. Nearly ruining my first date with Ryan. Triggering my transformation in front of him. It's always been me and the shadow of my magic calling out to find the missing piece of me I assumed was my connection to land. But maybe it was me calling to the one soul who could help me find the piece of me stolen and lost to the sea.

And now that my dad is no longer king, no longer fighting

to protect the colonies by any means necessary, my spark calls to the ocean like the ocean calls to me. Especially in the dangers of pirate waters.

There was a reason my dad fought so desperately to keep our secret. He was protecting us as a species, but his over-protectiveness hindered us. It hindered me. I could only see the ocean as it was around him. And now, I feel it. It's deep inside me, reminding me of who I am. The daughter of a queen who gave everything for not only the sea but also the surface. She dreamed of a better world, and I must help fulfill her legacy. My legacy.

Starting with this pirate ship with my pirate prince mate.

I fan my tail, keeping my head above water, though I want to dip back under to silence the cacophonous noise trickling from the yacht. "People make mistakes if they don't know any better, and no one knew the consequences until the ocean swallowed the boat, Tide. Now, please. Let me handle this. If I feel I can't, I'll call for you."

"I think you should wait for Queen Ava to return from relocating the other humans."

I frown at him. Ava should not be in this position. It's my fault the Ocean's King is here. She's dealt with enough already, and my mom was right about being her advisor and her ally. This is my calling. My duty. "Tide, Ava would trust me to handle this. You should trust me."

"I do, but I vowed to protect you at all costs."

I might be a princess, and he would usually listen to my

command, but it's different now. The guard knows the true danger the surface faces. And I'm afraid Tide and the rest of the guard might not let me pass.

"You have my word that I'll keep Luna safe," Ryan says from over my shoulder, finally speaking up. "I vow on my life. She's the most important person to me, and no harm will come to her."

Tide disappears from the surface, swimming to seek guidance from the others. They block me from their conversation, and I motion for Ryan to remain on the surface so I can plead with them. Because I can't wait any longer. I fear if I do, things will turn from fear to hostility, and I know what Wren is capable of. I feel badly enough as it is that Ava's had to handle the humans I brought to the island, when I know she intended never to use the cove as a prison.

"Tide, please. This is my problem to handle," I say.

Sailor, another of the guard, swims up to me and holds my shoulders in her hands. She kisses each of my cheeks and looks into my eyes for a long moment. "I agree with you, Princess Luna. You're capable like your mom. Give me a moment to assure the others."

I smile in appreciation. It's not often other merpeople bring up my mom to me, and they never speak of my dad now. But I feel the shift. The merpeople feel my mom's magic, and they're finally seeing things beyond the safety of the colonies as they embrace and adapt to the changing tides.

"Princess Luna, your mate," another voice calls into my

mind.

I spin away from Sailor and tip my head toward the surface. Ryan swims from his spot and toward the Ocean's King. He's returning to the yacht whether or not the guard thinks it's a good idea.

"What do we do?" Tide asks, swimming up next to me. "He was as much a prisoner as you. Allow us to assist."

I shake my head. "No, he knows what he's doing." If there is one person in the world who can handle Wren, it's Ryan. I trust in him to help me and to fulfill his promise to me. This is more than my journey. It's both of ours. We're a team.

"But—"

Tide doesn't have a chance to argue. Ryan closes the space to the Ocean's King, and I watch as he boards without interference. My heart picks up pace, and I stare at the clear surface rippling above me.

Slowly, I flick my tail and break through the water. Another whistle sounds out, and I meet Ryan's gaze. He stands with his arms crossed, dripping water on the bathing platform. Titus points a knife at him, yelling words I can't understand through the heat of his anger. I think he's accusing him of something.

Titus takes a step forward while Ryan takes one back. My mate holds his hands in the air, trying to get in a word, but the angry pirate continues to come at him. And no one does anything. Not even Wren. In fact, I don't see the pirate king at all.

Darting forward, I propel myself through the ocean, riding on a current of my fury. Titus has always had something against me—against Ryan—since the moment I laid eyes on him after the Kings' gala the night we left from La Tortuga Point to head to San Francisco. I think it far exceeds having his pride hurt by me, but I can't figure it out. He's the reason I ended up locked away on the Storm. He's the reason Wren acted so suddenly. And now, he's using the situation to his advantage.

I watch Titus swipe his blade at Ryan again, cornering him in a spot against the garage in a place he can't jump back into the sea. Panic laces around my heart, pushing me to move faster than I have ever swum before. I breach from the ocean and fly through the balmy air. Someone yells out, but Titus is too slow to turn his gaze from Ryan.

I collide into the pirate, sending us both sprawling forward. The sheer weight of my expansive tail traps him under me, and his knife clatters on the deck near Ryan's feet. Ryan scoops it up, gripping it in his hand, and I dig my nails into Titus's back, keeping him down.

"Stop fighting," I say, pressing him harder into the deck. "No one wants to hurt you."

Titus thrashes under me, yelling for someone to help him, but silence greets him. Anyone previously on the deck disappears within the boat instead of gaping in shock at me now emerged from the sea in my mermaid form.

"I will kill you!" Titus yells, trying to buck his whole body.

"Why?" I ask. I can't help it. How could someone make such a threat? It hurts my very essence to even think about. His vendetta grows by the second, burning hot through his narrowed gaze. "Why threaten such a thing? I'm not going to hurt you. You were the one to attack my mate."

"You're a damn monster. The old woman was right," Titus says, growling. "Everything about what happened to Nalani makes sense now. And Wren couldn't see past your damn charm all because you reminded him of Nalani, but you ain't like her. She was good and your kind dragged her under. I will kill you and feed you to the sharks like the animal you are."

I'm stunned speechless, hearing him shout about Ryan's mom. I haven't even had a chance to tell Ryan that Nalani isn't even dead, that no one had hurt her. And I can't tell him now. Not like this. Not in front of a man who clearly has some sort of bond to the Reyes family that surpasses being part of the crew. But it's not there for Ryan. I'd have felt it, and he shares no love or loyalty for Titus.

Ryan stomps forward, locks his fingers onto Titus's arms, and drags him out from under me. He does it so quickly that all I can do is roll onto my back and sit up. I stare wide eyed as Ryan holds up the knife, sending my insides twisting.

"Don't say another word," Ryan says, reacting to Titus in a way I've never seen him act before. "I will show you what a true monster looks like if you do."

"Ryan, please. Not like this," I whisper, trying to break through his hardened façade. His muscles flex on his arms, and Titus grips his arms, still fighting. I'm afraid if he manages to break his arms free, Ryan might get hurt.

Ryan finally meets my gaze, but he doesn't move.

I bring my hands to my chest, cupping them together over my heart. "This isn't you. He can threaten me and call me whatever he wants, but don't let him drag you down to his level. He might be able to live his pathetic life, but you deserve more."

Ryan nods, relaxing his hold on the knife. Titus takes advantage of the situation and jerks his elbow back to ram it into Ryan's stomach. Pain rushes through me at the sight. Darkness seeps into my heart, dimming the light blinking in my chest. Titus grabs onto Ryan's shirt, attempting to hold him in place to punch him.

I snap. I can't handle seeing the vile pirate touch my mate.

I thrust back, lifting my tail into the air, and swing it as hard as I can, slapping Titus with my fin. He and Ryan fall onto the swimming platform and roll into the sea. Titus screams out, his voice piercing my ears, and one of the guards drags him under.

Ryan pops to the surface, gasping for breath. He swims to the ladder and pulls himself onto the yacht. He rushes to my side, running his fingers over my body, making sure I'm okay before hugging me. We stare at each other for a moment, listening to the silence around us. With six of the crew now on the island, it leaves only a handful more, depending on how many came from the Storm. That still leaves the rest of Wren's fleet still out on the seas, probably wondering what happened to their king.

Shaking his wet hair from his face, Ryan kneels at my side,

and runs his hand over my hair, pushing it from my shoulder to get a better look at me.

"I'm sorry," he says. "I couldn't stop myself. I just—Titus—I couldn't let him threaten you like that."

I nod, knowing enough about the protectiveness of mermen to understand Ryan's protectiveness over me. I swallow to stop myself from tearing up at the reminder of what he'll never be and shift on my tail to expand my caudal fin out to inspect a few patches of my scales missing from my fluke from rubbing on the rough deck.

"I understand more than you know. Seeing him hurt you..." I can't admit how much it got to me out loud. Because I'd have dragged Titus under myself had the guard not. "Are you okay? Did he hurt you?"

He runs his fingers over my fin. "I'll be all right. I've been worse."

Ryan gets to his feet and scoops me into his arms and off the deck. He peers around the empty ocean around us and shuffles his way to the platform to lower me into the water. If he'd let me, I'd sink him back under with me while I transform, but he straightens his back to peer around.

"I'm going to get you something to wear," he says. "I'll be right back."

The second I dip underwater, Sailor greets me, holding out a waterproof bag to me. "Here, Princess Luna. Take mine."

I graciously accept her offer and transform into a human, pulling the garments out to change underwater even though everything gets wet. I don't like the silence of the vessel, knowing that everyone is waiting and watching. Sailor flicks her strong fin and helps me aboard the Ocean's King by tossing me on the platform. I sit for a moment, dangling my feet in the water, watching the guards circle the vessel a few dozen feet below.

Footsteps tap on the deck, and I shift to my knees to stand up. Ryan steps from the saloon, holding a shirt in his hands, but he drops it at the sight of me. I dash to him, practically knocking him over, forcing him to back into the wall. I can't help it. I feel like even though I'm breathing air, I haven't had a chance to breathe, and all I want to do is breathe in Ryan, kiss him, feel the weight of his fingers digging into my skin. To know he's really okay and here. And we're together.

He releases a breathless laugh into my mouth. "Hawk says my dad locked himself in his quarters and won't respond to anyone."

My eyebrows pinch together. "Not so tough now that the sea fought back."

"He doesn't know I'm alive."

"Oh." I pout my bottom lip. How can I feel bad even after everything?

Wren's not hiding away scared. He's grieving. I know how much Ryan means to him, even if he doesn't show it how he should. Even if it's bad for Ryan. And after all the horrible stuff he put us through, I realize that this was exactly how it was supposed to be. Because change doesn't just happen. Wren was never going to wake up and realize he's sailed so far off course that he's lost his way. He'd have continued the voyage and pretended he didn't make the mistake and that he knew where he was going. He's no different than my dad.

Ryan brushes his lips to mine, pulling me against him again. "I know what you're thinking, and I love your compassion, but don't feel bad for him, Luna. He doesn't deserve it. He should deal with the consequences of his actions."

But it's not Wren Reyes I feel bad for. It's for Ryan. Because I know what it feels like to be the heir of an ocean shunned king. Even though Wren resides on the surface, he still lives and breathes on the sea. Like me, Ryan will have to deal with the aftermath. But I know that together, we can pick up the pieces of our lives and rebuild them into the beautiful place of our dreams.

"Come on," I say, instead of revealing my thoughts. "Let's get this over with."

Tugging me along, Ryan guides me to the upper deck to the captain's suite. We pass through the dining terrace where the rest of the crew gathers, and they stare at us with wide eyes.

"Ryan?" Skull asks from his place. "What the hell?"

Ryan raises his hand. "Everyone pack a bag. You're disembarking. This vessel no longer belongs to Wren Reyes."

"You gotta be fu—"

"It belongs to Ryan and me," I say, straightening my shoulders.

"I don—" The vessel rocks on a sudden swell, and Skull shuts his mouth, staring at the other crew members with questioning eyes, like he doesn't believe this is happening, silently asking one of the others to stand up to me, but no one else argues.

"Go," Ryan says, waving his hand at them. "If you don't fight, you'll all be fine."

They'll be fine even if they do fight, but they don't have to know that. My dad used fear as a motivator to keep merpeople from venturing on land until they adapted to believe that my dad was protecting them. I see that now. I hate that I'm doing the same. I never want people to fear the sea. They should love it. Fear births rash actions and ugly outcomes where love blooms hope and promise and new beginnings, making it easier to embrace.

The crew scatters, disappearing down the stairs. I follow Ryan the rest of the way to Wren's quarters. Soft music hums through the wooden door. My heartbeat slows as my muscles relax. A pirate king who listens to a soft ballad doesn't exactly ignite fear in me.

"Dad?" Ryan calls out, tapping his knuckles on the door. "It's me."

The music cuts off before the door swings open. Wren stands in the doorway, his narrow, red-rimmed eyes flicking from Ryan to me and back to Ryan. He darts his hand out and grips Ryan's shoulder, making me tense.

But he doesn't pull him inside or try to hurt his son. All he does is gives him a good shake. "I can't tell if the sea has gotten to my head or if you're really here."

I twist my lips to the side. "We're really here."

Opening his arms, Wren swings them around Ryan and drags him back into the room. His deep laugh bellows through the air, and I stand in shock, seeing emotions I never imagined I'd see on a hardened pirate's face before.

Ryan doesn't reciprocate Wren's hug and clenches his fingers at his sides. He manages to pull away and backs into me, and I step between the two of them. Wren's lips twist downwards, his eyes burning through me, returning the fire Ryan had snuffed out a moment ago.

I step closer and point my finger, jabbing him in the chest. "You have no right to look at me like I'm the monster here."

"You're seizing my ship."

"You nearly cost us our lives."

"Do not blame the attack on me. It was your crew. Your submarines that took the Storm."

"What?" Ryan and I say in unison. This is unbelievable. Submarines?

"Take me to your captain, Luna. He has no idea what he's gotten himself into. I have an entire fleet at my disposal. Taking my ship will do nothing. All it does is pisses me off," he snaps. "Now, I think we can come to some sort of agreement that'll benefit us all."

I blink the confusion from my face. He still has no idea what's going on, only that he lost one of his boats and now he's trapped here because of some underwater force he believes is man-made.

"Luna doesn't answer to a captain," Ryan says, speaking up for me.

"You expect me to believe that? Luna might be a talented diver, but she does not have the ruthlessness it takes to bring down a vessel."

"The Storm capsizing was your fault!" Ryan's voice rises, startling me. "This is all your damn fault."

I slide my fingers through Ryan's, drawing his attention away from Wren. As much as I want to let him unleash his anger at his dad, I hate how it burns through me in the moment. I can't stand it any longer, knowing that the Storm sunk on my behalf even with Wren responsible. "There's no point in casting blame, Ryan. It is what it is now. We have too much else to worry about to hold onto the anger. Just let it go. I don't like feeling it."

And I feel it as hotly as I feel Giselle's worry drifting to me from the waves. I don't have to gaze at the cove to know she stands with Sun on the beach. I can feel her in my essence, wishing I'd return to land.

Ryan's face softens, and he nods his head. "I didn't realize you could still feel me at all."

It's never been strong like the official bond between mates, but being with him in every way imaginable left me in tune with his body and soul. He still feels like a part of me separate from myself as much as Giselle does. "I'm as confused as you are, but I'm not going to question it. You're still my intended, Ryan."

"What the hell are you both talking about?" Wren asks, raising his voice. He fists his hands, standing straighter like the extra inch will intimidate us. If my dad can't intimidate me with his size, neither can Wren. No one, really.

I swivel back to look at him dead on. "Pack a bag. Now. I don't want to have one of my warriors drag you off the ship."

"I—"

"Just do it, Wren." Dara's hardened voice cuts through the room, sounding as ferocious as Wren does. "Listen to the mermaid before the ocean rises to swallow you and this damn ship whole." I wish she'd use my name and not what I am.

Wren blinks without reacting. His expression gives nothing away. He doesn't realize the truth to her words, but he's about to find out. The guard will only take the pirates to shore one way in this moment—the way they feel most powerful—and it's not going to be by boat, gliding across the surface.

"Fine, I'll pack a bag for you. Go with Dara and wait with the others." I motion to the door. If he doesn't move, I'll have to push him myself.

"And give me your keys, Dad. We're taking everything you've stolen from Luna back." Ryan holds out his hand until Wren reluctantly hands a set of keys over.

"Won't get you into the safe," he remarks, glowering at me in protest.

I roll my eyes. "I have patience and an heiress that'll help me figure out how."

Wren doesn't move until Dara strolls behind him and gives

him a shove for me. "Did Luna get into your head, too?" He lets his mom push him toward the door. "You'd have never put up with this shit before."

Dara meets my gaze. "Not Luna. It was the sea. It's different here. Can't you feel it?"

He mutters under his breath, and I know he can, even if he denies it. The sea no longer belongs to Wren Reyes. The sea is free. We're no longer in pirate waters. We're not even in mermaid waters anymore. These are magic waters, and the tides speak to me. They roar.

I offer a small smile to Dara as she nudges Wren out with Ryan following behind to make sure his dad listens. "Hey, Dara?"

She turns to look at me from over her shoulder.

"Welcome to Celestiana Cove. I think you'll like it here."

POD SECRETS

THE CREW STANDS WITH their backs against the wall as far from the swimming platform and the ocean as possible. I can't help wondering what happened to the once vulgar and fearless pirates who graced me with their disgusting presences for the last few weeks. Each of them stares at me with an array of expressions—from annoyance to panic and to rage and one smile from Hawk, who gets elbowed by Skull for not glowering at me.

I stroll next to Ryan, adjusting the waterproof bag with all of the documents I could find and my mom's journal on my shoulder. I wonder what else is hidden in the secret safe in

Wren's stateroom. Ryan told me mostly money and valuables, but I think it's where he hid the map of my mom's, too. And whatever is in the safe isn't even all of it. The Reyes Empire spreads throughout the world on land and in sea. I'm sure to find out the full extent soon enough. For now, all I want to do is get these people off the boat and possibly return to the last place I dove to see what we left behind when Sun got injured trying to save us.

"Dara," I say to Ryan's grandmother, who sits on a step, dangling her feet in the water. "Would you like me to retrieve a boat for you?" She's the only one I'm willing to grant such a request to.

"I'd like you to get a boat," Skull says.

Hawk punches his arm. "What's the fun in that? You scared?"

I roll my eyes. I can't help it. "Just get in and show everyone how brave you are." As much as I want to toss everyone overboard and give them a scare, I know it'll only make things worse and bring me to their level, a place I never want to find myself in.

He yanks his shirt over his head, showing off his tattoos and muscles, and wags his eyebrows at me. Stepping to the edge of the platform, he stretches his arms over his head, cracking his neck, being a total show off. I smirk at Ryan, whose face stays creased with anger and won't change until I can get him close enough to kiss without anyone else watching. The others stare at Hawk in shock, and Skull tells him to stop being a dumbass and that there are monsters in the water. Hawk ignores everyone and dives in, sending a splash over Dara's legs.

He pops to the surface, smiling wide enough at me to see his fillings before looking at Skull again. "Water's warm. Come on, brother. Get your ass in."

Skull doesn't move, and neither does anyone else for that matter, and I heave a sigh and jump in next to Hawk. I take a moment to transform into a mermaid and motion for the royal guard to swim closer to me.

"Will you surface with me?" I ask. "They're disarmed, and I want the rest of them to join the others on shore."

Tide swims up to me first and propels us both to the surface. The other guards remain in wait below for his word. I pop through first, holding my arms up to Ryan, and Tide pushes me the rest of the way up onto the platform even though I can tell he'd prefer to tread with me on his shoulder.

Yells pierce my ears, making me cringe, and it takes Tide sending a wave of water cascading through the air to get everyone to freeze. The pirates react more harshly than I anticipated. The few people I revealed myself to were surprised and not outraged like my existence somehow makes things worse. And maybe it does. Maybe they'd rather believe they were being seized by the daughter of a pirate and not a mermaid princess.

"I don't believe it. Is this a joke?" Wren asks, stepping forward and speaking up for the first time. Ryan raises his palm, keeping his dad back, but Wren pushes closer even with Ryan. "The stories are true." He's not asking, just accepting whatever stories he was told were based on fact. That merpeople exist.

"Sort of," I say, slapping my fin on the surface. "But we're not monsters. No harm will come to any of you. Now will you just get in the water so we can go to shore?"

Wren's face morphs from surprise to rage, and even Ryan can't stop him as he charges toward me, grabbing me by the wrists to hoist me up from the platform. He gathers strength from the depths of his sudden hatred, and I can't fight him off. Flailing my body, I whack my tail on the deck, but he hooks his arm over my chest and uses me as a shield, squeezing me tight enough that I can't move. He yanks my hand up to his face and peers at the sea stone ring on my finger, darting his eyes to Tide now dragging himself closer. But I know he's not looking at Tide as a merman. He's peering at the ring on Tide's hand that matches mine.

"It was never pirates," Wren hisses, his fingers gripping my arm hard enough to make me wince.

Ryan launches himself forward, but Wren spins me in his arms, ripping something from his belt at the same time. Cold metal touches my neck, sending panic through me. The boat rocks on a swell, and a few more of the guards pop to the surface, preparing to fight.

"Everyone calm down," I say, doing my best to keep my voice even. "Please, Wren. Let me go. I can explain."

"You murdered my wife!" he yells, his hot breath heating my ear. Silence falls over the sea, everyone waiting for the ruthless pirate king to prove himself worthy of his name.

I was hoping I'd still have a chance to tell Ryan that a merman didn't murder his mom without an audience. He should hear it from me in private where he can process that Nalani chose the mermaid life, and my dad's rule guaranteed she wouldn't have been able to emerge from the ocean. But now? I don't think I'll have the luxury of preparing and protecting Ryan. Wren's out of control. He's blinded by the grief she left him in. Ryan, too.

"Wren let her go," Dara says, speaking up, saving me from spilling the truth in front of everyone. "The girl had nothing to do with Nalani's disappearance and you know it. She's a child."

Wren tightens his hold even more, his hand shaking enough to knick my skin with his knife. I close my eyes, trying to remain calm. If the ocean reacts, I could get seriously injured. So could others.

"Please, Wren," I whisper. "I can explain."

He jostles me in his arms, his body shuddering, fighting to hold himself back. "First my damn ship and now this. I don't want an explanation from you. I want revenge!"

"But you don't," I say. "Please, if you did, you'd have done it already. I know you're hurting—"

"Shut up!" He shifts his other arm, covering my mouth with his hand. One sudden movement could ruin everything, and now I can't even say what I need to say. "I need to think."

"Dad," Ryan pleads. "Don't do this. I love her. She wasn't responsible. I know that."

"She ruined everything. Her kind stole your mom from

me, and now she's trying to steal you. I won't lose you, kid."

"Hurting her won't change anything. It'll make it worse. You'll lose any chance to make things right."

Ryan's fear mingles with mine. Wren tenses, and the edges of my vision shadow, making my head spin. I expect to feel pain at any moment. I expect the sea to rise up to fight back, to break me away from the brutal pirate king. But all Wren does is loosen his hold on me.

Rushing forward, Ryan steals me from his dad's arms before he can drop me, not giving me the chance to tell them both the truth about Nalani, the mate of one of the sea's warriors who very well might be nearby. And if he is, it would mean she is, too. If Nalani's like Ava, she'll have kept her human bonds despite the laws of the sea at the time of her transformation. Now that her land family is in Celestiana Cove, she will surely come to shore for a family reunion I can't imagine going well. Unlike me, who understands the call of the sea, I'm not so sure Ryan will. Wren definitely won't. Things might end badly.

I blink the tears from my eyes, trying my best to compose myself before I break down. Because though it pains me to know Ryan will hurt and suffer trying to understand his mom's reason for leaving, I believe he can find the happiness I feel knowing Nalani is alive and that she wasn't murdered because of the unjust laws of my dad's reign. That he'll have the chance to strengthen the bond he had to cut to protect himself all those years ago. He gets what I yearn for still feeling my mom's magic swirling through the water here, and I'm grateful he does. He deserves the chance, especially after everything.

"Princess Luna, are you okay?" Sailor asks me telepathically from her spot in the water. The guards wait for my command, and all I can think about is getting everyone away so I can tell Ryan.

"Yes," I think to her from Ryan's arms, "but please, I need you to take the pirate king to shore for me. I don't know if he'll go willingly."

Wren doesn't even have a chance to prepare himself before Sailor launches from the water. I flick my tail, knocking him back into the guardrail, and she hooks her arm across his chest, yanking him back and into the sea. Ryan crosses the deck, peering into the water to watch Sailor drag Wren away from the boat. With the way she grips him with her warrior's strength, he won't be able to put up a fight.

Ryan's heart beats into my shoulder, and he turns his gaze from the ocean and to me. Running his finger across my cheek, he combs my hair from my face and leans in to kiss me like it's all he can do to calm himself. I sink into him, cradling my head into his chest, just wanting to get to land and breathe for a moment.

"Ryan," I say, watching as Tide motions for the rest of the crew to enter the water. "I have something I need to tell you."

He shifts me in his arms and looks at me. "He's screwed, isn't he? The merpeople won't feel safe with the anger he carries. This is your island."

I blink a few times, my eyes glassing over at what he implies. "Oh, Ryan, no. We'll work it out. But this isn't about your dad."

He rubs his lips together, his eyes darkening with his thoughts. "It's not?"

I rest my head on his shoulder, hoping my snuggling will get him to release the tension knotting his muscles. "It's about your mom."

He shifts my weight again, the vein on his neck pulsing, his jaw tightening as he clenches his teeth. I know the weight of my tail can't be comfortable as the boat gently rocks on the water, but he still refuses to put me down. "She's alive, isn't she?" He doesn't have to read my mind to know.

Bobbing my head, I confirm his thoughts, feeling his sudden rush of confusion rising in him. "I was going to tell you when I saw her picture in your dad's quarters but—I'm sorry. It wasn't supposed to be like this."

"You don't have to apologize, Luna," he whispers, strolling to the end of the platform. He carefully sets me on the edge to join me, automatically pulling me back into his lap to hug me. "None of this was your fault."

"You must be so confused and hurt by her leaving you."

He presses his lips together, turning his gaze from my eyes to peer at the hairline cut on my neck his dad inflicted on me. He glares at the wound, and I shift my hair over it to bring his attention back to me.

"But we're going to get through this," I add when he doesn't respond. "I know what it's like to have your world shaken with unbelievable revelations."

Groaning, he rests his head on my shoulder. "I can't think about this right now. You're more important."

I frown. "Never. This is our life together. My magic can wait another day while we sort this out."

"I—I almost don't believe it, you know. I mean, about my mom. I fully believe you're the most magical being in existence."

I smile. "I can take you to her—"

He shakes his head. "No, not yet. Can we—" Gulping a breath of air, he nestles his face into the crook of my shoulder. "Can we go for a swim?"

After everything, I wasn't so sure he'd want to return to the water with me, but now that he mentions it, all I can think about is swimming. "Of course. Anything you want."

"You," he responds. "You're all I need."

I roll onto my back, my chest heaving from exhaustion. Ryan slides his arm under me and pulls me from the waves before they draw me back into the bay. The only noises humming through the air consist of the gentle breeze and a few birds chirping from the branches of the fruit trees.

"I wish we never had to come back to land," I say, immediately regretting my words. Because that would be impossible. The reminder hurts my heart more than it should. Ryan remaining human shouldn't matter to me. It was always a possibility that he could have decided not to go through with the transformation ceremony. I should've prepared myself more, but this is worse. It's not Ryan denying me. It's the sea. The world.

Ryan plops into the sand with me. "And miss the chance to hide away on this island with you? No way." He smiles as he says it, brushing off my comment without letting it get to him while also making me feel better. "I hear there might be some hot showers around here somewhere. And beds. Can't make blanket forts in the sea."

I sink into him. "That sounds amazing. Can I sleep for a year, please?"

"I'd miss you."

I laugh. "You know, it should be me making you smile."

Ryan sweeps my sandy hair away from my shoulder and brushes his lips to my skin. Trailing his finger over my thigh, he traces an invisible line down my leg toward my knee. "You already do."

Voices hum through the air, drawing my attention away from Ryan. We both sigh and then laugh, tipping our heads together to kiss like our lips can somehow freeze the world around us. It'd be so easy to pull him back into the water for another swim, but it's already been two, and I know Ava's waiting for me. She told me to take as much time as I needed, but there isn't enough of it in the world. Better to get things over with.

Ryan pulls me from the sand and picks me up into his arms, letting me curl my legs around him to carry me instead of walking. I nestle my face into the crook of his neck, caressing my lips to his skin, making him shiver.

"We couldn't do this in the sea, either," he muses.

I frown and tilt my head back. "What are you talking about? Couples carry—"

Blush tints his cheeks, and he releases a moan from his throat and kisses me again. "I meant wrap your legs around me, but saying it out loud makes it sound—"

"Like something I don't want to give up," I say cutting him off with a smile. I've missed the flush that used to constantly cross his face with his desire to be with me. Being on the Ocean's King around so many people who wanted nothing more than to throw me overboard forced Ryan to hide a lot of things from me, and now I can't wait for him to let his guard down more.

"Definitely not." Trudging through the sand, he carries me all the way down the beach to where people gather around fire pits, burning as bright as the setting sun casting pinks and purples through the sky.

"Princess Luna," Sun calls, waving his hand. Giselle holds onto his arm, whispering something to stop him from running to me.

Ava and Carter appear from their cottage, one made especially for them as a gift from the colonies for helping to create such a paradise, and I close the space between us. Talia rushes out of the house from behind them and throws her arms around me, knocking us both to the sand. She presses into me, rocking me in her arms, half-sobbing into my hair.

"You have no idea how happy I am to see you. I was so worried you wouldn't come back to shore," she says.

I pull away from her and frown. "You don't have to worry about that. My mate will never be able to breathe water." My voice hitches as I say it, making Talia hug me again.

"I'm so sorry, Luna." Talia leans back, holding my shoulders.

I swallow the burning in my throat. "I'm not. I can't live without Giselle as much as I can't live without you or Ryan."

She slowly nods. "Just like Marina. But you know what? Charles still had an amazing life. He never regretted it. I can show you. Come on. Let's go inside."

I puff air through my lips, because there's nothing more I want to do than to go inside and sit with the people I love. "I need to go to the pirates."

"Luna," Ava's soft voice says over the pounding in my ears. She waves her hand at me, motioning me closer. "Everything is under control for now. Talia's right. You should come inside. You always work so hard to make sure everything is okay for everyone else, and now I'm commanding you as your queen to take a moment to let your pod care for you. We've missed you. I need to make sure you're okay."

Her words stir love within me, and I relent to her suggestion and let Talia pull me to my feet. Giselle and Sun meet the rest of us at the door, and I peer once at the merpeople that have come to shore, hanging out in the sand, just taking a moment to enjoy the balmy oncoming night.

"Hungry?" Ava asks, motioning to the table filled with fruits, bread, and an array of cookies that smell like she just baked them. "Carter can hunt for something from the bay if you'd like."

I drop into the chair and shake my head. "This is great."

Taking a bite of one of the cookies, I savor the sweetness in my mouth, but I'm too anxious and tired, more confused than I've ever been, to consider eating anything more. The others join me at the table, and Giselle remarks about how she needs Sun to take her somewhere more civilized to drop her professors an email.

Ava and Carter whisper to each other, leaning their heads together, but don't include me in what they plan. It's like everyone's afraid to say anything or mention the fact that none of us should be sitting around this dining table eating cookies.

I heave a deep breath and lean my elbows on the table, the whispers getting to me. "Can we all stop pretending that this is a normal day after the full moon? Can we stop treating everything like it's going to be okay?"

My loud voice startles everyone, and all eyes fall on me.

I bang my head on the table. "I mean, look at the mess I made. There's a bunch of angry pirates down the beach. I sunk a ship. I transformed Giselle into a mermaid. And now according to my mom, who somehow managed to get into both mine and Ryan's heads, says I need to find the ocean magic she stole from me or else the surface is doomed."

Lifting my head, I finally meet everyone's faces, lit with a mixture of emotions from surprise to sadness. Ava pulls her hands from her lap to rest them on the table, studying me from her seat, all words lost to her as she processes the bomb of information I just set off to shake the whole island.

"You forgot that my dad wants to kill everyone because he thinks merpeople murdered my mom," Ryan adds, smirking at me. I don't know how he can manage to smile, but the gesture is enough to make me laugh—not a real laugh, but something that sounds like there's a cat fighting a dolphin in my throat.

Ava covers her mouth. "Oh, no. Luna, I—"

"Ocean, yes," I say, cutting her off. "But she's not dead."

Carter comes up behind Ava. "You mean—"

I nod. "Nalani of Reefaria."

Ava's eyebrows shoot up on her forehead. "Sandy's mate?"

"Oh, crap," Giselle says. "What the hell? I thought Ava getting dragged into the ocean and getting prophesized to unite the sand and sea was crazy, but now you and a pirate—lost magic? Damn. I swear to God the ocean better not try anything funny with me."

I release a loud laugh, shaking my shoulders before tears burst from my eyes. Giselle's right. This is so incredibly absurd and complicated. I don't even know how I'm to handle it all. Word will travel as fast as the currents.

Ava narrows her eyes at Giselle. "You're not helping."

"I'm try—"

"Come on, my beautiful soon-to-be mermaid. Queen Ava

and Princess Luna need a moment," Sun says, lacing his fingers through Giselle's.

"But—"

He cups her face in his hands. "Okay, then *I* need a moment with you."

Ava watches them leave and motions for me to follow her into the bedroom, leaving Carter and Ryan with Talia at the kitchen table. Before I have a chance to open my mouth, she throws her arms around me and hugs me so tightly that I can barely breathe. And then she rocks me back and forth until my hands stop trembling.

I blink tears from my eyes. "I need to get access to Wren's safe on the Ocean's King for the map. As soon as I'm rested enough, I plan to swim to where we had last dove to retrieve what I didn't get a chance to find before...this disaster."

"We're going to get through all of this," she says. "You were there for me in one of the worst moments of my life, and now I'm here for you. I know it's all overwhelming and crappy, and feels like nothing will ever turn the way you want it, but it's all temporary. The tides change."

"Except things with Ryan. He's forever human."

She pouts her bottom lip and hugs me again. "Like your great-grandfather." Of course Ava knows that. She's the one who shared the memory with me, gifted to her from my mom and the magic in the sea when she was chosen to reign.

"My great-grandmer gave her spark to save her best friend, too," I whisper. "Carter's great-grandmother."

Ava's eyes widen in surprise. "I knew he came from a human-born but—"

"The tides feel like they're rising because of all my pod's secrets."

After catching Ava up on everything through sharing my memory with her, she hugs me for the tenth time. Something about this moment, hugging Ava and sharing with her the part of my life I just discovered, makes me feel like no matter what, I'll be okay. Because she has hope, and she gives it to me. Like Ryan gives me hope. And Giselle. All of these people who make up the pod I grew up without make me realize how my future isn't lost. How even if I didn't imagine things to turn out this way doesn't mean it isn't how I want them. I just didn't know of the possibility.

"So first thing in the morning, we'll all go dive together," Ava says. "After that, I'll travel back to Azure Waters and see about getting someone to help with the safe. You have me and the whole sea behind you."

"Except the pirates," I mutter, groaning.

"They'll come around."

"Can't we just pretend they don't exist?"

She giggles, crinkling her nose. "Come on, you helped me take on a scary merman king."

"You're right. I guess I'll figure out how to tame some pirates."

6

SCATTERED LIFE

SUNBEAMS CUT THROUGH THE clear water, creating a vortex of glittering light that points toward the magical reef below. Ryan squeezes my shoulder, motioning for me to rise to the surface, and I flick my tail to breach completely.

His laughter echoes in my ear before he sucks in another deep breath and I dive us under, releasing him to kick up while I swim another few circles to wait for the others to make their way to me.

I surface with everyone, meeting Ryan's huge grin. I haven't seen him smile so much in a while. All I want to do is hook my arms around him and flip him through the air again.

I'll do anything to assure his happiness never fades.

"Are we in the right spot?" Ava asks, peering around the surface.

Sun disappears under, leaving Giselle treading next to Talia. Ryan clings to my shoulders, peering at Sun combing his fingers through the sand to pick something up. He darts back to the surface, shifting us with his current in the process.

"This is most definitely the spot, Queen Ava. Here's one of the spears one of the pirates pierced me with." Sun wraps the remaining line around the pointed metal rod and shoves it into the bag on Giselle's shoulders. He'll keep the spear as a reminder of his strength as a warrior for surviving such a battle. My dad used to collect all sorts of things to display.

"Sorry about that," Ryan says, speaking up.

"And I'm sorry for questioning the ocean about what you mean to Princess Luna," Sun says. Neither of us talked about what he said to me out of fear and anger, and I wasn't planning to bring it up, but Sun has never been one not to speak his mind, and I can tell he feels bad about it, though Ryan had no idea.

Ryan bobs his head, rocking me in the water. "It's cool. I question it mys—"

A wave of water crashes over our heads from Sun cutting his arm across the surface to splash Ryan in the face. Ryan spits out water, coughing, and Sun gives him a look that keeps my mate from saying anything else. Because I know mermen, I know Sun wasn't intending to be rude but stopping Ryan from talking badly about himself when we're technically still court-ing.

"Thanks, Sun," I say to the merman telepathically without letting anyone else hear my thoughts. "I know none of this is ideal with Giselle now—"

"My mate is alive with the heart of a princess. I owe you my life and will do whatever I can to help."

Water splashes my face again, this time from Giselle, and she bares her teeth at me in a smile. "No more silent talking un-til I can join you all. We have a mission, remember?"

"We?" Ava asks, smirking. "You said you were going to sunbathe on the surface and merman watch."

Giselle laughs. "Okay, you're right. There is no diving for me until the full moon, which I'm a little annoyed about if I might add. You should talk to the ocean or whatever and tell it that just because I missed my window—"

Sun picks Giselle up by her waist and tosses her through the air only to swim and catch her before she splashes under. He silences her with a kiss, and I puff air through my lips, spinning to face Ryan, holding him close enough that our stomachs touch.

"It's okay," he whispers, knowing that I'm torn about the whole situation.

I nod my head, brushing my lips to his before they tremble. "I know."

After getting Ryan, Talia, and Giselle situated with snorkel-ing gear, I dive down with Ryan on my back. Sun stays with

Giselle to keep watch on the surface, and Talia holds onto Carter's shoulders while Ava swims beside him, holding his hand.

"What do you think we're looking for?" Ava asks me telepathically.

I hover in the water, spinning to get a better look at the reef. "A merpeople house. The last two spots my mom left items were long abandoned homes she used magic on. But be careful. The last one was filled with air, and Ryan got hurt."

Ryan digs his fingers into my shoulder, drawing my attention to him, and he points to something below us. I dive us deeper with Ava, Carter, and Talia coming up beside me. Ryan lets go of my shoulders and swims to a shimmering rock with something metal, covered in rust, sticking out of it.

Ryan tugs on it, releasing a few bubbles into the water to float to the surface. I gaze to watch them ascend, noticing a shadow darkening the surface west of Giselle and Sun. Giselle watches Sun swim circles below her, too busy enjoying the ocean together.

"There's a boat, Sun," I say, meeting his gaze through the water.

He pops to the surface to tug Giselle down, and they wait a dozen feet below. I draw my attention back to Ryan, tugging on whatever he found, and in doing so, he releases another breath of air. He gives me a thumbs up signal to motion to me that he needs air, and I dart forward to grab onto him.

"Another boat," Sun says from above us. "That's unusual

for this area unless—"

"They're part of Wren's fleet," I say. "I think they're searching for their pirate king." Because even though the Storm had pulled anchor, the boat and the Ocean's King didn't go far. This spot was only a few hours swim from the cove, less with Sun and Carter, and a bit farther from Reefaria. The Storm lies sunken somewhere to the north.

"Give me Ryan," Carter says. "I'll take him and Talia up for air."

Another shadow cuts across the water, stopping him in place. The boat will pass in another moment, but I'm not sure Talia has one. Ryan soon won't either.

"I'll swim them out farther," he says, looking at Ava.

I frown. "There's another boat. I think they're searching for the Storm."

"It's not safe to surface yet," Sun says.

"But they need air," I say.

Ava jets next to me, stopping me from taking Ryan from Carter. "Only us. Not them."

I frown. "But we can breathe water."

"But we can create air, too," she says.

I realize what she wants me to do, and I dart to the surface with her with Carter and Sun bringing the others with them. I spin myself upside down with my head pointing to the ocean floor.

"Hurry," Ava says. "The boat's circling back."

Panic sends me flicking my tail at the surface, breaking

through to create huge bubbles that Ava freezes with her ocean magic. Ryan sucks in a breath of the air I brought in from the surface until the bubble shrinks in the water. The silhouette crosses over the surface, circling, creating a bubbling wake, and Sun and Carter prepare to push the boat off course.

Talia meets my eyes through the water, and I watch her inhale another bubble of oxygen before Giselle does the same. My heart pounds in my ears, the ocean frozen around us in Ava's magic, and I fear we won't be able to stay here much longer. The boat doesn't seem to be going anywhere, making it unsafe to continue to surface.

"What do you want to do, Luna?" Ava asks. "There are only enough bubbles for two more breaths for everyone, and they'll need one to swim away with us."

Ryan touches my cheek, drawing my attention to him, and he brushes his lips against mine, sending me an image of a rusty knife through my mind. Without having to ask him, I know it's what was sticking out from the rock.

"Swim them far enough away to surface," I finally say. "I'll catch up."

I dive down a dozen feet toward the bottom, wanting more than ever to find what my mom left me, so I can return to the safety of the cove and get out of the pirate-infested sea, now seemingly worse.

"Ryan's following you, Luna," Ava says. "He doesn't want to leave."

I peer up at Ryan descending to me. The others remain

near the surface, and I motion for Sun to take Giselle and Talia away to break the surface where it's clear. If Ryan wants to stay, I'll see to it he's safe. I should get used to our life as it is with him needing the surface and me needing the sea.

Ava gathers the remaining air pockets into a bubble and brings it closer with her ocean magic. Carter circles near the surface, keeping his eyes on the three boats still cutting around the water without dropping their anchors. Their navigation systems might experience interference with the three of us in merpeople form, making it less likely for them to leave. If anything, it might make the vessels call in more boats.

"I don't like this," Ava says. "It's usually easy to ignore the boats, but now that I know these aren't like the ones under the scrutiny of different coast guards, I'm a bit worried. I had no idea piracy was a problem."

"You're still new to the ocean," I tell her, situating Ryan on my back again. "And honestly, neither did I. It's taken a few eye-opening events to show me exactly what we're dealing with, and it's not good."

"We'll get it all under control," she says. "Especially with your ocean magic."

Ryan releases me, and Ava helps him inhale another breath of the air bubble. We make our way back to the rock with the knife sunk into it. Ava brushes her fingers on the hilt but doesn't rip it free.

I lock my fingers around the rusty hilt, jerking it back and forth. It takes Ava hitting it with a magical current to dislodge it. An air bubble drifts from the hole where the knife cut into the rock, and I lean down and press my hands into the sturdy boulder, hidden deep in the sand. It shifts under my sudden pressure, falling out from under my hands.

I don't have a chance to move out of the way when a huge pocket of air clouds the water around us too quickly for Ava to control. It drifts me a few feet up, and I peer through the haze, feeling Ryan pinch my shoulders.

"Get out of the way," Carter calls from above.

He dives down to us as the water shudders, the hole now sucking the sea around us into it. Ava holds her hands out, fighting the current of the water plunging into the hole while the rest of the air trails to the surface. I sink down, caught in the strange current.

I lose my hold on Ryan, and he yells out in the water, releasing his breath. He's dragged toward the hole faster than me, getting caught in a sudden whirlpool that disappears into a place dark enough that I can't see the glowing light usually present in dark waters.

"Carter, help!" I call out. "We're getting sucked in."

I thrash in the current, knocking myself into Ryan, and he manages to lock his arms around me. Flicking my tail, I fight against the whirlpool the best I can. Carter swims around us in the opposite direction, trying to break the current, and Ava keeps her hands out, her ocean magic seeming to vanish from her fingers without helping me.

Hugging Ryan to me, I brace to get dragged into some

abyss, terrified Ryan won't be able to survive the depth of what lies through the cavernous hole shrouded in dark waters. My tail skims the edge of the rock, scraping my scales free, and I reach out to cling onto the rock, but the current suddenly releases me and Ryan, and I propel us up a few dozen feet, my heart pounding in my ears.

"Luna, you okay?" Carter asks from beneath me.

I push a bubble through my lips. "I—I think so."

Ryan squeezes my shoulder, and I spin to face his reddening face.

"But I have to break the surface," I say.

"Be quick while the boats are distracted," Ava says. "I caught as much as I could, but I wasn't ready."

I frown, jetting Ryan to the surface. He inhales a deep breath, gripping onto me like I'd even consider letting him go. Voices hum through the air, and a net drops across the water nearby startling me.

"Dive," Ryan says into my ear. "It's not s-safe here." He gasps another breath, waiting for me to take him under, but all I can do is peer at a collection of papers—money—littering the sea as the pirates skim the water to pick it up.

A whistle sounds through the air, and someone shouts to suit up, and I realize the vessels are about to send a few divers into the water. I don't know if it's the sudden appearance of money or that they know the Ocean's King wasn't far from here just days ago, but either way, they're searching the water, and the last thing I need is to bring more pirates to the cove.

Sinking under with Ryan, I return to Ava, still in the same spot I left her, and I catch sight of Carter gathering things from the sea. I realize Ava's ocean magic didn't stop us for a reason. She was using it to save what she could from rising to the surface to end up in the hands of the pirates.

"Oh, Ocean," I say, plucking a necklace from the water to cup it in my hands.

"Is that—"

I shake my head. "It belonged to my grandmer." I collect a few more items from the water and hold them to my chest. "These are their land things. My mom said in her journal that she took what she could to sea after they died on land. I never knew them."

"I think I got what's important," Carter says, swimming up to me.

"I don't think my magic's here. I think I'd feel it, and all I feel is like returning to shore." I shift Ryan to face me in the water. My heart hurts not being able to tell him anything telepathically, so I just shrug my shoulders and kiss him to send an image of the cove to him.

Concern crosses his face, and he motions to the pirates scouring the water above us. Again, I lift and drop my shoulders. All we can do in this moment is head to land and try to piece together my scattered life the best we can.

PIRATE INFESTATION

SANDRA SITS ON THE porch of the beach cottage she shares with Darren. She's the only human apart from my biological dad to remain on Celestiana Cove since the colonies started emerging from the sea. I haven't talked much with her, but I do know she stays due to her lack of human ties in the civilized world.

Ryan kicks through the sand next to me, carrying the items we managed to intercept from the hands of the pirates. Sandra stands from her hand-made by a mermaid wooden chair and holds her arms wide.

"I was wondering when you were going to stop by," she

says, wrapping me in a hug and greeting me with a kiss to each of my cheeks in the customary fashion of merpeople. "You two hungry? Darren should be back any minute."

"Oh, I'm okay. Maybe Ryan, though. Thanks, Sandra," I say, shifting on my feet. "Is it okay if we wait?"

Sandra nods her head and motions us inside. "You bet. Help yourself to whatever you like, Ryan."

Ryan sets my stuff on the small dining room table and takes a plate from Sandra, who brings me a glass of yellow liquid. I take a sip of the fruit juice before gulping the whole glass, making her smile.

"You mermaids sure have a sweet tooth," she says, pouring me another.

"It's all the salt," I say, spinning the knife Ryan had pulled from the underwater rock on the table.

Commotion sounds outside, and I watch through the open door as Tide sets Darren on his feet. The two of them shake water from their hair, and Tide shakes Darren's hand before strolling the beach in the other direction.

Darren grabs a towel from a chest on the porch and rubs it over his head, greeting me with a smile. His forehead wrinkles even more, weathered from his years living on the cove, making him look older than any of my human friends' parents on land. I get up from my seat and cross the room, wrapping my arms around him before kissing his scruffy cheeks.

"What a nice surprise, Luna," he says. "Looks like you found yourself some treasure. How was the swim?"

I puff air through my lips. "A disaster. Pirates showed up."

Darren twists his mouth. "Was afraid of that. The ones on shore are smug as heck, clinging onto hope that they'll be rescued."

Ryan clears his throat. "You saw my dad?" Ryan hasn't said much about Wren, and I know he's conflicted by his love and dislike of him, something I haven't pushed much about. The royal guards wanted to give them all time to cool off.

"Quiet guy," Darren says. "At least compared to some of them. The others act exactly how I remember from the few months I spent at sea. Hated it, but it was the only way to see your mom after your grandparents died. I thought I could get rich quick and help her return to land, but then... You know what? None of that matters now. I'm just glad you're here. I'll do what I can to help the royal guard deal with them."

I blink a few times. I knew Darren had joined a ship's crew, but I had assumed a fishing vessel. Then again, he wouldn't have had access to the waters near Pearlestria. I want so badly to beg him to tell me more, but he plops down at the table with Ryan and peers over the stuff I brought to shore.

"Hey, I recognize this knife," Darren says, picking up the rusted weapon to inspect it. "Marlin gave it to me on my eighteenth birthday and suggested I use it to bring your mom the biggest tuna I could wrangle from the ocean. You can imagine how confused I was over that."

Ryan chuckles from his seat. "So did you?"

Darren sets the knife back down and laughs. "Not until I

had my beautiful mermaid take me. And it was the size of my arm. But you know what? It wasn't the fish that impressed Tiana. It was the fact that I tried. If Luna ever asks you fishing, you bet your ass you better go. It'll be the best time of your life. You don't need a tail either. Fish will come right to you."

Tears trickle from my eyes, splashing on my cheeks as I listen to Darren share his experience of loving my mom with Ryan. And Tiana? I never heard anyone call her that before. It makes me feel closer to Darren than ever, getting to listen to the memories he has of my mom that no one but him can share with me.

"I plan to do lots of that," Ryan says, reaching out to touch my cheek, smearing my tears with his finger without pointing out the fact that I'm crying. Darren and Sandra don't say anything either, and Darren continues to fill the silence, telling me what he remembers from living next to a house full of merpeople.

Talia knocks on the doorframe, drawing my attention away from Darren, and I squeeze Ryan's hand once before excusing myself to join my cousin. A few of the guards' mates hang out on shore, sunbathing, and I peer around, half expecting to see Ryan's mom, but she's not here. I won't call to her either, not until Ryan's ready.

Talia bumps her shoulder with mine. "You holding up okay? I know it's been hectic since we've come to shore. This place is beautiful."

I nod. "It is. I can tell Ryan likes it."

"What about you?" she asks.

I shrug. "Is it weird that I can't see myself staying? I'm already antsy to leave. It's just—"

"The whole island reminds you of everything wrong in your life? I mean, that's how I'd feel."

"I just want to get everything under control and get the map back," I say.

"You know, we don't need the map." Talia swings her arm in the same rhythm as I do, and I watch my cousin in my peripheral vision. She stares into the horizon, her black hair blowing behind her. Sunlight sparkles in her light blue eyes, shining bright against her complexion. I might be a Lazaro like Darren, but I still feel very much a Torres as well, strolling with my cousin, seeing part of my mom in her pretty face. "I've spent so much time looking at it that I could probably recreate it from memory."

I stop in the sand and turn to face her. "You have a photographic memory, too?"

She lifts and drops her shoulders. "I guess you could call it that. I was pretty obsessed. And lonely. I'm just—" Talia throws her arms around me, hugging me to her. "I'm so happy you're okay. I was pretty mad at you for abandoning me like you did."

I pull back and nod my head. "I'm sorry. So, so sorry. I was so afraid of losing you when I just got you. I wanted to protect you."

"But I've been pretty good at protecting myself all my life," she says. "And I could've protected you, too. I still want to help you if you let me."

I bob my head, my hair bouncing with the movement. I never knew I wanted something so badly than to have Talia help me and Ryan find the rest of the pieces of my mom's life she left behind.

"I do. So much," I say. "But you know it might be dangerous."

"Wouldn't be anything new to me."

A huge wave of water surprises the two of us, nearly knocking us off our feet. I hit the sand while Talia lands in the arms of Tide, and he offers her a smile I'm not sure I've ever seen on his face, but it speaks to my mermaid essence.

I raise my eyebrows, meeting Tide's gaze, ready to say something, but Talia laughs, using his shoulders to get to her feet. She offers a hand to help me to mine, and I stare at her as she stares at Tide with her own smile.

"That's one way to sweep someone off their feet," she teases him.

"You're the catch of my day," he muses.

She laughs and shifts on her feet. I wonder if she even realizes that the sea's messenger might summon the courage to ask her to court him. I can see the wonder on Tide's face looking at Talia, reminding me of the same curiosity I thought about when I first laid eyes on Ryan.

Tide forces his gaze to leave Talia to look at me, and he adds, "I didn't mean to interrupt you and your beautiful cousin while you bond, princess, but there's a problem."

"A problem?" My sudden thoughts about the possibility of Talia and Tide, whose names even sound perfect together, being interested in each other washes out to the waves with his words.

"The pirates came across Attilonious," he says.

"Oh, Ocean. Is he—"

"It's the pirates I'm concerned over. Attilonious is outraged by the new inhabitants."

Talia mumbles something under her breath I can't make out, but whatever she says makes Tide grin and say, "I can escort you with the princess if you'd like."

Talia glances at me. "If you want to stay here, I can handle everyone for you."

"It'd be my honor to assist," Tide says, speaking up.

I sigh and shake my head. "It's my dad and Ryan's. We should really handle this."

"I'd still like to come."

I can only nod. "Let's go tell the others."

Looks like I can't ignore the pirate infestation much longer.

REUNION

"NONE OF YOU HAVE to come," I say, handing Ryan the waterproof bag to carry on his shoulders. "The royal guard will emerge if I need them."

"Oh, but I do. Wren deserves to be sucker punched in the face, and I'm going to be the one to do it," Giselle says, cracking her knuckles.

Talia folds her arms. "And I'm taking the second spot."

Sun smiles from behind Giselle. "You'll be gifted with many talents, my love. And I'll teach you many more. You're a warrior in the making already."

"Dang right I am," she says, tipping her head back to look

at him upside down. "I better get a badass red tail or something, too."

Sun kisses her forehead. "You'll be as stunning as a fiery sunset regardless."

Ryan chuckles from next to me despite my friends strategizing the punishment they feel Ryan's dad deserves. I'm not sure he doesn't, but the news I'm about to deliver might be worse than anything anyone could come up with.

"No one's punching anyone," I say, sighing. "He's not worth hurting either of your hands over."

"And how would you know it hurts to punch someone?" Giselle asks.

Ryan rests his hands on my shoulders. "My mate has a better punch than I do."

Giselle releases a high-pitched squeal that makes even herself wince. "I have to see!"

"You sure Giselle's not going to transform into a dolphin instead of a mermaid on the full moon?" Talia asks.

I can't stop the laughter from escaping my lips. Even though I'm super nervous about hitting the water to swim to the other side of the island to face Ryan's dad's fury, it doesn't seem so scary with my friends by my side.

Giselle sticks out her tongue. "Well, at least we know I'm not a siren with the sudden urge to lure men with my voice to their watery graves."

"Really, Gi?" Carter asks, strolling next to Ava in the sand.

Ava swings their hands between them, raising her eyebrows

at Giselle. "We're trying to shed the whole murderous mermaid persona."

My gaze falls on the crown on her head, sparkling in the sunlight. Ava's loose blond hair cascades around her shoulders, and even only wearing a bikini with a sarong, she's stunning. Digging into the bag strung over Carter's shoulder, she pulls out another crown made from twisted silver, sparkling in the sunlight with aquamarine stones the same color as Talia's—and my mom's—eyes. It's one of my mom's crowns from the castle in Pearlestria, and I can't help wondering why we're supposed to wear pieces that don't matter on the land.

Ava plops the crown on my head. "Darren suggested we wear them. Pirates interpret wealth as a form of power, and I don't want to have to summon a tidal wave to prove a point if I don't have to."

"My dad might not care, but it might help with the others," Ryan says, sweeping my hair behind my ears to straighten the crown. Sparkles from the silver and jewels dance across his face, and he shades his eyes.

"I still think you should allow Sun to summon the guards," Giselle whispers. "Nothing scarier than a bunch of buff people strolling out of the water with abs hard enough to scrub laundry on—speaking of—when are we getting a washer and dryer here?"

I snort and cover my mouth with my hand. "You're thinking about laundry?"

She glances at Sun, trailing her gaze down his bare chest

and stomach. "Among other things. It's better than the alternative."

Heat washes through me, and my cheeks uncontrollably warm under the influence of Giselle's emotions. Carter and Ava share a look, their faces morphing through several expressions I can't decipher, and then Carter rubs his hands down his cheeks.

Ava clears her throat. "Giselle, do I need to summon a cold current? Because if Luna's making that face for the reason I think she is, you need to figure out how to control your new bond to her."

Giselle's lust washes into confusion.

Crossing the space between us, I wrap my arms around Giselle for a moment and then pull away, still holding onto her shoulders. "You're fine. I will manage. I've prepared all my life to experience someone having a part of my essence. It's just a little weird getting used to because, well, you really love your mate."

Giselle's hand flies to her mouth, her eyes turning into two saucers. Sun chuckles from behind her, but not in a way that he's laughing at her. He's enjoying my admission about Giselle's feelings for him.

A wave of her embarrassment hits me next. "Oh, God. We have to break this bond."

I frown. "What? But Giselle—"

"Oh, God," she repeats. Tears blur her eyes. "Aw, man. No, I didn't mean—" She gasps. "Crap. I can feel you, too. And I'm the worst soul sister ever. I didn't mean to hurt your feelings. I love that our flashlight hearts blink together. I can't wait to get back to dancing in our condo to our new strobes."

I giggle and pull her close again. "I like the sound of that. But first—"

"Punching pirates," she finishes for me.

I blow strands of hair from my face. "Whatever makes you happy. You'll fit right in. They apparently like that sort of thing."

"Oh, jeez. And to think I thought you'd come back a hardened criminal. You're still so blissfully innocent, my beautiful, life-saving princess."

I blush.

She laughs. "Who still loves cheesy compliments."

Ava and Talia join the two of us, and we stroll into the waves with our mates trailing behind us, whispering to each other. Ryan grins at me when our eyes meet, and he and Giselle wait with Talia on the surface.

The swim to the other side of the island turns into a race between Sun and Carter, and Ava creates a current strong enough to zoom us past them, making both of them laugh in my mind. The place the royal guard dropped the pirates off at is as far from the cove as one could get, has enough fruit and plant life to eat if they fail to hunt fish, and a waterfall roars in walking distance inland, which is the same reason my dad ended up nearby. No wonder they ran into each other.

I don't think anyone considered the fact that my dad is better off alone, and especially away from the pirates he seems to despise more than even regular humans. He's probably as territorial as ever, claiming this section as his own prison kingdom.

Yells muffle from the surface, sending my heart racing. I flick my tail and dart to the surface with Ryan. Sun and Giselle pop up next to us along with Talia and Carter, followed by Ava. The ocean swells around us, and Ava shifts her gaze to mine.

"Luna, is that you?" she asks. "I know it's not me, but I also know the water here likes to do what it wants."

I throw my hands up. "Maybe? My mom said the ocean reacts to me, but I can't control it at all. Not without my magic."

"This is amazing," she whispers.

"You mean dangerous."

Ava brings her hand to the surface and pulls the wave higher, taking control of it. "I can't wait to see how even more amazing you are. Don't get me wrong. I appreciate what the sea gives me, but I'll be so grateful when you can help me with things no one else can. Like now, when I need to break up a fight."

"You should let them take care of themselves," Talia quips, her voice deepening as she grips onto Carter's shoulders.

My dad lifts Titus off his feet by his neck while both Skull and Ali attempt to stop him. Gopi looks like he wants nothing to do with anyone, and Hawk sprawls out in the sand with his T-shirt over his head. A few other men crouch in the shade just watching the fight unfold. But the closer I get, the more I realize Titus wasn't the first one to get in front of my dad's anger.

The crew looks roughed up more than I remember. Compared to the pirates, my dad towers nearly a foot over the tallest of the group and probably wouldn't tire even if they all attacked him at once.

Sun swims a few feet closer to shore. "Attilonious still has quite the power, even without the sea."

"Nothing compared to my incredible queen of a mate," Carter says.

Ava flicks her fingers and sends the swell crashing toward the shore. It knocks everyone off their feet, sending a few pirates scattering while others tumble in the tide rolling back to us. Dad stands back up, peers at the water, and strides away to lean his broad back against a palm tree.

"See?" Carter adds. "Even Attilonious backs down."

I duck underwater and transform before everyone else. Swimming ahead, Ryan and I wash onto the beach, and he helps me to my feet. The pirate crew doesn't notice us emerge except for Wren. He doesn't leave his spot in the sand next to Dara. She grabs his hand and shakes her head, guaranteeing that he doesn't rush us.

I wrap the sarong Ava gave me around my body and step forward, clearing my throat to draw everyone's attention to me. But a scream sounds out behind me, startling me. I don't even have a chance to react as Talia runs from the waves and on the beach.

"Attilonious!" she yells. "Come here and face me!"

Ryan swears under his breath, and I get my legs to cooperate and dash behind her. Dad straightens his shoulders and saunters from his spot against the tree. His gray-streaked hair blows behind him in a breeze, and his dark sapphire eyes flick from Talia to me.

A strange look crosses his face, his hard features softening. He takes an automatic step back as Talia flies forward.

"Celes—"

Before my dad can utter what I think is about to be my mom's name, Talia bends her knees, jumping up, and swings her fist out, clocking my dad in the jaw. He stumbles back, touching his chin, but he doesn't react as she goes after him again.

"Talia, stop," I say, closing the space between us. I grab her by her arm and pull her back even though my dad doesn't do anything except stand there. "Please, you're bleeding."

She cups her injured fist in her free hand and glowers past me. "I'm sorry, Luna. He deserved it."

"She's totally right," Giselle says from behind us.

I hold my hands up. "Just—" I turn my gaze to my dad. "Go away, please."

"Luna..."

"Please," I whisper again. I didn't account for Talia's feelings toward my dad, and I wish I would've realized this might have been the reason she wanted to venture to this side of the island after what my dad did to our land family—her own dad. He's responsible for the fear Talia carried toward merpeople all her life. But going after my dad now doesn't change anything, and I can't stand the thought that she'll hurt herself trying to feel better. It's best to give her as much love as she needs so that she can't summon the hate anymore. But for now, all I can do is ask my dad to leave. Another consequence he must live with for his actions.

His already saddened face twists into a deeper frown, and he spins and heads down the beach and toward the cliffs that will prevent him from taking the shoreline all the way to the cove. My heart thrashes against my ribcage, and my own hurt washes over me, but seeing Talia's reaction makes me not want to be around him. Not now. Not after our last conversation and not after everything my mom went through.

I don't have the energy to deal with trying to summon forgiveness in me while summoning the strength to face the pirates. Hawk gets to his feet and steps forward in the sand, kicking his way over to me. Sun blocks his way, using his sheer size as a shield. He doesn't know Hawk's on our side, and neither do the other pirates, because some of the crew shout that Hawk can take on Sun.

"It's okay, Sun," I say stepping around him.

I surprise Hawk with a hug, holding his hands in mine for a moment. "I'm glad to see you're okay. Did the guards treat you all right?"

"Tide offered to take me back to the cove, but I thought I might be needed here with this bunch of assholes," he says, jerking his neck to peer at the other crewmembers.

"Ya bastard!" Skull yells. "If we were still at sea, I'd feed your traitor ass to the sharks, brother."

Anger courses through me, and I spin on my feet and stride toward the heavily tattooed pirate. He leers at me, his lips stretching at the corners, daring me to do something he can react to. Straightening his back, he attempts to stand taller than me, but I still manage to meet him at eye level.

I jab my index finger in his chest. "First of all, sharks don't eat people, and it's mean of you to try to bait them to do so."

He raises his eyebrows without a word.

"And second, you will not threaten my new friend. Hawk is a true pirate and will be rewarded by the sea for his loyalty to me."

"Like this island? Sorry, princess. Pretty trees don't cut it for me."

"Oh, this isn't the reward. It's your punishment. You're stuck here for however long it takes." I shift my gaze to stare at the others. "That goes for all of you. Except for Dara and Hawk. They get to come with me."

Titus charges toward me, his hands curled into fists. "You can't do this, you little b—"

A swell rises and whips into him, cutting off his words and knocking his feet out from under him. His back thuds into the sturdy trunk of a palm tree, making him wheeze a breath. Ryan drags him to his feet, swinging his arm back. I touch his fist and stop him. I know it's how Ryan has survived all these years, using his fists against people who go out of their way to make the lives of others miserable, but it must stop.

"Not like this," I say, sliding my arm across Ryan's bare chest. "I will not scare them into complying. That's what my dad would've done."

Ryan releases Titus, shoving him back into the sand, still glowering. "We are not our fathers," he whispers so quietly only I can hear the breath of his words in my ear.

Wren clears his throat from his spot on the sand. Everyone falls silent, still giving the man who they show respect as their captain their undivided attention. I even give him mine, curious as to what he has to say and how he plans to get out of the position he's in.

"You will fail," Wren says, locking his dark gaze to mine. "Love and dreams don't garner respect and compliance. Ruthless authority and threats do. How do you plan to take the surface? With hugs? With promises of a better future?"

My brows pucker together. "I don't need to promise a better future."

He scoffs at me. "You think turbulent water and stormy seas will keep the fearless at bay?"

"It did you, didn't it?" I ask.

He smiles—but not in a bright and cheerful way. His eyes hold a darkness that leaves a chill deep in my heart despite the humid air. "You think the threat of dragging us to the deepest part of the sea will do?"

I remain expressionless.

"Because you will have to prove a point, *princess*. It'll come down to them or you. Like with the Storm. You think your friends will see this through when you put your life above theirs? When the sea doesn't give you a choice? I know that's why my ship sank."

"You have no idea."

"But I do."

I kick through the sand to get into Wren's face, fury and despair washing through me as he reminds me of what the call of the sea, the whisper of the magic begging to return to me had done. It wasn't Wren who had put my friends' lives—Ryan's life—in jeopardy. It was me. It was me and the ocean.

"You know I had hope for you? I hoped that we could change the world together. That you could make up for everything you put Ryan through."

"I've made him stronger."

"No wonder the ocean called to Nalani. No wonder she—"

Wren launches from the sand at me, knocking me back before anyone else can intervene. "No one come any closer," he says, spitting in my face.

I cringe, stiffening under his hot hands. "This is why the ocean sent me to you." I can't stop the words from coming from my mouth. "This is why it gave me Ryan. So that I could save him from you. Like it saved Nalani from you."

Wren pulls back his arm, and I close my eyes, bracing myself for what's to come. A shadow darkens my eyelids, and I expect the ocean to wash over the both of us to pull me from his painful grip. Water droplets splash across my face, making me flutter open my eyes.

"Release her, Wren," a soft voice says.

I peer at a figure haloed in sunlight. "Nalani? You didn't have to come to shore."

"Queen Ava said the same thing, but I'm glad I did. It's been too long since I've seen my land family."

Wren falls back into the sand and stares at one of the best healers I know in Reefaria. She kneels in the sand next to me, lifting my hair and checking out my skin to make sure I'm okay before turning to Ryan.

"My son," she whispers. "The intended mate of a princess. I never imagined I could be this happy."

Ryan doesn't move. He doesn't say anything. He doesn't take his eyes off mine.

I sit up and get to my feet, putting space between me and Wren. Ryan takes me in his arms, cupping my face, sharing a thousand silent thoughts with me.

He wasn't ready for this reunion, especially for it to happen in front of his dad. His eyes beg me to help him stay in control. To stop him from reacting.

Leaning in, I brush my lips to his, kissing him until he finally releases a deep breath. "It's okay," I say to him. "Come on. I'll take you to the water."

He shakes his head, swallowing and watching his parents stare one another down.

"I—I don't understand," Wren says, his voice low. "Nalani, you're alive."

She offers him a tight smile and nods. "Not alive. Reborn.

And you, Wren, are just as I remember. Handsome and brutal. The cause of my human undoing."

MOON STONE

NALANI TRAIPSES THROUGH THE sand next to me, guiding me away from the stunned and silent pirates. Something shifted in Ryan's dad, causing him to shut down and lose himself in his thoughts. I had expected more from the fallen pirate king—rage, ruthlessness, some sort of fight for the woman who fell into a different current to take her into a life of magic far from the dangers of the surface—but all he did was shut his mouth and turn away.

I squeeze Ryan's fingers as he walks on the other side of me in a silence different than his dad's. His hurt washes over me, and I know how abandoned he feels. Because before he knew his mom was alive, he thought she was gone and not by her own freewill—but he wouldn't understand. The same idea still applies. She never stood a chance any other way regardless of her ties to land. The call of the sea is strong, so strong even a fear of the ocean can't keep it away—and the laws my dad enforced would not have let Nalani have a life any other way. She had to leave part of her heart on the surface with Ryan, with Wren even, because even a strong-willed human can't fight against the strength of the ocean—especially one as unforgiving as my dad, controlled by his magic.

"You're angry with me, Ryan," his mom says, reading the hard lines of his expression. "But I hope you can find it in you to forgive me. I never had the intention to leave you. I never even planned to follow my heart into the sea. But—"

Ryan pulls me to a stop to face his mom. "You don't have to explain, Mom."

"But I do. I've been drowning in my guilt from the moment I gave my last breath and took Sandy's."

"Your mate?" he asks.

She nods. "I'd love for you to meet him."

Ryan falls silent, turning to the sea. Several merpeople from the guard swim in the shallows, but none of them surface. Sandy wouldn't unless invited by Nalani or ordered by me.

I open my mouth to tell Ryan how nice the merman is, how important he is to the colonies, acting as the right hand to Sun and currently taking his place as head of the Reefaria guards while Sun courts Giselle, but I refrain from saying any of those things. I know what it's like to find out that part of your life is a lie, and he's already been through so much—we've been through so much—I know he just needs to let it sink in.

Ryan kicks his foot into the sand, dusting it over my feet. "Maybe some other time. It's a lot to take in. I thought you were dead. And finding out you have the kind of life I want with Luna—I—I'm sorry, Mom." He swivels on his feet and strides a few feet away, linking his hands on the back of his head.

Tears burn my eyes by the unexpectedness of his words. I knew Ryan envisioned a future together with him transforming into a merman. I knew he wanted a life of adventure, exploring the seas by my side, following me wherever I led him. And even though he swears that he doesn't care where the sea has taken us, and he would never be angry that I saved my best friend, he's hurt that our choice was taken away, and we'll never get that life. He already thought he wasn't good enough to be my mate, and knowing the sea gave his mom such an existence— one that left him in the hands of his dad—wears down on him.

Strolling forward, I hug Ryan from behind, resting my chin on his shoulder. His tense muscles relax, and he spins in my arms to face me, his eyes glassing over but tears never falling as he blinks them away. "I'm sorry," he whispers. "I didn't mean that our life now isn't what I want. We're still going to have an amazing life."

I touch his cheek, running my fingers along his jaw. "I know. I can't wait to plan our adventure."

"And you will. I just know it." Nalani smiles at me, her green eyes sparkling in the sun against her dark tan complexion. Her black hair hangs in an intricate braid down her back, glimmering with a strand of pearls on fishing line wound through the tresses. Her ears sparkle with human earrings, and I wonder if they were something she took to sea. I didn't attend her transformation ceremony, and now that I think about it, I wonder why. I can't remember what would've kept me away besides my dad.

I return her smile with one of my own. "I promise to always take care of your son, no matter the land or sea."

"I know you will. I've dreamed of it. I always knew that even if I left Ryan, the ocean would see to it to bring me back to him. It's what led me into the deep, princess."

I blink a few times at her words. "The ocean spoke to you?"

She glances at Ryan, now watching the both of us, listening intently to his mom. "I believe so—through my dreams. I dreamed of a beautiful mermaid with a silver tail and eyes like the seas in the shallows off the shores of islands. She rose to the surface, her skin sparkling like it was dusted in gold or pearl, and she held out her arms to Ryan, taking him in her embrace, making him smile. I'll never forget the stone glittering on her neck, and how Ryan ripped it free."

My breath catches, listening to her recount a dream she's held onto all these years. One that makes my heart race thinking about.

"And I dropped it in the sea," Ryan whispers.

"You remember," Nalani says, grinning at her son.

"The Mahina Stone." He draws his gaze to mine, his brows pinching together, wrinkling his forehead. "The Moon Stone. Luna's stone."

"And the prince set sail, fighting the rough waves and vicious pirates to find the missing princess's necklace."

Ryan stiffens, his Adam's apple popping up and down in his throat. "It wasn't her necklace. It was her heart."

Nalani reaches out and squeezes his shoulder. "That's right. It was never really a jewel after all. And it looks like you've found it washed ashore just like I imagined."

"So you left me because of a dream." It's not a question. Ryan's low voice blends with the roar of the ocean. "You left with a hope to see me again."

Her dreamy gaze shines in the light. "It wasn't hope."

"You couldn't have known."

"I'm sorry," she whispers. "I know it doesn't make up for anything. But it was one of many sacrifices I had to make. If I had stayed with your dad on that ship, I was afraid you'd have stayed right along with me."

"You don't know that."

"But I do—the sea—"

"To hell with the sea!" he yells, shocking me.

Tears trickle from Nalani's eyes, splashing on her cheeks. Silently, she steps away from Ryan, letting go of his hand before turning to me. My heart aches, seeing the pain growing within both of them, feeling the throb in my chest coming from Ryan, but I don't know what to do. I don't know how to deal with this circumstance.

Nalani reaches out and touches her fingers to my chest where my heart flickers against the hot sun. I hold her hand against me for a moment in silence, reading her quiet thoughts, knowing she must return to the water so Ryan can process.

She leaves us on the beach and saunters into the waves. Ryan exhales a long breath when she disappears in the surf. Stepping forward, I wrap my arms around Ryan and hug him, running my hand over the tight muscles of his back. He sinks into me without a word, his body begging me just to hold him and never let him go.

"The mermaid with the silver tail and blue eyes," he whispers. "I was only a kid when she told me that story, and I forgot about it. It used to make me so mad. I blamed myself for losing the princess's heart, and now that I think about it, what if it wasn't a dream?"

"You didn't lose my heart, Ryan."

"But I kind of did." He's talking about the fact that I gave part of my essence to Giselle. He doesn't say it in a bad way, just like it's a fact. And it's kind of true. But he didn't lose it. I didn't lose it, either. It lights up my best friend's chest, reminding me how thankful I am that Ryan gave his chance to transform for something so very important to me.

I don't try to argue with him. Instead, I say, "Then I guess you'll just have to let me take yours. I promise to be careful."

He rests his head on mine. "I'll give you anything."

"Just you. You and your heart."

"Forever."

I smile. "Forever?"

"I promise."

The moon hovers above the glowing ocean stretching before us. I rest my back on Ryan's chest, and he hugs me against him in the sand. The warm fire keeps the chill of the cool night away, and I slide my fingers up and down through his, playing absently with our hands.

"I started on the map, Luna," Talia says from the doorway to Ava and Carter's house.

"And we brought back anything that looked remotely valuable from the Ocean's King." Giselle's voice hums over the sound of the waves. Sun carries her on his shoulders, her legs dangling on his chest, and they create a long shadow across the sand. "And dang it, I can't wait until the next full moon. The sun just had to rise to stop me from embracing my mermazingness."

Sun lifts Giselle off his shoulders and sets her onto her feet in the sand. "Which is a good thing, my love. You have a few weeks of class until summer vacation."

She groans. "God, I'm not looking forward to telling my mom. Her dang slogan turned into school first, mermaid later when I told her about you, babe."

He chuckles. "We'll manage. Right, Princess Luna?"

I swallow. "Right." Because Giselle is technically my responsibility. It's been the tradition of the sea, at least, until she officially couples with Sun. And if Giselle is anything like Ava was... "I will remain by your side until you're ready."

Giselle's eyebrows lower on her forehead, and she brushes her sopping dark hair over her shoulder. "Um, what about Ryan? I was planning to stay with Sun in Reefaria."

"And Luna can take the royal reef," Sun says.

"Oh, no she can't—"

"My love, Luna transformed you."

"And you're my soon-to-be mate."

"But tradition says—"

Meeting me with her wild eyes, she stares at me for a moment before glancing to Sun and then to Ryan. "Ava! Carter!" she yells, placing her hands on her hips while strutting toward where Ava appears from behind Talia. "We have a problem. Can you explain to that handsome ass merman boyfriend of mine that Luna has done enough by saving my life, and I don't need her to be my mer-mom. He is capable of handling me."

Ava's gaze flicks to mine. It's obvious from her expression that she has no idea what to do or how to handle the situation. This is something she'd ask me. As for Giselle, I want to be there for her. I want to teach her everything she needs to know like she showed me how to live on land. I can help her, because I can feel everything she's experiencing through our bond, and that won't change. Sun might feel a muffled version of her—at least, I think—but until they officially couple, I'd be better.

Carter whispers something into Ava's ear, and even though

Giselle can't hear it, annoyance and guilt rush through her to me. I don't have to ask her to know that she suspects they might agree with Sun.

Ava reaches for Giselle. "I'll help, too. We're in this together."

"But you have plans this summer to help your sister with her wedding. It's unfair for Luna to have to leave Ryan on shore." She throws her hands up. "You know what? I got this. I don't need to be treated like a dang merbabe learning to swim."

Sun smirks at me. "My love, there's no doubt that you can do this, but you shouldn't have to be alone. If Princess Luna—"

"I am a strong, independent woman. I've survived the rule of Attilonious. I've kept up a land identity for my best friend. I survived an island prison. I sort of survived pirates, which is close enough. I will survive my first full moon as a mermaid. Like I said, I got this."

I step closer. "Gi."

She raises her hand at me. "No, Luna. No arguing. I'm good. You are not invited to Reefaria. And I'm taking the royal reef. Alone. Because I got this, and those bone-hard abs of my sexy ass boyfriend can't be comfortable as a pillow."

Sun chuckles. "But my arms might do."

She fake glares at him. "We'll see."

He smirks. "Whatever you want, my love. My feisty soon-to-be mermaid princess."

"Princess?" she asks, looking at me.

I shrug. "Technically."

"Damn straight I'm a princess." She attempts to hold her face serious when her voice shakes with oncoming laughter. "And I command everyone to stop worrying about me and focus on more important things. Like Luna's magic."

Ryan curses under his breath, turning my attention to him. "And the pirate problem."

I frown. "That's handled."

Shaking his head, he points at the dark ocean. "I'm not so sure. Do you see that?"

I squint my eyes like it'll help me narrow in on the light on the horizon. And not just a light. Another ship. "It won't come closer."

"There's another," Talia says, strolling from the door to the beach to stand next to me.

"Over there, too," Giselle adds.

Ryan groans. "This isn't good."

"They're searching for your dad, but they can't get any closer." I study the few boats, knowing the truth to my words. "The magic here will capsize any unwelcome boat."

Sliding his hand through mine, Ryan tugs me a few feet toward the water, staring at the fleet of boats peppering the distant dark horizon. "If they think the Ocean's King is missing and my dad is lost to the ocean, there will be a shift in power. There will be a fight over who gets to take over the sea."

10

A MERMAID'S HEART

"THEY'RE DISPERSING." I PUSH the thought through the sea to Sun, Ava, and Carter.

"Good, because that's five ships too many so close to the cove and a lot of people to rescue," Ava says, swimming up beside me to watch the wakes of the vessels glitter from the light of the moon.

"And control," Carter adds. "These aren't innocent people we'd be saving. On land, they have the advantage, and it could put the cove at risk. Having Attilonious and the crew of the Ocean's King is bad enough."

"There are other ways." Sun flicks his tail, jetting up closer to the surface. "Queen Ava, we must think of the colonies first. We cannot risk our lives for those who will be so quick to destroy us."

Ava's face twists into a frown at the thought, but she doesn't respond out loud. It's obvious from her eyes shifting to Carter's that they're having a private conversation.

"We know," Carter says, speaking up for Ava. "But we can't make and act on rash decisions."

I swim closer to Sun and touch him on the shoulder. "Carter is right. There are other ways. Other islands. There's hope."

Sun looks at me, his long blond hair floating between us. "But there's also danger, Princess Luna. You cannot deny the atrocious acts upon us."

"Give me a day to talk to Ryan. He knows the surface. He knows the pirate ways," I say, meeting Ava's gaze.

She releases a small bubble through her lips, and it travels toward the surface. "I don't see the harm in that. I'll double check the magic before Carter and I leave to arrange more supplies. You can send Tide for me if you need to, but I think giving it the rest of the week until we get back will allow for things to settle. As long as the vessels keep away from here, we'll be okay. I'll force the currents on them if they don't leave by the time we get back, but the last thing I want is to attract more attention."

"But Queen—"

Carter reaches out and squeezes Sun's shoulder. "Trust Luna and her mate to decide. Pirates have caused havoc on the surface forever. And Ava's right, as long as they stay away, we'll be fine and can still manage safe passage with the supply boat. My mate will assure it."

"So will I," I say.

"Focus on Giselle, Sun. Your intended mate needs you to be by her side to help prepare her for the transition. You need to get her back to La Tortuga Point because Luna can't right now. She must act on my behalf during my absence as my advisor," Ava says. "We'll be gone until next weekend."

I blink a few times at her words. "Are you sure you want to leave me in charge, even though I messed everything up?"

Flicking her tail, she closes the distance and hugs me. "You messed nothing up, understand? We all have tough decisions to make, and you made them to the best of your ability."

Her words make me smile, though my heart still overflows with guilt. I can't help wondering what could have been if I had known about the secrets of my pod sooner. If I had known that my mom had taken my magic for safekeeping. I can't help worrying that I might never find it, and that my adventure with Ryan will end with us here, treading the surface, because he needs the land and I need the sea.

A wave of worry washes over me, coming from the shore. Ava must sense that my mind wanders back to the shallows, because she links our fingers together and tugs me along without waiting for me to say anything else.

Ryan, Giselle, and Talia wait for us in the sand, and Ryan

picks me up from the cresting waves and hugs me in the surf. I rest my head on his shoulder and watch Ava and Giselle stroll from the beach with their mates behind them. Talia remains on the shore in the sand, watching the horizon.

"Everything okay?" she asks, hugging herself while still looking at the water. "Are we still good to go tomorrow?"

I release a long breath into Ryan's shirt, and he slowly pulls himself away but doesn't let go of my hand. His eyes speak volumes, and I know without having to ask that he worries about bringing her deeper into the dangerous surface world, especially if Wren's fleet of pirates will be fighting to steal the reign of the Ocean's King.

But I can't let pirates stop me from continuing on my current. My mom said I'd need my magic. Nalani's story said we'd have to face ruthless pirates. Even if it scares me to bring her, I know she accepts my excuse not to, and I know she can handle it—maybe better than I can.

"Of course," I say, instead of telling her no. "This was always supposed to be our adventure anyway. My mom left everything to us."

Talia must sense Ryan's hesitation, because she says, "And you could definitely use someone like me to defend our boat, especially with what we're up against. You know, I've prepared all my life for the dangers of the sea."

"I could tell. That punch you gave Luna's dad... It's safe to say I feel pretty safe around the both of you." Ryan smirks, glancing from Talia to me.

She grins at me. "No pirate stands a chance. Th' booty be ours."

"Definitely." I laugh as she attempts to speak like one of the pirates I've seen on TV. Things have evolved on the water, and it's even more dangerous now. Wren's reach extends past the seas. He has ties and help from people on shore.

Though uncertainty still clings to all of us, it feels nice to laugh and joke, to lighten the dark mood that hangs over me like the moon overhead. If I ignore the fact that Ryan will never be a merman or that his dad and my dad will be hanging out here together for who knows how long, I can pretend this is exactly how I imagined things to be—treasure hunting with Talia, finding adventure with Ryan, enjoying both the land and the sea.

Ryan and I follow Talia toward the fire pits lighting the small beach community, now humming with life as some of the guards come to shore to greet Ava and Carter. When we enter the house, my eyes widen at all the papers Talia had laid out before I had to swim to sea to check on the boats cluttering the surface just past the line of magic protecting Celestiana Cove.

"What do you think?" Talia asks, waving her hand over the table where the map is.

I step closer and run my fingers across the pictures she pulled from my mom's journal to scatter across the top. But there are more now. Some I haven't seen before. It's probably one of the reasons Wren thought I was working for another pirate crew with a few of Darren.

"The pictures have coordinates written on the backs," she says. "Some match what I memorized."

Ryan picks up and flips over a picture of my mom smiling in her human form. It was like fate that Wren didn't find the journal with a merbabe picture of me in it. Because all the pictures I haven't seen are of my mom and Darren.

"Look," Ryan says, pointing to a picture of my mom. She's wearing not only the diamond that anchored her ocean magic around her neck but something else. "I think that's your heart." He pokes his finger to a stone on fishing line around her neck reflecting the light of the sun so much I can't tell the true shape or color.

It's strange to hear Ryan say the words like the glowing stone is actually my heart, though I feel it racing in my chest, beating so quickly it wants to hammer through to spill across the pictures and map. But I think it's because my mermaid essence recognizes the stone in the photo. It yearns for the piece of me taken to be returned.

I pick up the picture and stare at it, brushing my fingers across my mom's face. It's one of the few she isn't smiling in, just gazing at the turquoise water stretching out next to her. I flip it over and peer at the coordinates. My breath catches, and I drop the photo to the ground to peer at the map.

"This isn't far, Ryan," I say, combing my fingers into my hair to braid a few strands together to stop my hands from trembling. "And it's the only photo where my mom wears it. It has to be it, right?"

It's then that I realize someone had to have taken some of these pictures.

I swipe my hands across the photos, gathering them up, and spin on my feet to rush from the small beach cottage. Ryan and Talia both call my name, but I don't wait for them. I kick through the sand toward the last beach cottage at the end of the community.

Darren sits on a chair on his porch, the hum of his generator almost louder than the crashing waves he watches. Soft light trickles from his window cutout, a curtain pulled across the opening to provide privacy.

He greets me with a smile but doesn't get up from his spot. Instead, he pats the seat next to him, inviting me to join him. I plop down, dropping the pictures of my mom in the process. Darren bends down, collecting them before I have a chance to do so myself. He flips one over and freezes, staring at my mom's smiling face.

"She's still just as beautiful," he whispers.

"Still?" I ask.

Bobbing his head, he hands me the picture. "I dream of her all the time. Your mom might've coupled with Attilonious, but part of her heart belongs to me. Always has, always will. She was the most magical, mesmerizing being in the whole world."

"A lot of good that did her," I whisper.

"You're angry."

"I'm trying not to be. I just—" Tears spill from my eyes, splashing across the collection of pictures on my lap. "I feel like nothing will ever be right for me. How could you manage when Mom was at sea? And me. How can you sit here and talk so lovingly of her when she abandoned the both of us. Do you ever think of the life we could've had?" It's a life I've been trying so hard not to think about, because it's something that'll never be.

"Your mom might not be here, but she's never left us. Can't you feel it? These magic waters carry her very essence even now."

"It's not the same."

"You're right. It's not. I still regret to this day that I didn't fight harder to keep your mom from returning to sea when your grandparents died in that car accident. You know, that's how I found out she was a mermaid. She came knocking on my window and asked me for help because she didn't want to leave the land."

"But she surfaced to see you," I whisper.

"And I took a deckhand position on a pirate ship. Maybe even one of those out there now, terrorizing the water. Attilonious assumed she snuck to land to see me when it was Talia's dad. Washed away the house I grew up in."

I let his words sink in. I couldn't imagine going through what my mom did with her parents or the rest of her family. What Darren went through. It's rare for a merperson to lose their life, especially at the age my grandparents had. But that's the risk of a life on land. The sea isn't always there to protect you. And even so, my heart hurts even more knowing that my mom had to leave her intended mate on land, and that she felt she had to choose my dad to help the seas.

"Oh, Darren. This is all so—" I can't put my thoughts out loud. This is all a story to me and will never compare to the life he lived. What my dad stole from him. From the sea. Even from me.

Darren slides his arm over my shoulders and hugs me. I twist to face him and embrace him, burying my face into his shoulder, feeling his love for my mom radiating through him still—or maybe it's the bond ignited through me.

"Why don't you come inside, and we can talk about happier things. There's nothing that hurts my heart more than seeing a mermaid cry, especially you."

"Oh, I wish I could, but I came here for a reason," I say.

"The pictures?"

I nod. "Did you take them?"

I hand them over and Darren flips through them, his eyes softening the more he looks over the photos of my mom. He removes a couple of them and hands them to me. "These ones. Funny she marked the coordinates. That's how she would meet me." Squinting, he studies the back of the photos. "Actually, I think these might be exactly some of the places we used to meet. They were all close enough for her to swim from one of the colonies she was staying at while following Attilonious around."

I pull out the photo of my mom wearing the Mahina Stone. "This one?"

He scrunches his brows. "I definitely remember this one. It

was the last time I ever got to leave the cove."

"When she renounced her mermaid essence?"

His eyes shine with unshed tears. "And promised me the best life she could ever give me. And look around. What more could I have asked for?"

Something about his words, about the way he looks at the sea, makes me feel like everything's going to be okay. If Darren manages to still find happiness after everything, it gives me the hope to believe I will, too.

An idea strikes me as I stare at Darren, and he stares at the pictures of my mom. "How about some time with me? I'm leaving the cove tomorrow with Ryan and Talia, and I would love for you to join us." Something about this moment with Darren, asking him to join me on an adventure, feels like fate. Like the ocean—or my mom—might have prepared him to help me. He has experience with pirates like Ryan. He knows the magic waters. He's a person I never knew I had missed all my life looking at the surface from the glimmering walls of Pearlestria.

Darren's brows scrunch together, and he turns his gaze from the picture he clutches to the sea and finally to me. "You sure you want me? I don't know how much use I'll be to you, Luna. I'm not as quick on my feet anymore. Haven't been to sea since..." His voice trails off, and he swallows. "I don't know."

I suck in my top lip. "Will you at least think about it? We're leaving at first light."

Puffing a long breath through his lips, he nods. "To hell

with it. I'll come."

"You will?" I ask, my eyes lighting up with the blink of my spark.

He bobs his head again. "Anything for my daughter."

LIFE TOGETHER

RYAN'S WARM BREATH TICKLES my shoulder before his lips do, and he trails whisper-soft kisses to my neck. It seems like it's been forever since I could just be with him without worrying about the world sinking around us.

I smile into my pillow, enjoying the heat blossoming across my skin. The salty air trickles in through the window cutout, and I shift in his arms to meet his eager lips with mine.

"You know we only have a few hours of night left," I whisper into his lips, kissing him again.

He groans, resting his head in the crook of my neck, sneaking another kiss against my collarbone. Pressing his weight into me, he meets my lips again. Goosebumps prickle over my skin as he sends me a memory from only a few hours ago, showing me again why he loves my legs.

"But I think we'll survive," I add.

Ryan chuckles, his soft laugh vibrating over my skin, sending tingles through my body with a wave of his desire. Everything has been so overwhelming the last few days that just being with Ryan, exploring his body with my fingers and letting him do the same with mine, losing myself in his kiss, his caresses—it's these little moments that make me feel like I can continue to breathe air. With Ryan, I'm not suffocating.

Pulling me closer, Ryan rests his legs between mine, framing both of our heads with his arms as he runs his fingers through my hair. His tongue glides over mine, and he kisses me deeper with enough passion that I gasp, my body exploding with a wave of love and lust and need unlike anything I felt before.

He rolls completely on top of me, pressing his hips against mine. His fingers hook onto the hem of my tank top, and he pulls it over my head, kissing my clavicle and then my throat before meeting my lips once again.

Ryan showers me with a dozen more images, sending heat cascading over my body in a wave I want to dive into and never emerge from. He thinks about moments of us together on land, like the first time we gave ourselves to each other in San Francisco and then of us kissing in the shower after I revealed myself as a mermaid to him.

And then he creates a new image—one not from any moment we've shared together. It's of one we'll never get to—one of us in merpeople form, kissing underwater below the surface in the light of a full moon.

I pant, needing more air, and pull away, touching my fingers to my lips. Blinking my eyes, I try to suppress the oncoming tears, but it's too late. They streak down my temples into my hair too fast to hide. Disappointment snuffs out the flame of lust and love and everything good swirling through my spark, leaving my chest heaving.

Ryan rests on top of me, his weight sinking us into the mattress. He hides his face in the pillow and releases a long-winded breath. "I'm sorry," he whispers.

I hold him, rubbing my fingers into the skin over his taut muscles tense with the stress from this whole situation. "No, I'm sorry. I didn't mean to react as I did. It's okay to fantasize of a life like that. Merpeople always take the form of their mates if they can, and you're still my intended mate, so it's natural to desire being a merman with me, especially when we're this close."

I've imagined him as a merman myself a dozen times, wondering what color tail he'd have had or how our bodies would be made for each other in the sea. Of being able to hear him in my mind and know one another on all levels across the forms we take. I just didn't realize how much my love for Ryan, the bond I created with him the moment I saw him, would affect him. I don't even know how my mom or my great-grandma survived a life separate from their other halves. I don't know how I'll even survive, split in three. Though I don't want to feel whole. It's bittersweet to give away parts of me to those I love, no matter the type of bond.

"I just can't stop thinking about what life could've been like." He shifts off of me. "And it makes me feel like shit, because I'm angry, and I know I shouldn't be. I wouldn't change things if it was this or the alternative. Can't we ask Sun to give me part of his spark or whatever? He's a cool dude. It'd only be slightly weird to feel his emotions, but I'd do it to be with you. I know how he wants you to join them in Reefaria, and the thought of you leaving me..."

Reaching out, I brush my fingers through his dark hair. "Sun will still share his spark with Giselle when they officially couple, and I'm not willing to risk losing you if he should fail. You have to give your last breath."

"And I would for the chance, Luna. If there is even a tiny possibility that I could be with you on land or in the sea, I'll take it."

"Ryan, no. It's not worth it to me. If something were to happen to you—I'd—I don't want to even think about it, not after nearly losing you already."

"But what about me in all this? You worry about losing me, but I'm afraid of losing you. Look at everything I brought into your life." He tips his head back, staring at the wall behind us. He'll never understand that it was never his doing. Some things can't be controlled no matter how hard someone tries—like the sea. Ocean magic can only freeze a wave for so long before it must come crashing to shore.

"Ryan, you've only brought good into my life. You're not responsible for your family history. Look at your mom. You don't think she'd purposely leave you."

"That's the thing that bothers me most. You might not intend to leave me either, but with the talk about you following Giselle into the sea for her transition—what if you decide to stay? I know you love me, but look at what happened with your mom. With my mom. If you leave, I can't follow. I can't even put up a fight over it. I feel so damn helpless like I did on the full moon. I hate it."

"Ryan, being in the sea with Giselle isn't a permanent arrangement. She has family on land."

"So did my mom and your mom."

"Things are different now."

"But are they?"

I can't answer his question. I'm not certain enough to be honest, so I'd rather not say anything at all, especially with how adamant Sun was about doing what it takes to keep the colonies safe. And no matter how powerful Ava is or how strong her will is to do things her way, if it came down to it, she must pick our safeties. Pirates aren't like most innocent people. Even my dad doesn't think they can be redeemed.

But I do. I'll do what it takes.

I shift onto my side, running my fingers across his bare chest to place my hand over his thumping heart. "I promise you that I will never leave you."

"Luna."

"What happened to your trust in me?"

"It's not that—I just—I don't want you to make that kind of promise to me. I don't want you to feel stuck on land when I know you love the sea. I see it every time you transform and how your whole heart lights up."

I sigh and sit up, raking my fingers through my hair to brush it off my shoulders. "I don't care if you don't want me to, I'm still promising you."

Swinging my legs off the bed, I push to my feet and saunter across the room. The weight of Ryan's stare warms my back, and I peek over my shoulder once to catch him watching my every move. I offer him a smile, pushing away all the hurt and anger trying to mess with my head. His hard features soften, and he can't resist returning my smirk.

"What are you doing?" he asks. "Just come back to bed. We don't have to talk about any of this anymore. Cuddle with me instead."

I shake my head. "No."

He frowns, sitting up on his elbows. "No?"

Another smile pulls at my mouth. "That's right. I have something I need to do first. I know that no matter what I say or promise, you're never going to get it into that human head of yours that you're my one, and I don't care that you'll never be a merman. I love the land, but especially because you're on it."

He smiles at me. "I swear I'm going to work on holding my

breath longer."

I dig into my small bag of belongings Sun and Giselle retrieved from the Ocean's King and pull out a small chain. I unclasp it and tug off the sea stone ring my mom had left for me to find, one my great-grandmer had planned to give my grandfather—the same ring that had been passed to my grandmer and then to my mom for Darren. But Mom never gave it to Darren. Instead, she hid it for me.

"Good, because you're going to have to get to at least nine minutes, and right now you're coming up a little short."

He chuckles. "Nine minutes for what exactly? I can use a tank."

I shake my head. "No tank. Now sit up."

Ryan scoots to the end of the bed, and I close the distance between us. His brows pinch together when I don't fall into his outstretched arms and instead drop to my knees like every romantic movie I've cried in happiness over the last four months from the permanent indent I created on Giselle's couch.

"I—"

I touch my fingers to his lips, cutting off his words. "I'm going to say it again. I love you. I love everything about you, and you're the one being in the universe I want to share this existence with."

Ryan studies my face, his eyes searching mine. "Luna, is this what I think it is?"

I straighten my shoulders. "It is. And I'm serious, so you better think with your heart and not let your head make you say something you'll kick yourself over, because I know how much you do that."

He holds his smile and brings his hand up to touch my cheek. "I love you, you know. No matter what. You, me, and a boat on the sea."

I lean in and kiss him softly, just enough to tease him and widen his smile. "I'm glad you say that because I want to make this official. Because why wait? You don't have to decide to give me your last breath anymore, and I'm never leaving you no matter what you think. So, Ryan Reyes of the Ocean's King, son of Wren Reyes and Nalani of Reefaria, will you be my official mate and couple with me under the light of the next full moon with the colonies and the ocean as our witnesses?"

He swallows, his smile fading to something more serious, the intensity of it making my heart flicker so fast I can no longer see the pauses between beats. He must see it too, because his hand drops from my cheek to my chest, and he rests his fingers over my heart.

His lack of response leaves me leaning closer, holding my breath, studying his eyes for any indication of an answer, and fear trickles through me. Because what if he can't get past his human rationale? What if he denies my love, thinking it's what's best for me? Or if he thinks it's what's best for him?

But then he slowly nods. "Under one condition."

I blink in surprise. "A condition, but Ryan—"

"I want you to marry me on land, too."

My mouth drops open at his words, and I don't respond.

"Because I love you, and you're the one person who has ever made me feel good about myself. Even if I can't be with you in the sea, you can still be with me on the land, and it's what I want. Us together no matter what."

My head catches up to my heart, and I scramble to my feet and tackle him, showering him with dozens of kisses that leave him laughing before he turns serious and kisses me unlike he's ever kissed me before. It's a kiss so full of promise that it steals my breath away and gives me the ability to breathe. A kiss that brings us together as we agree to a life on the land and in the sea as mates, treading the surface. It's a kiss we share with each other to prove that nothing in this world, nothing on land or sea, nothing even in the stars or the magic of the full moon can ever keep us apart.

It's the moment I've dreamed about since I was little. A moment I had expected to wait years for because Ryan is human. But even if he must stay above water, the ocean flows through his veins, and our hearts will drift to sea together.

He pulls back and cups my face in his hands, his chest heaving and a smile lighting his entire face brighter than the spark in my chest, beating solely for him. "So, it's a yes?"

I nod and laugh, running my fingers on the bed next to him until I find the sea stone ring I had dropped. Taking his hand in mine, I slide the ring on his finger, the ring that matches mine, and then I brush my lips across his knuckles. "It's a thousand yeses. Possibly a million. An infinite amount even."

"Good, now come here. I feel like a part of me is missing

with you a foot away."

I sigh in happiness, hearing him say things a merman would say—no, actually. It's all Ryan. He's who makes my essence sing to the rhythmic thrum of my spark.

I cuddle against him, fitting perfectly to his side, my leg sprawled over his as his arm cushions my head. "Better?"

He shakes his head, grinning. "Not quite. I want to dream about my life together with you."

Titling my chin up to him, I caress my lips to his, sending him a dozen images about moments yet to happen. His arms tighten around me, and he leans back and smiles, and then closes the space between us again. I sink into him, letting him take over, creating everything he'll fight for to happen in our future. And I know our life together will be better than either of us can ever imagine.

Because it's me, him, and everywhere else. Always. No matter what.

12

OFFICIAL

I DON'T WANT TO get out of bed. I don't want to remember what life outside of Ryan's arms is like. But a loud laugh sounds through the air, stirring Ryan from sleep, and he turns over and covers his head with the pillow.

He groans, his voice muffled by the mattress. "Tell the world to go away."

I bury into the blankets next to him, sticking my head under his pillow. Our noses touch, and I nuzzle mine to his before I kiss him. He slides his arms around me, pressing his warm body into mine. Tingles rush from my heart to my toes, and our promise to each other swirls through my mind, pulling everything amazing from me.

More voices hum through the air as the community rises with the oncoming dawn. Someone says my name, and then a knock bangs against the door. I attempt to move from Ryan's arms to get out of bed, but he holds me tighter, silencing me with a kiss that has me yanking him on top of me, still under the blankets where we can pretend the world isn't demanding our attention.

I don't feel like a piece of me is missing with my arms around Ryan and our hearts thudding together. I don't even care that we're supposed to set sail in search of the magic my mom had taken from me. Because I don't need magic. Everything about my life is magical. Now more than ever.

When the banging persists, Ryan props up on his arms. "Go away, world! I want another day alone with my fiancée."

"Did you just say your *fiancée*?" Giselle's voice rises over the roar of the ocean not far from the cottage.

"He did," I call out, grinning into Ryan's chest. "We're officially coupling on the next full moon."

"And getting married sometime after," Ryan adds.

"What in the actual hell?" Footsteps thud against the wood floor. "I'm starting to think that mer-marriages are contagious, and I need to swim as far and as fast as I can away from you before I get any ideas. My mom's already going to flip the heck out."

"Wait until you transform and—"

"Luna Torres-Lazaro, princess of Pearlestria, and apparently soon-to-be Mrs. Ryan Reyes. I need you to shut your mouth, get your emotions under control, and get out of that bed to take a deep breath of the sea air and remember there's more to life than pillow forts and cuddles. Thar be pirates on these waters and danger afoot, ye mermaid princess."

Ryan laughs. "We better listen to her. She used all your names."

"Why does the use of all my names mean we have to listen?" I ask, replaying the list of names she said. I never imagined I'd ever be more than Luna of Pearlestria.

Giselle throws her hands up and sighs. "It means I'm serious."

"You're just jealous of our fort," I say, grinning. "I can feel it."

She rolls her eyes at my joke, because the only emotions I feel pouring through her are love and happiness, excitement, too—all for me and Ryan. "Needs work. Sun and I build blanket mansions."

Ryan slides his arm around my chest and uses his other one to point at the door. "All right. Now it's on. Out. We're definitely making the world wait."

"Oh, we'll see about that." Giselle struts from the cottage and starts shouting our news to whoever is in listening distance on the beach. Her voice nearly screeches loud enough that I bet even the pirates and my dad can hear the announcement on the other side of the island.

I rest my head on Ryan's shoulder. "We should probably

get dressed before the royal guard attempts to parade us around."

"What?"

I shrug and giggle. "Merpeople love to celebrate."

Commotion sounds through our window cutout, drawing our attention away from each other. Someone yells, and not in the excited way I had expected from hearing my news. Ryan tugs his shirt over his head and crosses the room to peek outside. He stiffens, gripping the window frame, sending panic crashing over me.

"It's Titus," Ryan says, his low voice barely reaching me over the yelling.

"How did he get here?" I ask.

Ryan curls his fingers into fists. "Stay here. I'm gonna find out."

I don't stay.

Throwing on a dress, I rush behind Ryan into the sand. He realizes I'm next to him and takes my hand, protectively pulling me closer. A small crowd of merpeople stands around, some in bathing suits, a few in the nude, fresh from the bay. Titus kneels on the beach, dripping water from his hair. He digs his hands into the sand, gulping in breaths of air.

"Princess Luna, we found him swimming along the barrier," Tide says, shaking the seawater from his dark hair.

"Can't a man get some exercise?" Titus asks.

"Not when he is hollering at the top of his lungs, trying to get the attention of a vessel that dropped anchor."

Ryan pulls me with him. "Where?"

Tide folds his arms across his chest. "East, a mile outside the barrier. Another one was spotted speeding north."

"They must be tracking the last location of the Ocean's King," Ryan says.

I squeeze Ryan's hand, turning him away from Titus in the process. "I thought you said they would give up and fight over the waters."

"Give up on our captain?" Titus asks, smiling with a cocky grin on his face. "Never. Who do you think pays them? Who do you think has ties to governments around the world? Who do you think makes all this possible? If you thought the surface was dangerous before, you have no idea."

I stomp forward and glare at Titus. "I guess I'll sink the Ocean's King just like I sank the Storm. But maybe my royal guards are right. I should put you back on it."

"You don't have it in you, *princess.*"

I don't know what comes over me, but all I can think about is how my life spiraled out of control because this man told Wren I was trying to hurt him when in actuality I was trying to save everyone. A fury unlike anything I've ever experienced arises inside me like a hurricane storming over an active volcano. Grabbing the front of Titus's shirt, I drag him so quickly to the waves that he can't even find his footing to fight me off. I push him back, and a swell rises with my anger, crashing over the both of us. Voices yell, some cheer, but the rising sea mutes the surface world. I transform into a mermaid—one the shunned king of the ocean would be proud of.

Titus thrashes in the water, struggling against my powerful hold. I drag him to the bottom of the bay, holding him away from me so I don't have to look at his face. This cruel man has spent all of Ryan's life tormenting him along with his dad. He's been trying to break and mold him into the same monsters the rest of the pirate crew is. Titus has helped murder people. He's hurt Ryan on more than one occasion. He's why Giselle lost her human life. He's stolen everything he could ever get his hands on and shows no mercy.

This ruthless pirate deserves to fall by the ocean's waves because he's done nothing to make the sea a better place. He's done everything he can to keep the land and sea apart as my dad had. And I won't stand for it any longer. I won't risk the damage he could do to my future with Ryan. He will surely try to hurt us before he ever gives in to doing what is right for the world. This man only cares about what is right for him. At least with Ryan's dad, I can see his love for his family. But Titus is empty. He's worthless.

Now, after last night, I have more than the ocean to protect. I have my mate—my fiancé. I only thought mermen had the intense need to protect their mates at all costs, but as it turns out, so do mermaids. So do I.

I guess I'm not much different from my dad.

"Princess Luna, please stop," a soft voice says, trickling into my mind. "This isn't who you are."

Nalani swims up in front of me, and Titus jerks in my

hold, reaching for the mermaid who hovers in front of us. Her dark hair veils the space between us, and her green eyes glitter exactly how I imagine Ryan's would have if he—the thought angers me even more, and I shake my head.

"But it is who I am," I say. "And I'd rather have this on me than risk the seas another day. I can't risk my pod—or Ryan."

Nalani closes the distance. "He's Ryan's uncle, Luna. You know the familial bond, do you not?"

No one ever told me Titus was related to my mate. Maybe Ryan doesn't consider him family. I know I wouldn't, not with the way he's been treated by him. Hurt by his hand. "It is my duty to protect my mate."

"And it is mine to protect my children, and Luna, you're my daughter. I know you'll regret this. I know how much it hurts your heart that you've been put in so many unfair positions, but this one can be changed. Let me have him."

Nalani tugs Titus from my arms, and I let her. I don't fight as she swims him up toward the surface and releases him. He kicks for a breath of air, flailing above us. Instead of swimming him to shore, Nalani returns to me.

She wraps her arms around me, drawing me in for a hug. "I have dreamed of this moment every day since I took my last breath as a human. Do you remember when you were a merbabe, and you had come to visit Reefaria all on your own?"

The memory is faint, but it sneaks into my mind. That was one of the first times my dad had ever yelled at me. "My dad was furious, thinking I had attempted to go to land without permission. Like I even had a sea stone ring," I say.

She nods. "All you wanted was to meet the mermaid who was born on land."

I had forgotten about the first time I had met Nalani. My dad had kept me away during her transformation ceremony, and now I know why. She would've been the first human I'd ever seen in real life, but Dad had stolen that opportunity from me. I only ever knew of humans from the minds of others until the moment I met Ava and convinced her to take me to land for an adventure. Giselle was the first human I met, and the first one I bonded with as a friend. Who knew I'd be the reason she's a mermaid. It was friendship at first sight.

"And you insisted I show you everything about the land, about humans," she adds. "You were so curious, and I couldn't resist the princess who looked like the one from my dreams with her pale blue eyes and cascading black hair—a beautiful silver tail that sparkled like rainbow prisms were embedded in your scales. You were the first merbabe I ever met, and I..." Her voice trails off as she loses herself in her memory. I must've still been so young if she claims I had looked like my mom. No one talks about the change that occurred with me, and I wonder now if my dad commanded everyone to forget I looked like my mom.

I blink a few times, wishing I could remember more. I don't remember much of any of this except that I learned to never swim the currents alone without permission, which Dad didn't grant until I was reaching maturity and desired to find a mate. "And you what?"

"I fell in love with you. You were the perfect little princess I needed for my grieving heart as I adjusted to my new life in the sea. And after I showed you my memories of Ryan—" Grinning, she pets my dark hair out of the water between us, pushing it behind my ear. "I'll never forget what you called me. You touched my cheek, nestled into me, and called me Mom. Sandy thought it was because I reminded you of Celestiana, but I knew deep down that my dreams were right and that one day you'd bring my Ryan back to me."

I study her eyes, trying to recall this moment she shares with me, drawing up a blank. It's the exact feeling I get when I try to think of the memories of my mom as a merbabe, but all I hold onto are the ones given to me by other people.

"Why can't I remember any of this? Why didn't you tell me more when I was older? When my dad was bringing prospects of a mate to me?" The words whisper through my mind, drifting out to sea.

"It's all so complicated, my beautiful princess. Attilonious was always so adamant that he knew what was best. I was forbidden from talking about the land with you and your wandering heart."

Of course my dad is responsible. He went to the extent to change my physical appearance to match his. He tried to guarantee I'd never leave the sea. And I'm so angry. As angry at my dad as I am Ryan's or Titus. Even the ocean.

I cover my face with my hands. "You could've told me after

he was shunned."

Nalani cups my face in her hands. "And risk disappointing you if I was wrong? You've been through so much. The last thing I wanted was to break your heart, and I knew you'd find your way to shore like I found my way to sea."

Nalani releases me but doesn't let go of my hands. Together, we propel back to the surface where Titus swims past the reef that surrounds the island with the protective magic used to keep the rest of the world out.

I pop up in front of Titus, making him holler. He splashes me with water and attempts to swim in the other direction. If he gets much farther, the sea will pull him under, but I let him try. All I do is swim next to him, gliding along the surface like he could out swim me.

Nalani breaks through and spits water over his head, clearing her lungs. "My brother, you were never one to give up, were you?"

Titus stops swimming, bobbing up and down in the calm waters of the expansive bay. "I have nothing to say to you, Nalani. You're a traitor and a monster."

"But I have something to say to you," she says.

Titus heaves a breath and turns his gaze away from the Ocean's King anchored not far from us on the other side of the reef but still within the magical invisible walls of Celestiana Cove. "Go on. Tell me I'm a piece a shit you were glad to get away from after everything I did for you. I've heard worse."

She pouts her bottom lip, and something softens in Titus's

scowl. The longer I look at them, the more I see the sibling bond. Nalani swims closer and grabs onto Titus because he keeps sinking under. "I'm not sorry for choosing the sea, but I am sorry for abandoning my son to grow up with you. But I'm also sorry it had to be this way. You're my brother, Titus. I still love you. You're my land family, but this life you helped Wren create was not the life we had dreamed together when we headed to sea."

"It's better than that crap boat we worked on," he says. "You damn messed up leaving Wren, Nalani. That man would have stolen the world for you."

"The world is not meant to be stolen. It is meant to be shared. And that is what my children are trying to do. I will not let you get in the way."

"So drag me back under then."

Nalani releases Titus, flicking her tail to rock the water around us. Titus sinks back under, caught up in the current she creates. He flies a few feet through the sea until he manages to break free to swim to the surface a dozen feet away. The ocean doesn't drag him down now that he's far enough away from the magic, but it doesn't mean he's free.

I swim to close the space between us and grab onto Titus's shoulders. He recoils, turning his head away. "Is that what you want? You would rather the sea claim you than do something better with your life? Why insist on leaving destruction in your wake? The ocean is your home as much as it is mine. It gives to those who do what they can to protect it."

"I'll use it if I damn well want to. It took my home. My parents. It took my sister. I won't let it take everything else."

"I'm sorry for that, but I'm sure it wasn't the ocean," I say. "And I won't let you cause any more damage. I love your sister, and I love your nephew. He's everything despite how you tried to ruin him. I will fight to give him everything good he deserves that you took away or destroyed along with his dad."

"The kid will disappoint you," he says. "You don't know him like I do."

I release a scream as I shake him. "You don't know him! You don't know anything."

Titus leers at me, swinging his arms to grab hold of me. Fear sparks in my chest at the shift in his features. Something dark flits through his eyes, and I try to yank away from him but he grips me tighter.

Nalani yells my name.

I flick my tail, sinking us under, but a net blankets over me. I don't have time to transform back into a human before I'm dragged from the sea with Titus and dropped on the deck of a fishing boat. My tail scratches on the rough surface, and I cry out, trying to drag myself away and back to the ocean.

Titus locks his arms around me, yanking me from the deck. "Don't fight, princess. This doesn't have to end badly for you."

"Let me go!" I scream, trying to dig my sharp nails into his skin. Peering around, I wait for the sea to rise to sink the vessel. But it doesn't happen. The waters are as calm as ever.

"Someone clear the livewell," Titus shouts. The livewell? A man swears under his breath at the sight of me, and I watch him yank a huge fish from what looks almost like a tank. And I realize what's happening.

Panic squeezes my chest, and the boat starts rocking. Titus leans us over the railing to peer into the sea. "Nalani, knock it off. I'll gut her if the boat so much as rocks again. Go get the Ocean's King and bring it to me."

Titus shifts me in his arms, carrying me toward the livewell, a space too small for me to completely submerge to transform back into a human.

"Please," I beg. "You can't do this."

Titus holds me out, his muscles bulging from my weight. "Someone grab my knife."

Oh, Ocean. Help me.

A man rushes from below, his eyes widening when they land on me. The knife in his hand reflects the sun sparkling overhead. He freezes in shock and doesn't see Nalani breach out of the water. She collides into him, making him yell, and Titus drops me into the livewell. The vessel sways on a swell the same time a loud pop pierces my ears, and fiberglass fragments pepper the side of my face. They're armed and unafraid to use their weapons.

I stare in shock at the damage to the wall only inches from my head.

"Luna, get out of here!" Nalani screams.

My gaze turns toward her as she presses her weight into a

man. The boat rises on another swell again, making Titus side-step to grab onto the railing. I take the chance and hoist myself out of the gross water of the livewell and onto the deck. The ocean waits for me a few feet away, and I drag myself across the deck, ripping my scales along the way.

"Don't let her escape," Titus yells, attempting to rush to me.

The fishing boat bobs again on another wave, sending him toward Nalani and the man. He collides into them, knocking Nalani off, but instead of coming after me, he yanks his sister against him.

"Luna, go!" she yells.

Titus hoists Nalani up with him, holding a knife to her throat. His wild eyes hold mine in a stare that leaves my whole body shivering.

"I don't care who I take. Go get me the Ocean's King. If you try anything stupid, I have more boats waiting. You won't stand a chance against us. The waves can't protect all of you."

I don't get the chance to think about it. A swell rises up, spilling over the side of the boat. It washes me toward the stern, and I flop over the side and dive head first into the water. The boat's engine sends bubbles scattering as it cuts across the water, leaving me in its wake with Nalani still on board.

"I'm taking my crew back, too," he calls out through a megaphone, now far enough that the swells stop rocking the boat. "Except Wren. You can tell him I'm taking over the Ocean's King."

13

RUTHLESS PIRATES

"SINK THE VESSEL!" A masculine voice calls through my mind in the sea. A dozen powerful forms dart through the ocean from the bay in perfect warrior formation.

I flick my tail, swimming as fast as I can toward the royal guard now led by Sandy as they head toward the fishing boat with Titus and Nalani. Panic crashes over me, and I can't stop thinking about what Titus said about hurting his own sister and whether or not I should let the guards risk it.

Sucking in a breath of the sea, I call out, "Wait! I command you to stop. You can't sink the vessel."

Sandy cuts away from the formation and closes the distance

between us so fast that his current thrusts me forward a dozen feet before his muscular arm encircles my waist, and he pulls me into him.

"My daughter, you must allow us to take the vessel. My mate is on board."

I blink a few times at his calling me his daughter. The moment Ryan agreed to officially be my mate, the bond between our families started to form. Of course Sandy would acknowledge the expansion and blending of our pods, even if Ryan is human. Nalani's blood runs through him.

I push the thought away. I don't have time to soak in the sudden shift in my feelings toward Sandy. "I know, and I'm getting her back, but they're expecting us to act. Her brother threatened to harm her if we do. It's not a risk I will take."

"But Princess Luna—"

I hug him tighter. "Trust me. I will not let anyone hurt her. Now, call off the guard. We need to meet on land. The pirate has demands."

The water quakes around me with the sudden shift in formation as the royal guard dives down to flip and head in our direction, following the silent command given by Sandy. He doesn't release me, swimming me so quickly to shore that I don't have time to transform as he drags us both on the beach.

"What happened? Where's my mom, Luna? Titus? Is he—" Ryan bats me with so many questions at once, it's hard to focus.

"The pirate kidnapped my mate," Sandy says, turning to the others on the beach. "Someone summon the queen."

"She's probably near home," Sun says, cutting in. "Princess Luna is in charge of the situation."

Sandy shifts next to me, his eyes wide and wild, glassy with more than the ocean spray wafting from the waves. "We need Queen Ava. She can control the sea. She must sink the vessels the moment we retrieve Nalani."

I blow out a breath of air. I never thought I'd ever be put in the position to make such tough decisions, but I know I must. Even if Ava hadn't left for home last night to make arrangements for the new additions on the island, she'd still turn to me for guidance as I know the workings of the guard more than anyone. I know the importance of keeping the colonies safe, but I also understand what we're trying to accomplish with the land and the sea—and sinking boats and taking the lives of humans won't help us. My dad's failed reign is proof enough.

"Tide, I would like you to stay with the vessel Nalani is on. Don't lose sight of it, but also don't act out against it. I do not trust the bond the pirate and Nalani share. He's far too removed and human to feel such a thing, and I do not want to risk her safety."

Sandy smacks his tail into the surf, sending water splashing over us. "It should be me."

I shake my head. "You must remain here. I know the strength of a mate's bond, and I know you'll do everything for Nalani, but I can't risk you getting hurt either. I want you to wait for my summons."

"Daughter—"

I turn to Giselle. "Will you please stay with Sandy?"

She blinks her eyes, nodding. "What are you planning to do?"

"I'm going to give Titus what he wants," I say.

Sun puffs out his chest. "You can't be serious, Princess Luna. He knows our secret. He kidnapped a mermaid, something that has never been done. He must be stopped. He cannot leave this cove."

I swipe my hands across my face, pulling the strands of sandy hair from my eyes. "I know, Sun, but he has Nalani, and it's the only way to get her back. But don't think I'd allow him to keep what he's trying to steal. I have a plan."

"What can I do?" Ryan asks, kneeling in the waves next to me.

"We will help, too," Talia says from next to Darren.

I nod my head, pressing my lips together. Feeling the love radiating from my pod is enough to push away my worry and doubt in my ability to take care of the colonies. I can do this. I know I can. I don't need to be a warrior or have ocean magic. All I need to be is me, full of love and hope, and the sheer will to see this through. I will not be known as the daughter of a shunned king and lost mermaid queen. I will rise with the tides, and the tides will rise with me.

Ryan clings onto my back as I swim him around the island to where both of our dads reside. I'm almost afraid to see what we'll return to. When Sandy summoned the guard for help, it left the pirate crew and my dad alone, and I'm not sure either can control themselves long enough to realize they better start getting along soon, because if things continue as they do, they're going to be neighbors until further notice.

I transform into a human in the shallows and swim with Ryan to shore. The back and forth changing is becoming annoying with having to keep putting my bottoms back on, so I don't. I wrap the sarong around me instead. I don't plan to stay on the beach long.

Someone releases a whistle, and a few figures step from the shade of the tree line. Ryan kicks forward through the sand ahead of me, still dripping seawater from his hair. His tense muscles ripple over his arms, and he surprises me by shoving someone into the sand. Not just someone—his dad.

"Did you know?" he asks, nearly yelling.

Wren pushes himself from the sand and smacks his hands on his dirty jeans. "Well, hello to you too, son. Nice that you remembered I'm on this godforsaken island."

Another figure emerges from the trees, and I turn my gaze to Dara, who refused to leave her son to return to the cove with us. She strolls past Wren and directly to Ryan, enveloping him in a hug he can't refuse.

"Are you here with news of Titus?" she asks, turning her attention to me. "We saw him taken under."

"Why didn't you stop him, Dad?" Ryan asks Wren, letting go of Dara to meet his dad face-to-face.

"He's a big boy and doesn't need me lookin' after him. If

he wanted to face these damn waters, then let him. It's not my life."

I ball my hands into fists and strut the distance to him. Ryan steps in front of me, blocking me, and I stand on my tip-toes and glower at Wren from over Ryan's shoulder, slightly annoyed my mate doesn't let me unleash my fury.

"He kidnapped Nalani!" I scream, nearly spitting the words. "He tried to put me in a tank."

Two of the crewmembers high-five each other, and I whip my head to burn a glare at them. They take a few steps back under the intensity of my eyes. All Wren does is cross his arms over his chest, glancing at the ship in the distance now gliding away, no longer anchored outside the magical barrier that blinds them toward seeing the island or the inhabitants. Titus must have called them.

"And you stuck us on this island," he says. "So, let's call it even."

"What?" I say. "You really are a heartless monster."

Dara slaps Wren's arm. "Oh, don't let him get to you, Luna. He knows Titus won't hurt Nalani."

"How are you so sure?"

"He asked for the Ocean's King and the crew back, right?" she asks.

I nod.

"Put someone in a bad position, and they'll do—"

"Shut up, Dara," Skull says from behind the old woman, drawing my attention to him.

Dara spins on her feet and clocks the man square in the jaw with her fist, surprising me. I cling onto Ryan, my hands trembling. No one's taking this seriously, which makes me more nervous. Because they don't see Titus as I do. They're too close to him, and from my moment with him on the boat, even with him in the water, I know he is capable of hurting people, even Nalani.

I swivel past Ryan, sidestepping his outstretched hand as he tries to pull me back into the safety of his arms. As princess and the mermaid in charge, it's my duty to face threats head on. I know Ryan wants to protect me, but he'll soon learn that as my mate, one of the ways he will take care of me is seeing to it I can take care of myself. He closes the space behind me, turning from my shield to my back up.

"If you seriously think Nalani is safe as a mermaid in Titus's hands, I will believe you and proceed as her mate desires and sink the boat. I will consider this war against the surface, and there will be no chance for you or your crew. Do you understand?"

Wren straightens his shoulders, his jaw tightening, but he doesn't respond right away. He's far too rational and calculated to do things on a whim.

"And if you think Titus will figure out how to come to your rescue, you are mistaken. He demanded I bring the crew to him and insisted you stay here."

Wren's face twists in a scowl, and he swings his arm out. Ryan jerks me back, but Wren wasn't trying to hit me. He punches Skull in the throat, sending the pirate to his knees. Another man flies forward, jumping on Wren's back, and I back up even more as some of these people turn against their captain. Actually, they're turning against each other.

Ryan pulls his grandma away from the fray of things, and the three of us watch in silence. I don't know what to do. We need their cooperation if we're going to get Nalani away from Titus. A giant shadow shades me, like a palm tree erupts from the water. I turn, expecting to see Sun or Tide on the beach, but my dad emerges, dropping a fish he caught to the sand.

He doesn't even stop to look at me and Ryan, charging past us toward the pirates. With a jerk of his long arm, he knocks three of the pirates off their feet and into the sand. Skull tries to scramble to his feet, but my dad is too quick and rips him from the ground by his shirt and throws him into the surf, where a wave drags him back.

"You will submit to the will of my daughter, or I'll force you to submit to the will of the sea." My dad's low voice vibrates through me, reminding me of the king he used to be in the water. But now he's standing up for me. For my mate. For Nalani.

Another pirate charges my dad, not taking him seriously. Dad doesn't even let him get a punch in before he raises him off his feet and spins him over his head, tossing the man into a nearby tree.

I cringe at the sound of his body breaking, his wails cutting through the air. It's enough to get my legs to work. I run to my dad, throwing myself in between him and another pirate. They both freeze in their tracks, and I realize a wave builds behind me, reacting to my fear. But it's uncontrolled, untamed, and out to sweep everyone away.

"Luna," Dad says, his eyes wide. "What is this?"

My brows furrow, my face contorting as I inhale breath after breath of the sea air to calm my nerves.

"You have ocean magic." My dad steps closer, outstretching his hand to touch me. He never knew. My mom hid it from him, and now, all the pieces fall into place as he puts everything together.

Neither of us sees Skull rush from the waves, and he launches at me, knocking me away from Ryan and Dad.

Yanking me off my feet, Skull hooks his arm around my throat, putting enough pressure on my airway to make it painful to breathe. His heart beats against my back, and I kick my legs, trying to break free, but all he does is squeeze harder.

"If you move a damn inch, I'll break her neck," he says, spitting his words next to my ear.

The hum of a boat engine cuts over the waves, and he twists to peer at another boat gliding across the surface too close for comfort, and then it crosses the barrier.

Oh, Ocean. I didn't think Titus would use Nalani to bring a boat over the barrier where ocean magic is most powerful. He must not have believed that I'd go through with his demands.

I can't even call for help without being in my mermaid form.

MAGIC WATERS

I can't tell the guards to sink the boat.

I can't do anything.

And then Skull drags me into the swelling sea.

14

BACK TO SEA

WATER ENGULFS US, SWIRLING around me in Skull's tight hold. If he squeezes any harder, I'll black out. He pops us to the surface, swimming with one arm the best he can in the rough water that only drags us farther away from the shore.

Yells sound through the air, and I catch sight of a boat speeding toward us. I shouldn't have underestimated Titus. Pirates are strategic. They plan a lot of things, and Titus has had a lot of free time to think about things. And now I know he must've realized that we were going to plan things too and boarded the new craft with Nalani. Tide's following the decoy fishing vessel floating on the sea.

A wave rises and crashes over our heads, and I inhale a deep breath of the sea, drinking it into my lungs to transform. There's no way I'm going to allow Skull to drag me onto another boat. Flicking my tail, I dive us under, taking Skull deeper into the surf. He was sorely mistaken to think he could get away with capturing me.

Instead of releasing me, he squeezes my throat tighter. The edges of my vision shadow, my gills struggling with the pressure he puts on my neck. Reaching behind me, I dig my sharp nails into his side hard enough that his voice bubbles through the water as he yells.

I elbow him in the nose, fighting him off, and a current separates us, pulling him down while sweeping me toward the surface. I break through, spitting out water, spinning around to see what's happening.

"Princess Luna," Sun says, calling my name through the sea. "A boat came through the barrier. They're armed, and we can't get close enough without risk. Nalani is our only healer present."

"I know. Don't try to approach them," I respond, diving under as the boat heads directly for me. "They're expecting it. They'll attack anything they see in the water."

A net expands over the ocean above me as the pirates attempt to capture me again. Because they now know of our existence, we're all at risk. The ocean can only do so much to protect us. They're trying to take over the waters here. They're trying to sever the union we've been working hard to establish between the land and the sea.

Summoning all my courage, I do the only thing I can think of. I swim toward the surface and break through. These pirates will continue to fight for the surface. They'll figure out how to take over the land here if I let them. And I can't. This is my mom's cove. This is our sanctuary.

"Sun, gather the guard. Go to the cove and protect the bay," I order.

"Princess Luna, what are you planning?" he asks. "Let me help you."

"No, you need to stay with Giselle. As soon as the pirates disperse, get her out of here. Go to La Tortuga Point. Tell everyone to return to the colonies where it's safe."

"I don't like this, princess," he says. His figure jets through the water, closing in on me. Something whizzes through the sea between us, startling me. Sun freezes a few feet away, armed with one of the spears for fishing in the shallows from the community.

"I know, but you have to trust me. I'm not going to let them ruin our sanctuary. I will get them out of here," I say.

"How?"

"I'm going to surface and give them what they want."

"What's that?"

"Me."

Before Sun can argue, I transform back into a human and kick up, allowing the pirates to throw another net over me. The world jostles around me, and I hit my hip hard on the deck, but

I don't move or fight.

I curl in on myself instead. "Please, don't hurt me. If you hurt me, this will be an act of war against the ocean."

A shadow falls over me, and Titus rushes me with a knife. The boat rocks on a swell. I flinch away from the scowling pirate, but he only cuts me free from the net. And then he pulls me to my feet, glancing around the quiet surface. The only sounds coming through the air are from the pirates on shore.

"You don't think we're prepared for a threat?" he asks, yanking my arms behind me. My sarong clings to my skin, dripping water on the deck.

"I'm sure you are, but is it worth it? I know you don't want to fight. I know all you want is to get out of here." Because it's true. It's what I'd want if our positions were switched. It's like when I was locked in the boat against my will after Wren accused me of trying to take over the Ocean's King.

"What I want is the wealth that comes with catching my very own mermaid," he says.

"And I will help you. But you have to call the fleet off. We don't have to be against each other. All I ever wanted was to work beside you. Pirates were always allowed to sail these protected waters because they kept the surface clear. It can continue to be that way."

His gaze flicks to the ocean around us and then to the land. A dozen silent thoughts swirl through his head. He knows how dangerous these waters are, and he doesn't have a clue of what he could possibly face. He has no idea that our colonies are small and even if it came down to it, we're no match against humankind. Ava wouldn't allow such a thing to happen. I wouldn't either. We love the land. We have family. Only my dad thought it okay to call everyone back to sea, and it's not a life I want to live, not with my mate forever a human.

"How do I know you won't turn against me?" he asks. "You sunk the Storm."

"I had no choice. It was a full moon."

"She's right, my brother. My daughter would have never risked the life of her mate and her land family." Nalani's soft voice trickles through the air, and I turn my gaze to the mermaid, sitting with her tail splashing the water circulating in from the sea through the livewell.

Titus's features remain hard, and he refuses to glance at his sister, keeping his glower on me. Finally, he bobs his head. "I need collateral."

"I will stay," I say, hugging myself. "But you have to promise I'll be in the sea the next full moon."

He shakes his head. "I need someone else."

"Ryan—"

"Ryan's already coming. His dad, too. But not as captain. I want your sister."

He means Talia. We look alike enough to be mistaken. But I can't allow such a thing. She doesn't deserve such a life. "No."

His lips twist into a scowl, and he stomps across the deck to Nalani, aiming the knife at her. Fear blossoms in my heart at the sight, but Nalani doesn't react. All she does is straighten her shoulders and meet her brother's eyes straight on.

"I want your sister," Titus repeats. "She'll be treated well."

"Don't do this, Titus. You dragged me down, but you don't have to do it again," Nalani says.

Titus jerks his arm down, stabbing Nalani in her glittering copper tail, causing her to scream. I stand in shock and horror. I thought Wren was ruthless, but he doesn't compare. The water sways around us, and I take a step back, inching toward the sea. I was wrong to think I could possibly get the pirates away peacefully. I was wrong to think I was strong enough to handle them. I was wrong to hope that we'd all get out of this un-scathed.

I back into a hard chest of a well-built man, and he hooks his arm across my shoulders, locking me in place. Titus reaches down, pulls the blade from Nalani, and shoves her off the side of the boat and into the water. I can feel their familial bond snap the instant she dives under. It cuts through me like a fro-zen dagger set out to snuff the spark from my chest.

"How could you?" I cry, trying to stand on my tiptoes to peer into the water. "She is your sister."

"My sister died. That thing is not my sister." Titus steps closer and locks his fingers onto my shoulder. "Be thankful I didn't kill it, because you monsters of the deep deserve nothing more than that."

I blink a few times, clearing my eyes of the tears I refuse to shed. I've never felt less than my entire life until this moment. Titus embodies the humans my dad warned me about. He's the kind of human the sea is supposed to protect me against, but here it is, only rocking with small swells when I want it to rise. I want it to swallow this man whole and rip him from my world. But the ocean doesn't bend to my will. It doesn't react to the shadow of magic in my spark.

Titus whistles through his fingers, and a small inflatable boat launches from the vessel to head toward the shore. I count six armed pirates all together, two on the tender boat, four on the deck, including Titus.

He glances over the side of the boat and into the water again for signs of merpeople, but no one swims nearby. Nalani would have swum as best she could've, and she'd have followed the orders I put in place to protect the colonies. Now, I'm alone on the dangerous, pirate-infested surface once more. But this time, I'm not at the mercy of a man who cared about his son— his family. I'm facing the wrath of another man who doesn't feel the bonds I do. The man who lived for himself and no one else. The man who might very well be responsible for destroying my future and the future of those I love.

I watch in silence as the two pirates threaten my dad on shore, keeping him away. It takes several trips to bring back the pirate crew, all except for Dara, who remains in her spot on the sand. No one bothers with the old woman, and I steel myself to face the pirate crew, now uncontrolled by Wren.

No one lets Ryan near me, and I stare in shock and fear as Titus hits him hard enough to knock him unconscious. I rush forward but don't get even a foot within reach of my mate.

Wren wraps his arms around me, pressing my face into his chest to muffle my screams.

"Do something," I beg, struggling in his hold. "You're the pirate king. This is your crew."

"Stop fighting, Luna," he whispers in my ear. "You're making things worse."

And he's right.

Wren once told me he could make things bad for me, but he was wrong. It was always going to be me to make things worse.

And this feels like it's only the beginning.

15

DETHRONED

I'M DESTINED TO NEVER leave the Ocean's King. My life's current seems to lead me right back to the place Ryan was born, the place Ryan grew up, the place more familiar and comforting than I care to admit, even with the odors of the cabins assaulting my nose. I've gone from princess to warrior to prisoner, and now all I can do is pray that the ocean sees me through this and no one gets hurt in the process.

I commanded the merpeople to return to the colonies, but as soon as Ava learns what has happened, she'll be required to make some decisions as reigning queen to fix what I've messed up. I'm afraid what Titus will do. The magic in Celestiana Cove is stronger than ever, but Titus can use me as a key. I must also face the fact that all these months I thought the ocean was rising by its own freewill to protect me, but now I'm not so sure since I know it's reacting to the shadow of magic in my spark the way it reacts to Ava. At least she has control.

If only I could help her make the decisions and be the ally and advisor she needs me to be. But I can't help her. I don't even know what to do. If the elders have a say, they'll revert to our old ways, because it's what they've known all their lives. It's what has kept us safe. Because who can trust pirates with our secret? Who's to say Titus won't try to reveal our existence to the world? What if he steals our magic waters and turns them into a place no merperson will ever swim in again? Everything everyone had gone through would have been for nothing.

The best I can do now is hold tight as long as I can. I must save Ava and the rest of the colonies from having to make these sorts of decisions. I need to use my experience with dealing with someone as stubborn and lethal, someone as brutal and commanding as my dad, to make things right again.

Footsteps sound on the stairs, drawing my attention away from my dirty hands and my thoughts of saving the sea—saving my home and world. Talia appears from the stairs, worry lining her light blue eyes, a beautiful contrast to her flawless skin. I get to my feet but don't make it far. A chain rattles on my ankle, and I stop in place and hold my arms open for her instead.

She rushes me, encasing me in her sinewy arms. Rocking me back and forth, she hugs me in a way she's never done—or had the chance to do—before. Her hug squeezes me in a burst of relief, the fractured pieces of me fusing together by the heat of my spark. I tighten my mouth to stop myself from crying, though it's all I've wanted to do. Tears won't help me in this situation. All they'll do is make things worse, especially because I can see Talia holding back her own. We're holding it together, so we both don't fall apart.

"Are you okay?" I ask, nestling my face into her hair to hide the sorrow in my expression. She smells of the plumeria flowers still clipped in her hair from the island, a welcomed scent I want to hold onto as long as possible to combat the smell of the filthy room around me. "No one hurt you, did they? I know how awful these people were under Wren's watch, and I've been so worried."

Instead of pulling away to answer, she speaks against my shoulder. "I'm fine. I can handle myself, Luna. Not everyone aboard is out to get us."

I groan, muffling my voice against her shirt. "You shouldn't have to. You shouldn't even be here. I'm angry you didn't put up a fight. The island was big enough to hide on. They would have assumed you had left." Instead, both Talia and Darren took matters into their own hands after word traveled about what Titus demanded. And now Darren is somewhere aboard this yacht, too. Titus couldn't pass up another working hand with ties to me. The three of them—Talia, Ryan, and Darren—will do what it takes to assure I'm safe, even locked away now.

But I still hate the thought and position they're in. I'd hate to see how far Titus could push them into doing what he wants. Because Ryan once sunk a boat for Wren to assure my safety and innocence when it came to the pirate life. Their love for me could put them in the same position or worse. It's possible Titus could very well destroy all the land family I have left in a matter of seconds, and there would be nothing I could do but sink the vessel and take everyone else down too.

"And give them more of a reason to attack the cove? Not everyone left. And of course I should be here for you. You know I'd have come if you'd have allowed me in the first place. This was our plan. Find the treasure left by your mom and—" She presses her lips to my ear. "Find your magic. Don't you see? I can help assure it. I know the maps. I can do what you can't. This is how it's supposed to be. Nalani said so."

Her words swirl my mind. She sounds like me with her talk of fate, of how she feels things are supposed to be with finding my magic and how she can help me when I can't help myself. With everything that has happened since this morning, the last thing I thought about was locating the Mahina Stone. A princess's heart. The story Nalani shared with me, one from Ryan's childhood, whirls through my head. The prince was supposed to set sail and fight rough waves and vicious pirates. Here I am—here we are—falling to the story prophesized through the dream of the land-born mermaid. And Talia's right. This is how I'm going to fix things.

I suck in a shuddering breath, thinking about Ryan's mom.

"Nalani's okay?"

Talia hums her confirmation. "She gave me everything I need to handle her brother, too. And I have to warn you—"

"Time's up, Talia," someone calls from above. I recognize the gruff voice belonging to Ali, one of the Ocean's King's best divers. He's also a man I saved from the water and has been kind to me. "Captain wants you to have dinner with him."

"Sure thing. Tell him I expect dessert, too," Talia calls up, surprising me. She squeezes my hand and bows her head to me. "Like I was saying, don't worry about me. I know how to handle myself. I've been doing it all my life. And I want you to remember that no matter what happens, we're still family."

I squeeze her again. "You'd make a fierce warrior."

"Oh, I'm already one. And I also know it might get worse before it gets better because I'm not letting anything happen to you. Ryan won't either. He asked me to tell you to remember his promise." To always protect me on land. I'd never forget.

"You talked to him?"

She nods. "He's going to try to sneak down lat—"

"Hurry up, Talia," Ali yells, his voice sounding forced. "I don't want to have to come down there."

"I'd tell you to be brave, but you're the bravest mermaid I know," she whispers.

I stand in my spot, my ankle aching against the metal shackle digging into my skin, until she disappears completely. Turning around, I meet Wren's stare from his place on the floor. He leans his back on the wall and darts his gaze between me and the stairs Talia ascended.

"What?" I ask him, dragging my chain back and forth with my swinging leg. "If you have something to say to me, then say it."

It's easy to forget he's been in the room with me all this time. He hasn't said one thing to me since we were both incarcerated in the unofficial brig. The only reason Ryan isn't shackled with us is because he's useful, and Titus threatened to harm me to get Ryan to comply. Keeping me safe on the land like he promised isn't the same as how he would in the ocean. He's not a merman after all. Things will always be different in our relationship compared to everyone else.

Wren shrugs without looking up, his dark hair damp with sweat on his forehead. "I don't understand you."

I purse my lips, rolling my eyes. Looking at Wren annoys me more than ever, because everything could've been different between us. He had it in him to make a difference, and now who knows what Titus plans. "Obviously."

My sarcasm gets a smile out of him, and I heave a breath of the stale air and return to my spot on the dingy cot. We continue to sit in silence as we have been for what feels like days, though I know it hasn't been more than hours, according to the wristwatch Wren glances at every hour on the hour like it'll somehow predict the future or give us answers.

Wren tilts his head forward before tipping it back, stretching his neck. "So, you really love my son." It's not a question, and his words surprise me. I thought by this point it was obvious to everyone how deeply and madly in love Ryan and I are. Neither of us would be in this position if we weren't. But instead of throwing all of that in Wren's face, I decide I have enough negative energy flowing inside me, and this room is bad enough that I don't need to add unnecessary tension to the mix. Wren knows what he's done. He's more aware than anyone about our dire situation as the dethroned king of the pirates.

Shifting, I summon all my love for Ryan to put into words the best I can. "Ryan's the most amazing being in existence, and I plan to create the best life possible for us. I'm willing to fight to make sure he gets everything incredible he deserves, even though things haven't turned out how we imagined, no thanks to you." I sigh, combing my fingers through my hair. I just couldn't help myself by blaming him to his face. Titus might be why we're here now, but Wren started all of this no matter where the ocean's waves pushed me. I could have done without the pirates in search of my ocean magic. I don't think my mom intended it to be this way, but she couldn't have known. No one could have.

"Me? You put yourself in this position," Wren says, making my anger worse. "I was providing a good life for my son. I was nice to you and tried to include you in my family even with all this—" He waves his hand at me, probably referring to my mermaid self. "You messed things up for yourself."

I snap, the dam controlling my fury smashing to pieces. I stomp my bare feet to the floor and throw myself up to tower over him. He's delusional and more removed from everything than I thought. I bet he blames me for his fate in all of this. "A good life? Look around, Wren. This is not even close to a good life. I've been called a monster, but these ruthless, horrible people are the real monsters. You're a monster."

"I do what I have to just like you, princess. I give many people lives they wouldn't have otherwise. I've given them a place to live, opportunities to travel the world, a family."

"A family of thieves and murderers. Sounds like the perfect group to make the world a better place." Clenching my hands into fists, I list the places Ryan taught me to punch people to take them down, and all I want to do is take Wren down and make him feel the pain he's inflicted on my heart. "You're not even doing things to help people. Even my dad had a better reason than you no matter how misguided he was."

Wren scowls at me but doesn't move a muscle, even when I lean into his face. He peers at me with his dark eyes, studying me like he can hear all the thoughts flooding my mind. "Well, we can't all have everything given to us. Some things we have to take."

I clench my jaw. "No, you don't."

"You're a hypocrite, Luna. It's exactly what you did. Sinking one of my boats and dragging us to some island. You said it yourself that you'd start a war if you had to. You live in this unrealistic dream world where you really believe you'll change things. But damn it, can't you see the reality? You might be a mermaid, but you're also no different than humans. We're all just trying to survive and make the best of it. There's no denying it. I see it in your eyes. Hear it in your words. You'll do whatever it takes to get what you want."

I turn away from him. "Not at the expense of others. What I want is to take care of the world you want to crush under your boots."

He grabs my arm, yanking my attention back to him. "Hey, I don't want to ruin the damn world. You think I like being in my position always facing some kind of trouble? I do it because the surface needs control. It needs someone willing to do things no one wants to. I protect the world as much as you think you do keeping my crew under control. But there's give and take. You gotta make some compromises and no one will be happy about everything."

He's right in a way about trying to survive, about his reasons for doing what he did. Because he's stopped men like Titus from taking over. But his way is the same as what my dad did. I want to do more than survive and control. More than sit behind my glittering palace walls, loving and living for a single soul. I want to love and live for many. I want to explore and help everyone I can. And I still know I can. When I'm swimming, and something blocks my way, I navigate around it. If I can't, I push it out of the way. And Wren's wrong. I'm not living in some dream world. I'm fighting my worst nightmare.

"I guess you're right. I was stupid to think that I could make a difference and help you do as you were intended. I was wrong to think that because you were my mate's dad that maybe we could build an amazing life as a family, helping the seas. I thought you'd want to see to it that your daughter's home was thriving. That your son's future in the water would be protected."

"My daughter?"

I hit my hands on my knees. He'll never see me as such. I'll always be the mermaid who got in his way and messed up everything he had going for him. "I'm talking about me. Out of all that I've said, that's what you focused on? For one second, can't you just believe in my existence? You're powerful, but you're also selfish and—this isn't how life should be."

"You think this is how I imagined life? Imprisoned by my own damn crew? Having a son that hates me? You know, if I were you, I'd sink the ship before it's too late. You can still have a chance to get my son away. Forget about all this and just live in your damn la-la land. I know you have the means to do so. Turn him into a merman and disappear. Leave the human world to take care of the surface."

I give up. I hate how much I want to continue to fight for this man and to get him on my side. I hate how invested I feel in the bond forming between us and how much he hurts me with every word he utters aloud.

"You sound like my dad." Rubbing the heels of my hands into my eyes, I finally sit back down and lean on the wall. "Oh, Ocean. Why does it feel like you've split part of my dad to make Wren? Why do this to me? Why do this to Ryan? It makes this all so hard. Is there a way to stop the bond forming?"

Wren stretches his legs out. "What the hell are you talking

about?"

I bow forward and glower. "I wasn't talking to you."

Raising his eyebrows, he looks at me like he thinks I'm the strangest person ever. It's the look many humans give me when I speak my mermaid mind instead of trying to sound human, something Ryan embraced about me. "Well, I don't give a shit who you were talking to. You make things more difficult than they have to be, Luna, and I'm sorry for how things turned out, okay? I like you for my son even with—I'm not even gonna say it—I like you and never wanted things to turn out like this. I was only trying to get you to comply not kill you when I locked you up with your friends. You pissed me off, and I—I'm sorry. I want to make up for this. I think I can manage to break you out. Take Ryan and go. Go live your magical life together like how you want."

"My magical life?" My voice rises through the air as I practically scream at his pathetic attempt of an apology to make things right with me. "Ryan will *never* get to feel the magic he deserves. You messed up the magical life we were building. And for some reason, I still care about you. Stupid bonds!"

All he does is shrug, which infuriates me enough to smack my hands on the cot. "Yelling ain't gonna help either of us, so calm down, will ya?" he asks.

I glower at him and shift away.

"And whatever bond you think is forming between us won't be your problem much longer, so stop sweating it, princess. You can all celebrate and swim on my watery grave."

My anger fizzles out with his words. "Grave? I might not appreciate that you'll be bonded to me as my dad on the next full moon when Ryan and I go through the coupling ceremony even if we can't see it through completely, but I don't want you dead. Neither does Ryan. Or Nalani, even."

He releases a wheeze of a laugh. "Guess I should've handed you control after all. It's too late now. I'm a dead man. The idea used not to bother me, but now that I know—" Shaking his head, he shuts his mouth without finishing his sentence.

"Know that Nalani's alive?"

"Damn it," he mutters. "Fu—rickin' life. All this time. You know when I met Ryan's mom, I knew that we didn't stand a chance at a good life together, but the hell I wasn't gonna try. She was...too good for me. I knew she hated the business, but I thought she'd stick around, especially after Ryan was born."

I rub my hands together without responding. I never in a million moons expected Wren to open up to me and bare his soul. It's like he truly believes his words about his fate, and he's now using me to confess everything he's been holding captive inside of him.

"I—" I snap my mouth shut. Nothing I can say will ever excuse the betrayal he feels toward Nalani. He'll never truly understand the call of the sea or the coupling of mates. Eternal bonds. And even though my mind screams that I have no reason to feel this way, my heart feels bad for the overthrown pirate king the same way I feel bad for my dad. But just because I feel bad, doesn't mean I think things should be different. Actions have consequences, even my own. And I'm facing them as much as he is.

He rubs his hands across his scruffy cheeks, taking them into his hair to push the damp strands up. "You probably think I deserve it. Hell, I probably do. But you can't back down or show weakness in this life, Luna. The sea isn't for the weak. It's for the strong."

I never expected Wren to give me any sort of fatherly advice, no matter how unnecessary it is. "But it's up to the strong to help those who can't help themselves," I whisper, leaning my elbows on my knees. "Not for the strong to destroy everything in their paths."

Wren shifts on the floor, pushing himself up to sit on the cot beside me. He keeps a foot of space between us, turning his knees toward mine and meeting my gaze instead of looking at the floor. "Ya know, I know this won't mean shit, but I *am* sorry you're here. I always thought something was different about you, and that you were too good for this place. I couldn't wrap my mind around the thought that you actually loved my son despite the no good family he came from and the asshole who raised him." His self-deprecation sounds like Ryan's, and I realize where my mate got it from. Pirates don't lift each other up. They step on each other, using those in their ways to climb up.

"I love him more than you could understand," I say. "He's my mate."

"Well, I hope it works out for you two. He'll make a damn good fish. Been swimming all his life. Could do so before he walked." Reaching out his hand, he rests it on my knee. "Wish I could see such a monstrous sight." He sounds like he means it in the best way possible, but it doesn't hurt me any less.

It takes everything in me not to yell at him that he just doesn't get it. That Ryan will never get the chance at a life as a merman. I want to tell him how he's at fault. He's the reason I'll forever have part of my heart on land. But Wren's shoulders droop, and he hangs his head.

"At least I can die knowing someone will look after him better than I ever could," he adds.

I frown at his words. "No one is dying. I put orders not to sink the boat. Once I get my magic back, I'll fix everything. Maybe we can start over, or you can join my dad on the island." I don't want to threaten him to get him to comply, but it seems pirates need a constant threat or reward to get anything done.

A small laugh escapes his mouth, more breathless and filled with disbelief than funny. "You really are naïve, Luna, aren't you?"

His words bother me for two different reasons. One, he has so little faith in the world. And two, he might be partially right about me. I might have traveled all the seas, but I'm not worldly. I have a hard time seeing things any other way than through the blurry mirrored view I get from staring at the surface from below it. "What is that supposed to mean?"

"I always thought Ryan was excessive in his need to protect your innocence, but I get it now," he says without answering my question. "It's cute."

I should know better by now that Wren takes nothing I say seriously. Still doesn't stop annoyance from washing over me. As quickly as the emotion comes, it morphs into something lighter, more peaceful. It takes me a second to realize the emotion doesn't belong to me at all. It's through my bond with Giselle. And I'm so thankful for her in this moment. Her new bond keeps me from losing it. "I'm well aware of the situation, Wren, but I still have faith that the ocean will assure things get righted. You have nothing to worry about with me around."

"Tell that to me when we anchor."

"I will."

He chuckles and shakes his head. "Naïve mermaid. I bet you make my kid feel all sorts of guilty. I bet he makes you blush."

I deadpan at his words, nearly opening my mouth to defend myself and say that it's me who makes Ryan blush. But I don't give in as he tries to get to me for his own amusement. I just wish he'd stop dancing around whatever is on his mind by trying to change the topic from his situation to Ryan's. "Stop calling me that and tell me what you think will happen. Help me understand why you think you're going to die."

He shifts, flaring his nostrils while burning a look at the stairs, though no one descends to us. "That asshole didn't drag me on board out of the goodness of his heart, Luna. If he was gonna show me mercy, he'd have left me to rot on that damn island. He's using me to make a point to my crew. He's assuring his position. Because no one can stand up for a dead man."

"You mean…" He thinks Titus is going to kill him, and I wouldn't put it past that vile pirate evil enough to stab his kin not to.

"Don't think I won't go down without a helluva fight," Wren adds. "I didn't get to my position and win the respect of people because I'm a nice guy."

"That jerk. He's worse than you. I don't even know how you could let him on board."

He chuckles and shrugs, but all it does is tightens my chest. It's the same feeling I got after the ocean stripped my dad of his ocean magic. I had assumed the worst, and that he wouldn't stop until he was dead, but the last thing I had expected was for the ocean to show him mercy, and I hope it'll do the same for Wren. He is Ryan's dad after all.

"I don't think the ocean will drown you," I muse out loud. "Your family has managed to survive all this time for a reason."

"Because we know how to defend ourselves." He sounds so sure of himself and his ability. I nearly roll my eyes at him again. He has no idea about anything.

"Partially, at least in regards to humans, but not because of the ocean." If he wasn't thinking about what he believes is his impending demise, I might rub in the fact that he was only ever the pirate king because my dad allowed it.

"Still won't help me. You think he'll let me enter the water?" He whips his head back and forth. "No damn way. He'll execute me first, making a show out of it."

Ice travels through my veins, streaming toward my heart.

The idea of such a horrifying end reminds me of how scary the human world is compared to my beloved ocean. Not only are humans fragile, but they face more dangers than I could have ever imagined from the safety of the palace walls of Pearlestria. Humans get sick, they have accidents, and they even hurt each other. It's things mermaids never really think about. But I've been thinking about it a lot lately. Because of Ryan. Do I want to live out the rest of my life on land with him, or would I return to my colony in the sea after...

I don't get time to think about it.

Heavy footsteps thud on the stairs, stealing away the last bit of the good emotions my bond with Giselle trickled into me. My hand takes on a mind of its own and automatically reaches for Wren. His warm fingers slide over mine for a second, and then he gets to his feet and moves to stand in front of me like Ryan has done what seems like a thousand times for me. His short chains don't allow him to move far, and he has a shackle on his wrist, but it doesn't stop him from turning his body into a wall that now blocks me from whoever's loud footsteps thunder through the quiet of our room.

"Get out of the way, Reyes," Skull says, lifting his arm to raise a knife in our direction. "Titus says I can visit with the princess."

"You're making a mistake, Aiden," Wren says, making Skull jerk his other hand forward to lock his fingers on Wren's shirt.

"Don't call me that shit."

"Then don't sign your damn death certificate by siding with a man who will throw you in the line of fire instead of protect you. How many times have I managed to get you out of jail? What about your dad? Your brother? Who will assure you could provide for you—"

Skull brings his blade up to Wren's throat, shaking him slightly. The scary tattooed man looks ready to end Wren's life right in front of me.

I step forward, raising my hands. "Stop it! Just stop. Don't hurt him. I'll come with you."

Skull turns to me, raising an eyebrow. "You really like the Reyes men, don't ya, princess?" He turns his full attention to me, pushing Wren back with this hand. "You know, maybe if I spent some time with you, I might understand what it is about you. I'm not as scary as I look. I'd treat ya right."

I shake my head, hearing his voice deepen. "Stay back."

"Aw, come on. Fish are my—" Skull charges forward at me, snapping his mouth shut, not finishing his sentence. The sudden movement sends a waterfall of panic washing over my head at the strange, demented look crossing his face. The same glint Titus has in his eyes when he hurts others also shines in Skull's narrowing gaze.

He reaches out his hand, trying to grab me. With my free hand, I attempt to punch him, but he squeezes my arm and pulls me closer.

I scream out, the noise startling me.

A shadow cuts across the floor and chains rattle. I meet

Wren's angry face, his lips twisted, his brows furrowed. He drags Skull back and sucker punches him in the jaw before spinning him to face me, still holding onto him from behind. Wren winds the short chain attaching his arm to the wall around Skull's neck. Skull's face turns a deep red, and he jerks around, reaching for the weapon on his belt.

I flinch away as Skull's fingers brush the holster. "Wren watch out—"

A bone in Skull's neck cracks, sending bile rising into my throat. The noise reverberates through me, and my ears ring at the loud pop though I know it wasn't loud at all. Skull slackens in Wren's hold, his arms dropping to his side.

Blinking, I stare in shock, my body frozen, my mind whirling. And then my body turns against me. For the first time in my life, my stomach—which can digest anything I put in it—betrays me. I throw up on the floor at the same time Skull's body slams into it. Wren kicks him into the nearest wall and stomps his boot into the dead pirate's stomach a few times, swearing words I've never heard of or understand.

I fly away from Wren, putting as much space between us as I can. I pant, the air hard to breathe. My spark flickers so quickly that I light up the whole room, making it clear that Skull isn't just knocked out as much as I hoped him to be.

"You killed him," I say, my voice squeaking. I bring my knees to my chest and bury my face into them, sucking another breath through the salty, sea-scented fabric of my sarong.

Wren straightens his shoulders and turns to me, his stone

expression scaring me as much as Skull had. Everything light he carried a moment ago, even talking about his own death, vanished like Skull's life. Wren looks like the man Ryan warned me about these last few weeks. He reminds me of a man who puts so little value into the lives of others. But he saved me, and I don't know how to feel about it. "You think I was gonna stand around and let some asshole lay a hand on my son's girlfriend?"

"Fiancée." I don't know why I have the need to correct him. It's like saying the words out loud stops me from curling in on myself and sobbing for a man who doesn't deserve my tears. But he didn't deserve to die, either.

"You mermaids fall fast. You sure you're not hypnotizing my son? I know the stories of sirens." He questions me like Skull's body doesn't lie feet away from us.

I gawk at him. "What?"

He shrugs. "Would make sense."

"I—" I don't know how to respond. It's easy to believe such tales since humans must give their last breaths, but our bond has nothing to do with hypnotizing or luring someone from land.

There's no point in defending myself because Wren says, "There. That did the trick. You stopped shaking. Pretty sure you won't cry now either. Question your love and it seems nothing else matters."

I sit in surprise, gaping at him. He was right, though. He distracted me enough that I manage to get my emotions and fear under control.

Wren moves on without another word, bending down to search Skull's body.

"You're stealing from a dead man?" I ask, clearing my burning throat. "I thought you were better than—"

"Save your moral bullshit for another time, Luna. I got the key," he says.

I blink. "The key?"

He waves his hand, ushering me to move closer. "We're getting out of here."

"And then what?"

Lowering his eyebrows, he gives me a look that makes me feel like I should already know everything. "Do I have to explain every detail to you?"

I don't respond no matter how much I want to answer his question with a yes, because I do want to know everything he's planning. Obviously he's no longer worried about Titus trying to murder him. He even smiles at me, showing off all his teeth.

Wren shakes his head and rips a set of keys from Skull's pocket. "Come on, princess. It's time to fight for your pirate prince."

I only nod my head.

"No one messes with the pirate king."

16

HOPE

"PLEASE DON'T TAKE ANOTHER life," I whisper, following behind Wren as he climbs the stairs.

I know he'll ignore my request, but I have to say it anyway. I can't act like I'm even a little okay with him killing someone again. He swore there was no other way, but he didn't even try. He saw Skull grab me and reacted with all the ruthlessness he's known for.

Wren looks at me in his peripheral vision. "I need you to get it into your head that he would have hurt you, Luna. I know Skull, and there's a reason he's on this boat and not on any of the others. It's not because he was one of my best men. He was one of my worst and needed to be kept in check. He was a risk to my operation more often than not, but he followed my orders and did good work."

Before experiencing the pirate life, I never thought much of the atrocities some humans were capable of. Everyone I had met up until boarding the Ocean's King was nice. They were caring, and they were worthy of the mermaid secret.

And Wren's words hit me hard, cracking the colored sea glass I've been staying behind in hopes that I can somehow change everything. But changing the future doesn't mean that the crimes committed and evil deeds are forgotten. My dad faces his consequences and surely more pirates will face theirs like Skull has—Wren, too.

Even knowing all this, it doesn't hurt me less. I'm one mermaid. The colonies are small, too. It's why it all comes down to a union between the land and the sea. I'll need Wren to help me as much as the idea brings an ache to my heart because of the way he does things—the necessary evils he believes are a part of surviving and the ones I know we're all capable of living without.

"There are other forms of punishment," I finally manage to say. "I'd like you to consider every option first."

"Oh, I did, but right now, we're going to do what we have to," he mutters. "I ain't dying today because you think you can go the lawful route. Law doesn't apply to these waters."

I stifle my groan. "Please, Wren. I don't think I can handle it. It hurts my soul. It can't be good for you, either."

"If I die, you're screwed, Luna. Ry is screwed. I told you time and time again that I care about my family, and if you're marrying my son, that makes you a Reyes. I know you're capable of being tough, so suck it up and deal with it."

"I'm not capable. I *am* tough," I whisper-hiss. "And I don't have to prove it to you or accept any of the wrongs of this situation."

He swears under his breath. "I thought Ryan was stubborn but damn. Listen to me, Luna. If it's them or us, it's going to be us who survives all this hell. Got it? You want the chance to change the world, then you better follow my lead."

All I do is nod. Because he's right. The ocean needs me more than ever, especially with the rising threat of pirates, and I can't allow those who seek to harm others have their way. I've been sheltered for too long. I'm sure every warrior in the colonies would agree with Wren. I just hate that I have to. At least for now.

Because I will make sure it doesn't stay like this forever even if it means giving up the ideals I've held onto all my life. Even if it means I'll not get the happily ever after I always imagined for me, Ryan, and the sea. If the pirates have their way, there won't be a place for us in this world anyway.

Wren halts in place just before the entrance to the main deck. He holds out his arm, stopping me from moving forward, and listens for an unnervingly long amount of time. I count over two hundred of my heartbeats while I grip the wall in fear. Someone might come looking for Skull, and they'll stumble upon us, forcing Wren to stay good on his word and me floundering as I fight to accept what my life above water has turned into.

Skull's dead body is forever imprinted in my memory. Without Wren talking, my mind automatically dwells on the moment I know I'll never forget just like I'll never forget seeing Titus stab Nalani's tail or the look of horror on all the innocent people's faces these pirates tormented since the moment I stepped aboard the Ocean's King. It haunts me as much as seeing Giselle take her last breath.

These painful moments feel like weights tied around my limbs. My whole being wants me to find an escape into the sea to sink under and never breathe air again—but I can't ever do that. Ryan holds the rope tied to the anchor around me, and he's far stronger than even the call of the sea. If only I could fall into his arms now instead of steeling myself by his dad's side.

"We're going to hole up until nightfall," Wren whispers, peering around the deck.

I stay close behind him, standing on my tiptoes to whisper into his ear. "No, we need to find an escape for you. I can swim you somewhere and return for Ryan and the rest of my family."

He mutters something I can't hear under his breath. "No. This ends now. I can't let my men think I'm a coward. This is my damn ship, and the only way I'm leaving is if I'm dead."

"And you complain I'm stubborn," I murmur. "You're not going to die."

Lifting and dropping his shoulders, he says, "The more you

say it, the more I start to believe it."

I offer his grin a ghost of a smile. It's like he's suddenly found hope at the death of another man. And maybe he has. It's possible he stole some of the hope I've been carrying. All I know is that he reminds me of the man I first met when he boarded Talia's boat to bring Ryan back to what he thinks is his son's home.

Wren nudges me forward without waiting for me to respond to his remark. "Come on. No man would dare step into Dara's quarters uninvited. Even now. If anyone's place is sacred to anyone aboard this boat, it's her room." Even Titus didn't have it in him to bring Dara from the island. I'm sure he left her behind not to risk people turning to her in place of Titus after his plan to dethrone Wren in the only way he knows how.

I glide across the deck in front of Wren, strolling as softly as I can on my bare feet. Voices hum from the galley, but there's no way one of the crew would get up from a meal and risk having their dinner stolen.

My stomach growls despite the knots tightening my insides. I can't remember the last time I ate. If I were in my mermaid form, it wouldn't be a huge deal, but my human body complains that I've ignored it for far too long.

Wren uses a key from the collection he stole from Skull and unlocks Dara's door. We both freeze at the sight of Ryan and Darren sitting at a table with their heads hunched over a blank map of the world similar to the one my mom marked up.

Ryan gets to his feet first, crossing the room. Wren shoves

me in when my feet don't cooperate and locks the door behind us. He sidesteps past me, heading toward the built-ins the same time Ryan envelops me in a tight hug that smothers the trembles coursing through my body.

Another pair of arms wraps around both me and Ryan, and I catch the familiar scent of the coconuts Darren favors from Celestiana Cove. My throat tightens with a sob. I muffle my voice with Ryan's chest, afraid someone will hear the noise that burns my insides to hold back even a second longer.

"No time for tears, Luna," Wren says from behind Ryan. "I don't know what the hell is going on, but if Ry and whoever the hell this is are in here, we gotta find somewhere else."

I blink and pull away from Ryan. "What?"

"This will be the first place someone will look now if they see we're missing," he says, digging through the room.

I meet Ryan's glassy gaze, and all he does is nod in agreement to his dad's words, making the sorrow rising in me even more intense. I never in a thousand sunsets thought that Ryan would go along with what his dad says, but here he is, and it hurts because I know they're both right.

"Titus took every weapon out," Ryan says, his voice low.

"What is he planning?" Wren asks.

Ryan pulls away to face his dad, but I close the distance, not letting any space between us. I'll hug him until I have to do something else. "A funeral celebration."

I gasp, the air unable to get in my throat fast enough. "He knows about Skull. Oh, no. He's going to search for us. We have to go now."

Ryan frowns, looking from me to his dad. "Skull? I was talking about my da—"

"You're welcome," Wren says. "I saved your fiancée. Now maybe you'll do something other than stand back and watch me die."

Ryan ignores his dad's remarks and steps away from me, still holding my hands, to give me a thorough once-over. He furrows his brows, staring at my eyes long enough that I almost lose myself in his, but then he breaks our stare and hugs me again. "Are you okay?"

All I can do is nod. "Wren did what he felt he had to."

Ryan hides his lips in a line and jerks his attention to his dad. I expect him to yell at him, to call him a monster. But all he says is, "Thank you."

My mouth drops open. "Ryan."

Darren touches my shoulder, waving his hand to coax me from my mate's arms. I relent when Ryan nods and joins his dad to help him pull up the bed. Darren slides his arm around my shoulders, turning me away as they tear the place apart in search of something, possibly a weapon, that wasn't taken.

"There is nothing right about taking a life," he says, keeping his voice a whisper.

"But?" I ask, expecting him to give me a reason for doing so anyway.

He shrugs. "That's all. I wanted you to know that you can feel however you want, and some people will disagree with you, but we're all trying to do what we think is best."

"For whom?"

"Depends who you ask," he says. "If I've learned one thing from your mother, it's that we sometimes have to make decisions we don't necessarily want to make."

I puff out my bottom lip, blowing air through my lips. "I wish I had my magic so I could be as strong as her."

"Her magic never made her strong, Luna. It was all her like your strength is all you."

Except I feel like I have no strength left. The last bit of power inside me drifted out to sea that even the waves no longer react to the shadow of magic supposedly in my spark.

"What the hell you two talking about? You sound like a sitcom, old man," Wren says, chucking a drawer he pried from the built-in on the floor.

Darren kicks it with his foot. "It's how you talk to a mermaid. My daughter needs a little light in all this damn darkness you've brought into her life like a hurricane destroying everything in its path, now shut the hell up and hurry up."

I stand in shock at Darren as he fists his hands, glaring at Wren. I never expected him to lash out at someone on my behalf, and it reminds me of how Dad stood up to the pirates on the beach for me.

"She don't need words of encouragement. She needs to face this reality. You both treat her like she's made of glass, but Luna's made of concrete and steel. That's good enough to protect whatever it is you're trying to shield her from."

Wren rips out a piece of wood from the bottom of the built-in and pumps his fist up with vigor because of what he finds. He pulls out a bag and rummages through it to pull out a knife and waves it around, stopping both Darren and Ryan from saying anything else on my behalf.

It leaves me to simmer on the words Wren said about me, and they dig into me in a good way. The words restore the hope I thought he stole from me. All he did was take my hope and grow it into something that gives me what I need to pull myself together. It helps me act like the daughter of a fierce mermaid queen and all the mermaids who came before her, passing on the same strength to one another and now to me.

"Let's go," Wren says, motioning for me to move.

I quickly hug Darren and kiss Ryan. "I'm sorry I can't stay. We have a plan, and I'll return for you. Stay safe."

"And out of the way. Get ready to fight or abandon ship."

Ryan stops his dad. "If anything happens to Luna—"

Wren waves the knife again. "I'll let you do the honors of sending me to the ocean's depths."

17

WARRIOR PRINCESS

"YOU EVER USE ONE of these, Luna?" Wren asks, holding out a pocket knife.

"No, but I have used a kitchen knife a few times." Giselle always did most of the cooking, and the only times I ever picked up a utensil that wasn't a spoon or fork was to cut a piece of one of the many cakes and pies Ava loves to bake.

Wren looks more disappointed than he should, like he assumes I'd be armed with secret murderous mermaid skills passed to me from my dad. But the only weapon my dad ever used was his magical scepter now long gone and broken. The sea finished many lives on his behalf.

"Let me show you the best—"

I raise my hand, cutting him off. "You are not teaching me how to kill some—"

"I'm teaching you how to defend yourself," he says, rudely interrupting me back. Being interrupted by Wren is far more annoying than when Ryan does it, probably because he kisses me first. Wren looks like he wants to give me a good shaking.

I poke him with my nail in the shoulder just hard enough to get him to step back and lower his arms. "I can impale a fish with my bare hands. I'm fine."

He raises his eyebrows and nods his head without commenting. All he does is touch the spot on his shoulder, which I realize I might have stabbed a little too hard, because a pinprick of blood seeps into the fabric of his T-shirt.

I puff air through my lips and scrunch my face at his sudden look of appreciation. "Of course that would be what impresses you." Pirates are the strangest people.

Wren chuckles, his shoulders shaking with the action, and I can't help thinking how similar he and Ryan sound. But where Ryan's laugh lifts me up, Wren's laugh makes the room drop in temperature like how the ocean feels when transforming from a mermaid and into a human.

"I'd like to see that when this is all over," he says, shoving his folded knife into the pocket of his jeans on the opposite side of the sheathed blade he found of Dara's in her room.

"Really?" His words, while not drenched in hope, give me a tiny bit of light because it's a plan he wouldn't have made not long ago while we were chained below. Now that we're both free, he thinks there's a chance for himself after all. And I'll do what I can to see to it. If only his questionable morality didn't ruin him. He'd be a great person otherwise. I just can't excuse his behavior. It's not right.

He shrugs. "Why not? I'd like to get to know the spitfire of a mermaid my son will spend his life with." His certainty surprises me. He doesn't say that Ryan wants to spend his life with me. He says that he *will* spend his life like there isn't another option, which I hope to be true.

"I had assumed we'd be parting ways," I say. "I honestly don't know what the ocean has in store for its pirate king or me for that matter."

He smirks at me instead of frowning. "I guess we'll find out."

A whistle sounds through the air, drawing our attention away from each other. It's the tell-tale sign that the watchman is letting the crew know that he caught sight of something. Usually it'd be a boat, but now I fear he saw something else.

I tense, listening for any signs of the pirates' weapons, seemingly doubled since we've left the cove. Before, there were only a few powerful weapons because Wren had his fleet nearby, keeping anyone away. The Ocean's King is what Ryan referred to as his dad's castle and the boat used to enter ports. Now, it seems Titus transformed it into a battleship ready to take out threats from below.

Wren holds onto the frame of the open garage door. The

stall, with direct access to the ocean where the yacht's tender boat can drive into, sloshes with seawater since the boat is missing. Peeking his head out, Wren listens to the commotion sounding above us. But it's not the sound of a fight.

I inch closer, staring at his back and then to the sea beyond. It could be so easy to knock him off the vessel and swim away with him, but I'm too afraid to go against his plan to lure the men siding with Titus out from the rest of the crew before "taking care of the problem," which I'm pretty sure means murdering Titus, something I still don't feel right about.

I know that Nalani would want me to try everything I can to assure Titus gets punished without it having to be his death sentence. Unlike how Titus doesn't consider Nalani his sister anymore because she's a mermaid, Nalani will always consider Titus her kin, despite how awful he is. It's just the merpeople way. But we've never had to deal with human connections until recently. It's an adjustment for everyone.

"There's a boat heading this way," he says to me, stepping away from the entrance where the crew can bring in small boats to easily board the vessel. I haven't seen this garage before. The last time Ryan and I left in a tender boat was from a hydraulic platform on the stern of the boat where it was waiting.

As I look around, I determine that the garage is nicer than the cabins. It's obviously where the crew and Wren's priorities lay. Their vessels are treated far better than humans, which is the strangest thing in the world to me to put an inanimate object before a life.

"Looks like we're also dropping anchor," he adds, closing the space between us.

"This is bad," I whisper. "Didn't you say—"

Before I can get the words out of my mouth, Wren stifles my voice with his hand, pulling me toward a storage compartment too small to fit the both of us. A beam of light cuts across the water outside of the vessel, and the hum of an engine purrs loudly enough to send my heart racing.

"Get in," Wren orders, opening the small door.

I have to hunch down to even get inside, bending my body in an uncomfortable position. Wren glances over his shoulder once and shuts the door without closing it completely. Voices hum through the air, and I peek through the crack to watch Wren soundlessly stride away to duck under a counter with what looks like a small bar with a fridge behind it. The garage looks like Wren used it to entertain guests in this portion of the yacht, maybe people of influence who stop by, but I'll never be sure unless I ask. And now, I don't really care. Not with the voices growing louder in volume.

Bright lights flash in my eyes, and I cling to the door, bracing myself as a small boat enters the garage. Water cascades from the stall and onto the deck to drain out again. The garage door automatically shuts, and I listen to the water sloshing in the stall now with the unfamiliar boat driven by strangers I've never seen before.

Rocco, one of the crew members I saved from drowning, appears next to the boat from the stairwell leading to the upper deck. I haven't seen him much, and he must've been one of the crew to have taken over the boat Wren had stolen from some hostages, because he wasn't on the island either.

"There's a lot of shit you need to hear about Captain Reyes," Rocco says, his voice low. Something about his tone stirs hope in me. He sounds like he disagrees with what Titus is doing, and he's exactly someone we could use on our side. "I think we need to stick together and make sure Titus—"

I flinch at the sound of a loud pop. Covering my ears with my hands, I lean farther back into the storage space, wishing I could sink into the wall. My mind can't process what I just saw. In a split second, the hope I gathered fell to the floor with a man I knew could have helped us—one who *would* have helped us.

My ears ring, making it hard to hear anything through the crack in the door, but I'm too afraid of what I'll see now. I can only hope that it was a warning to Rocco—letting him know that his place shouldn't be devoted to Wren as the rightful captain according to the strange people who have obviously sided with Titus. I know it's why they're here and probably why Rocco was one of the crew to be sent to welcome them.

"Katie, don't," another masculine voice pleads. "Come on, Justin. Tell her it don't gotta be like this. I got the message loud and—"

Another pop echoes out, stinging my ears, and I jerk back, losing my footing. I accidentally kick the storage door open, and two strange people—a woman and a man—gape at me from their position on the deck beside the stall. The garage door reopens behind them, and I train my gaze everywhere else but at the floor.

"Come on out, sweetheart. The bad men aren't gonna hurt you," the woman, Katie, says. She holsters her weapon under her dressy jacket with a button-up shirt underneath and raises both her hands to show me she is no longer armed to hurt me.

The man, Justin, who is older with cropped hair and glasses, follows her lead and offers me a smile. Neither is dressed like any pirate I've seen. They look like they would fit in with the Kings, Giselle's aunt and uncle, in Azure Waters in their elegant business attire. Diamonds glitter on Katie's ears, and the man's suit looks designer.

"You can trust me. Look how I stopped them." Katie points at the ground I refuse to gaze at. She then proceeds to kick her leg, shoving the toe of her heels into... Nope, I can't look to see who. "Dead like they deserve."

I'm taken aback by the air of brutality she carries under her lavish façade. There are a few women who are part of the crew, but Katie seems different. Scarier. I can only compare her to a warrior mermaid, but this pirate posing as someone else doesn't seem to have mercy. And she killed Rocco. He wasn't the bad man she claims he was.

"Come on now. It can't be comfortable in there. You're safe with us," Justin adds, turning to Katie, who subtly nods her approval.

But I don't feel safe. Panic rises in me with every breath,

especially as the two people step over the bodies on the floor. My breath quickens, my lungs working hard to intake air, making me crave the sea. Katie's heels click across the deck, and while Justin keeps his hands up, one of hers sneaks back into her jacket.

"Stay back," I warn, glancing around for Wren, but he remains hidden. "You killed those men. One of whom pled for you to show mercy, and the other you didn't even give a chance."

The people stop in their tracks, and Justin looks to Katie to take the lead again. She brushes her dark blond hair from her face and feels for something in her jacket pocket again, making me tense. "I'm Agent Harder. This is Agent Schauer. We're here to seize this vessel, okay? This ship is connected to some unauthorized activity. We do what we must to protect ourselves. Those men were armed and dangerous. Okay, sweetie? So, please. Don't pity the criminals. Be thankful we arrived when we did."

Justin steps even closer. "How long have you been on the boat anyway, princess?"

Out of all the things he could've called me, he just happened to choose the one name all the other pirates call me. The term rings an alarm inside me, making it completely obvious that my instincts are right. These people aren't who they claim to be, and they remind me of something Ryan told me when we first met. He said he could adapt to any social situation, and it wasn't until I stepped aboard this yacht that I discovered why.

Wren doesn't command just a bunch of tough pirates who destroy whatever comes in their paths. He runs an operation that requires more than brute force. He's intelligent. He has power and pays a lot of people off. And these people here? They remind me of him. They're the brains behind the muscle and twice as ruthless.

"You see that logo?" Katie points at the boat when I don't respond to her partner's question.

"Where are your badges?" I ask instead of answering once again. "What coast are we near? Who is the human authority of these waters?" To someone who doesn't know what I am, they might be thrown off by the way I worded things. "Where is the rest of your team? How come I haven't heard anything called out on a megaphone? This ship is full of pirates. Why isn't anyone rushing to see why another vessel boarded our craft?"

They both peer at each other, taken aback by my endless stream of questions. Justin loses his cool first and reaches into his jacket. At the same time they try to rush me, I scramble away from my spot and toward the bar where Wren was hiding.

But he's gone.

Fear crashes over me, and I swipe a glass bottle from a rack bolted to the counter and swing it as I spin back around. I hit Katie in the head, sending glass and sweet smelling liquid spraying everywhere. Justin yells and charges me, encircling me in his arms to lift me off my feet. I scratch my nails across his face in a quick swipe. He hollers again and drops me. I land hard on my feet in the broken glass, and I release a yelp from the pain. I force myself to move instead of staying in place as Katie now comes to her senses, pushing back to her feet.

Justin yanks his weapon free with one hand, still cupping his face with the other. "You little bi—" His words cut off, his eyes widening.

Wren stands behind Justin, holding one of his shoulders for a second before letting him drop to the floor. Blood coats Wren's hand, and I squeeze my eyes shut, willing this to be only a nightmare I'll wake up from at any second.

Boney fingers grab me from behind, forcing me to open my eyes. Katie locks her hand in my hair, twisting the strands to stop me from moving. A cold blade brushes my throat without cutting me, and I freeze, holding my breath, afraid that if I inhale or even swallow that the pirate will kill me.

"Drop the knife, Wren," Katie says, blatantly not calling him Captain Reyes. Very few people call Ryan's dad by his first name, and it's obvious by the scowl twisting Wren's face, that this woman isn't one of them.

"After everything I've done for you, you—"

"Watch it," Katie snaps. "You don't want me to slip accidentally."

"This is between you and me. Let the girl go."

Pulling my hair tighter, Katie forces my head back. "Titus thinks he's in charge, but it looks like he's going to be sorely mistaken. Now get on the boat."

I expect Wren to tell her off, to charge forward in an attempt to rescue me. I expect him to do a thousand different things before he resorts to getting in the small craft. But he does as Katie says and heads toward the boat, stepping over the bodies that seem to pile up by the second.

Dropping the knife from my neck, Katie shoves me forward. She guides me to where Wren stands crossed armed on the boat. The glowing ocean expands out as far as I can see with no signs of merpeople.

Katie shifts from behind me, and she throws a set of cuffs at Wren. "Cuff yourself to the rail."

"Why are you doing this?" I ask, wincing with every step I'm forced to take, my feet leaving drops of blood from the small cuts from stepping in glass.

"Shut up," Katie snaps, punching me between the shoulders hard enough to make me gasp.

"Please, you can't take me. Titus will—"

"I don't give a shit about that asshole. He was never going to last long, trying to take over the Ocean's King. It takes someone with connections to run—"

I stab her in the throat with my nails, cutting her words off. They don't sink deep enough to kill her, but it's enough to get her to release my hair. I rush forward to Wren, and he grabs my arms and swings me onto the other side of the stall. I brace myself on a bar on the wall, so I don't fall back into the boat.

Katie swears, her voice screeching through the garage, while reaching for the weapon tucked away under her jacket. She rips the gun free, but Wren's too fast and launches himself at the woman posing as an agent, and she drops the gun. It falls into the water of the stall and slides out the garage door and into the sea.

I tiptoe on the balls of my feet, wishing I could transform into a mermaid to help with the pain of the cuts. All I can do is get out of my corner to help Wren. Throwing punches faster than Wren can move, Katie overpowers the pirate king, and he stumbles back, his mouth and nose a bloody mess. While she's an excellent fighter compared to some of the men on this vessel, Katie doesn't look much better than Wren does, her lip split and her eye swelling shut. But I don't doubt that she has it in her to steal his power and become the pirate queen.

They both get to their feet, neither of them armed. Katie reacts first, bending forward to charge Wren. The fallen pirate king swivels out of the way, but he trips on the body of one of the dead pirates and lands on his back.

Katie tackles him, digging her hands into Wren's throat. Wren's face reddens at the sudden lack of air, and I beg the ocean to rise up to break them apart. My body freezes, fear stealing my ability to move. I pray for Wren to push Katie off. But he can't.

His body slackens, his eyes closing. Watching Ryan's dad slump beneath the woman ignites a fury inside me I've never experienced in my life, not even when I was left transforming in a room with no escape.

I break under the thought, my legs moving first as my mind catches up. Katie can't even get to her feet before I jump on her back. The vessel quivers, rising on a swell that sends my stomach into my throat and back down at the quick movement.

Latching her fingers around my back, Katie flips me over her head. The wind knocks from my lungs as my body hits the rough floor next to Wren. His closed eyes flutter for a second and then open, distracting me long enough that Katie climbs on top of me to pin me down with her hand on my neck.

Wren jerks up next to me, swinging his arm at Katie at the same time a glittering wave crashes over us, washing us apart. I roll a few times, the swell dragging me toward the stall where the boat rocks with the sloshing water. I grab onto the tie bar with one hand and catch sight of the ocean pulling Wren and Katie in my direction. With my free hand, I catch Wren by his shirt, bracing the both of us in the sparkling current heading to the open sea.

Fingers lock on my ankle, nearly causing me to lose my grip. Through the bubbling, rushing water, I spot Katie using me to anchor herself to the boat. A million thoughts rush through my mind, catching sight of the panic in the woman's eyes. If she loses her grip, she'll wash away and get sucked under by the ocean now desperate to protect me.

I remain still instead of shaking my leg to break her hold. The current dissipates as the wave drains back to sea. I gasp air at the same time Wren does, and he manages to grab hold of the tie bar next to me.

We lower in the stall, the water still sloshing around the boat.

"You're a damn monster," Katie says from her place at the

end of my leg.

I don't have time to react before she hooks her other hand around my leg, surprising me. She yanks me hard enough to break my hold on the tie rail, pulling me toward her. My head dips under the shallow water, and I scream out, accidentally inhaling. I can't believe she's still attacking me though I saved her life. And now I can't fight back.

A hand grabs my wrist, stopping Katie from pulling me away completely. I break through the surface of the shallow water in the boat stall and meet Katie's twisted features. She crawls toward me despite Wren drawing me closer to him, and I tense, preparing to be sandwiched in the middle of two ruthless pirates.

Gathering my strength, I kick my leg up as hard as I can, clocking Katie in the chin with my foot. She arches back at the force and lands in the water where another wave rises. Her yells mute as the ocean swallows her, dragging her into the sea.

Wren pulls me from the stall, gathering my trembling body into his arms, and he hugs me for the first time ever. "You're okay, kid," he whispers, combing my wet strands from my face. "I gotcha. Just take a breath."

My jaw quivers, ice dripping over me as I stare at the open garage. "She was right," I say, my voice barely sounding above my pounding heart. "I am a monster."

Wren embraces me again. "The hell you are. You're a damn warrior, princess."

18

MONSTROUS

"TELL ME THE PLAN again," Wren says, peering over his shoulder for the hundredth time as he drags the three dead pirates on the small boat still floating in the stall. He didn't bother asking me to help him, because he knew I wouldn't do it. My stomach barely stays inside me already. The tears in my eyes don't help much either, and I'm pretty sure my nose will never stop sniffling.

"You should take the boat and leave," I say. "You're the one with a death sentence. Not me." Because it's true. It's obvious what Titus will do, and after dealing with the vicious pirates, one dead in Wren's arms and the other now lost to the sea, I'm not sure Titus's plan will even work out for him. If Wren were to die, it'd be meaningless. Not that a meaningful death is much better. Especially if it benefits a man capable of being more monstrous than even Wren.

"Don't think that sparkly fin of yours makes you any safer, Luna," he says, waving at my legs like he can imagine my tail.

I place my hands on my hips, training my eyes on the sea instead of what Wren's doing inside the boat. "Safer than you."

Wren glowers at me for a second before turning back to his task. His jaw tightens and his muscles flex as he positions one of the bodies behind the wheel in the cockpit. Bile threatens to rise up my throat, but I wring my hands together, swallowing the dread inside me for the thousandth time in the last two minutes.

"Just tell me the plan. I wanna make sure you have it down," he says, grabbing the rope that keeps the boat tied in place in the stall.

I accidentally glance at the fake agent, now ready to set sail back to sea with how Wren ties him to the seat, and I squeeze my eyes shut, releasing another breath. "You'll finish situating the—"

"Your part," Wren says.

I slowly open my eyes, catching sight of Wren leaning over the side of the boat and into the cockpit. Averting my gaze, I narrow my eyes on the sea, praying it gives me the strength I need to follow through with the plan Wren guarantees will give us the chance we need to take back what is ours. *Ours*—I couldn't believe he included me, but now that he did, I fully trust him and his ability. He even promised not to kill anyone who surrenders. Not exactly the compromise I was hoping for, but it's better than acting the way that monster, Katie, acted toward Rocco and a pirate I'm too scared to ask Wren for his name.

"I use this lever to accelerate and scream as loud as I can." The plan is simple enough. If only it wasn't as gross as it is easy.

He nods. "Everyone aboard needs to hear you, all right? And don't be afraid when the bow starts to lift. It's normal. I'll really teach you how to drive the boat some other time. We just need to make everyone think the damn bastards are kidnapping us."

Anxiety tightens my chest, not at the idea of driving the boat—I've seen Ryan do it enough that I can manage—but because Wren really does mean that everyone aboard must think we're getting taken. "Ryan's going to—"

"Be fine. Better he flip his shit in front of everyone. Makes it authentic."

"You're cruel."

"You'll thank me, kid."

"That's a terrible assumption. Who would thank someone for putting another person—your son, if I might add—through something like this?"

"It's an expression," he mutters.

But even so. Instead of arguing, I stroll away from Wren to peer up the stairwell leading to the upper deck. It's late enough that those not given a task are inside their cabins or hanging out in the saloon, but it's only been minutes since the boat boarded. I know that if no one goes up soon, someone will come looking, and if they do… I suppress a groan at the thought. I'm on edge enough as it is because I also expect people to start yelling that we escaped from the brig. Titus obviously never thought we'd escape, and I hate to think what's keeping him preoccupied. I have to trust that Talia knows what she's doing when she said she knew how to handle the pirate.

"All right, Luna. I gotta put this on your head," Wren says, grabbing a cloth bag from a storage compartment. The sight of it freaks me out as much as having to sit in the boat while pretending the pirates accompanying me are still living.

I bite my lip to stop it from uncontrollably quivering. I don't want to do this. I can think of a million things I'd rather be doing than boarding a boat and using it as a decoy to get Titus to send a few of the crew members after us. The fewer aboard on his side, the better.

Wren cocks his head, studying my eyes. "Hey, don't do that. There's no time to break down now. You got this. Save those tears for my son to deal with."

A breathless laugh escapes my mouth at his words. He wags his eyebrows at me, proud at himself for stopping my oncoming tears. After pulling me into another surprise hug, Wren helps me climb into the boat. I sit on the floor near the steering wheel, crammed against the side close enough to push the lever forward to propel the boat from the garage. I'm just thankful it was backed into the stall to dock. I'm also grateful for the cover of night.

"Remember, take it as far as you can in five minutes." Without waiting for me to respond, Wren helps me start the engine and shows me how to accelerate quickly once more.

I tear holes in the bag with my nails to see out of and brace myself as I exit the Ocean's King and hit the still choppy water. Inhaling a deep breath of the fresh sea air, I release a loud scream until my voice gives out on me, and I have to gulp in another breath. Wind whips around me, whistling so loudly I can't tell if anyone heard my scream, but I can't shift and peer over the side of the boat yet.

"Please, let this work," I pray to the ocean, my body bouncing with the movement of the boat cutting across the water. The bow rises like Wren said it would as I gain speed, and I follow his quick directions, replaying a moment of watching Ryan plane the last tender boat we were in and manage to do the same from my position.

The seconds on Justin's watch tick by much slower than my racing heart. I can't take my eyes away from the faceplate, afraid if I do, my panic will get the best of me, and I'll throw myself overboard too soon to disappear into the deep.

And the most important thing for me to do is to swim as fast as I can back to the Ocean's King while all eyes are on the boat. Because if someone sees me, it'll put me at risk of getting hurt.

Thirty seconds pass, and I slide off the bag Wren put on

my head and ease up to peer over the edge. I catch sight of a few people from the crew launching from the yacht on jet skis exactly like Wren said they would. I didn't even know they were on board the Ocean's King, but how could I? I had barely left my room, and when I did, it was usually from the balcony when no one was watching.

Turning the wheel, I change the boat's direction to give me coverage to dive overboard and put it on autopilot like Wren showed me to keep it on course. I glance at Justin's wristwatch again, thirty more seconds passing, and then I gather my bravery, shift onto my feet, and throw myself over as fast as I can. I dive a dozen feet under as I take a breath of the sea and transform.

From my place, I watch the vessel skip over the water, leaving a trail of moonlight rippling behind it. The two jet skis fly across the surface, gaining speed faster than I thought possible, and I race in the opposite direction of the pirates and toward the Ocean's King.

I cling to my sarong, the currents pulling it back and forth around me. Flicking my tail, I cut through every swell, staying hopefully deep enough that no one will spot me. I ascend toward the surface, willing my transformation into a human to take hold, and as quietly as I can, I pop my head through the surface at the stern of the boat.

"What the hell are you doing?" a masculine voice hisses.

I reach my arm up toward Ali, the one pirate Wren told me I could trust and the one he knew would take guard at the stern.

"Hurry and help me."

He lifts me from the water, glancing at me up and down. "You should leave, Luna. Why would you come back?" This is probably the most he's ever said to me, usually staying quiet and obeying Wren's orders.

I gawk at him. "Why?" That's the weirdest question I've ever heard. There are a million reasons for me to come back here, the most important being my family and Ryan are aboard. I'd never abandon them.

Grabbing my arm, Ali pulls me with him away from the swimming platform and into the shadows of the small garage of the yacht. "Is Wren?" He doesn't ask his whole question, but I know what he's implying.

I shake my head. "He's okay and here. He also said that you'd help me."

Ali whistles through his teeth, cornering me in the garage like a shield made of taut muscle and bone. He's more fit than most on board, one of Wren's best divers and almost as good, if not equal in skill, to Ryan. He's the perfect candidate to remain on the crew after Wren gets control over the surface once again. If that's even possible.

"What do you need help with?" he asks, peering over his shoulder to check the deck around us again. "You know if I'm caught—"

"You can say you caught me," I say, knowing that even if Wren trusts Ali, the pirate won't put my life before his. He doesn't know me well enough, and I wouldn't expect him to, either. No one will get hurt or die on my behalf. I won't allow it.

He bows his head, staring at the deck. I half expect him to deny me my request for help and to yell out that he found me and that I asked him to pretend to be captured. I mean, I wouldn't blame him. I know the rules of the boat and how Wren molded his crew, but Wren's no longer captain. Ali now has more to lose if Titus were to find out that he's still on Wren's side.

"Please," I whisper, my soft voice disappearing with the salty breeze. "Just hear me out. I'm not asking you to stand up and fight. Just to make sure no one hurts me as I get to my cousin. I need to get her before things go down." Because not only do I want to protect Talia, I need to make sure she doesn't share her knowledge with Titus about the map and coordinates where I'll find my magic.

Ali releases a breath and reluctantly nods. "I think you're being reckless, Luna. Talia's safe enough. Better for you to get away now and leave the others. Your fate will be much worse than theirs." The fact that he doesn't mock me by calling me princess speaks volumes to me. He could have turned me away, thrown me overboard, or even handed me over to Titus, but he's treating me better than most have, and his kindness won't be taken for granted.

"I'm not worried about me," I say. "I'm worried about my family and the rest of my colonies. We don't want to end things with violence. I'm trying to stop a war. And to do so, I need my cousin and to get into Wren's safe for the map. My mom hid something important to me."

He groans. "A war?" It's probably all I'd care about if I were him, too.

I nod. "Do you honestly think the ocean will allow you to keep us away from the surface forever? That it'll allow you to hold knowledge that others would use against us?"

He pales at the thought but doesn't respond.

"All I want is to return the surface to how it should be. Pirates are supposed to protect the oceans from those who intend to do it harm not be the ones harming everyone and doing anything for your own self-gain."

Ali's eyes flick to the sea and back to me. "I'm only aboard the Ocean's King because I have no place on land. I like the sea. I love diving. Wren made that possible."

"And if Titus gets away—"

"Okay, I'm in. I'll do whatever you want. If Wren needs me to fight, I'll do that, too." He reaches for the weapon on his belt.

I stop him from pulling his knife free. "Let's start by finding Talia."

"Got it. Stay behind me, okay?" he says, strolling from the shadows. "She's exactly where you need to go for the map, anyway."

I nod.

Glancing over his shoulder, he adds, "If someone catches us—"

"No killing anyone," I say, cutting him off.

He puffs air through his lips. "Good, because I don't think I could."

His admission lights hope within me. For the first time, in someone other than Ryan, I realize that maybe not all pirates are bad.

There's hope for the ocean.

There's hope for me.

19

FALLING APART

"OH GOD, LUNA. WHAT are you doing here?" Talia asks, her bright eyes widening at the sight of me. "If Titus catches you—"

"Come on. We don't have much time." When Talia's not quick enough to move, I slide past her and into the captain's suite. Ali stays outside to keep watch, and I peer around the room.

It hasn't changed much since the one time I was in here, except the portrait of Nalani and Ryan has been removed from the wall and shredded into a pile of trash still littering the floor. Wren's clothes lay strewn across the bed and floor like someone was searching for something, but other than that, it's cleaner than most of the living spaces on the vessel.

Talia hugs herself, glancing at the door. "I told you I'd handle this. Titus promised me that he wouldn't hurt you as long as—"

"You cannot trust him," I say, rushing to the safe on the wall where Wren told me it would be. It looks like Titus unsuccessfully tried to open it.

"I have something he wants." She combs her fingers through her hair, pulling it out of her face. "Because he doesn't think Wren will cooperate and give him access to the map."

I blink a few times. "You told him you have it memorized?" I should've known. He probably suspected as much and Talia's his backup plan for if he can't get Wren to open the safe. Using Talia is easier than going through the trouble of breaking a safe, especially when other pirates will be after him.

Titus is smart. He's been watching Wren for years. But he's also full of himself.

"It's what's keeping everyone safe until we find what we're looking for," she says.

"Not everyone. Titus plans on—"

"Hurry, Luna. Someone's coming," Ali says, knocking on the door.

Pulling myself away from Talia, I rush to the safe and pound in the combination Wren told me. The lock beeps and I listen to the gears shift as the safe pops open, revealing more money and jewels than I have ever seen in person.

Voices sound out in the hallway, and something smashes against the door, startling me. Ali yells out my name, and I kick my body into action and rummage through the shelves on the left side of the safe where Wren told me he stored the map.

Talia latches her fingers on my arms. "You have to close it."

"I need the map."

"Luna, please. Titus can't know you have the combination. It'll—"

I spot the map, rolled among other documents, and pull it free. Talia drags me from the safe and shuts it, activating the lock. A crash on the door shudders the wood on its hinges, and I refold the map to place it between my skin and the strap of my bikini top under my sarong.

More commotion sounds out in the hallway, and I turn to Talia. "Are you ready to fight?"

She blinks a few times without responding. I realize that no amount of self-assurance can prepare either of us to fight the pirates no matter how much Talia says she can take care of herself.

Taking her hand, I hold it to me. "I know this is scary, but I need you to summon the fierceness you used against me when we first met, okay?"

"Please, just hide. Let me handle all this," Talia says. "I'll make sure you stay safe. We don't have to fight. I can see something different in your eyes already, Luna."

I straighten my shoulders. "I can't stand back and hope the

ocean takes care of things. Dealing with Ryan's dad was one thing, but Titus? No, I can't allow this to continue. I have to fight."

"But—"

"I know I haven't been all that great at protecting you, but can you trust me now? I'm not leaving you here. I need you with me." I study Talia's face as she gives nothing away. "I know you might not feel our bond yet, but just—"

"You're all I have left. Why do you think I'm here? Of course I feel our bond."

I throw my arms around her, hugging her to me. "So, come with me."

She nods. "We're in this together."

Together. Exactly how I always wanted.

The door to the suite flies open, and a man with a long beard tumbles across the floor. Ali falls on top of him, throwing punches as the man yells out. If he continues to holler, the rest of the yacht will come looking to see what's going on.

"Luna, go!" Ali yells, wrestling the man down.

I wave my hand. "Hurry, Talia."

More voices sound from the hallway, sending panic through my spark to lace around my chest. I grab Talia's hand and rush to the door, but I spot another pirate charging in our direction. I spent too much time talking to Talia. Wren warned me—in and out—and I didn't listen. Now we're going to get caught before I have a chance to get to Ryan and Darren.

The whole ship will know that I'm back on board much

sooner than they were supposed to. We should've had more time with the people chasing after the boat they were to think kidnapped us.

"Luna, the balcony," Talia says, motioning me to the glass door with a view of the glowing sea meeting the black of night. "We can jump."

I pant, tensing, trying to figure out what to do. "I can't leave Ryan."

Talia doesn't give me a choice. Tightening her hold on me, she drags me toward the balcony. Whistles sound from several places on the boat, and more yells echo through the air. My chest heaves, and I nearly trip on the rung to send me overboard and into the sea before I'm ready.

Talia steadies me and helps me to the other side. A few pops blast through the air, stealing my breath. I hook my arms around Talia and launch us from the balcony, the world whooshing by us.

I dive deep, holding onto my cousin as tightly as I can while I transform. Without any gear, Talia must rely on me to get her away. And right now, I have no idea what I'm doing or where I am yet. I don't get the chance to look. Talia pinches my shoulder, indicating she needs to surface for air.

She gasps for breath, brushing her legs against my tail, and she clings onto me. "Are you okay?"

I can only nod my head in response. I swim us in a circle and peer at the Ocean's King far enough away that someone would have to have binoculars to see us but still close enough to hear the faint commotion of a crew turning on themselves as they choose sides.

And they're not the only ones. Lights flicker in the distance, more boats heading in our direction. Chaos will surely ensue as Wren's fleet gathers. Titus probably summoned them all to see that their reigning pirate king will be no more. But he underestimated us. He underestimated me.

I'd never allow Titus to reign. And Wren? That's still to be determined no matter if he helped me. All I know is that I must find my magic and stop this violence. I must learn to control the pirates, and quickly, before the sea takes control of the situation for me, leaving sunken ships and waters too dangerous for even the innocent to cross, which will surely not go well in the human world. The colonies will revert to the ways of before with only those with connection to the lands surfacing. We'll be worse off, and it'll all be my fault.

"You need to swim us farther away before another boat spots us," Talia says, dragging my attention away from the fray of the battle aboard the Ocean's King.

My heart hangs heavy with worry, and I search the decks for signs of Ryan. Being out here with Talia leaves him and Darren vulnerable. The only thing that stops me from asking Talia to wait here while I return to the boat is that I know Ryan and Darren are used to facing the worst in the world. They can handle themselves.

"Give me a minute," I say, sinking under.

Peering around the sea, I take in the sparkling reefs teeming with nightlife. We're not as far from Celestiana Cove as I thought. It's a half day's swim from here. If I left with Talia now, I can get her to safety and return by sunrise. I can bring a boat and—

What am I even thinking? There might be nothing left come sunrise. This isn't me rescuing hostages from a crew that works together. This is me trying to stop the crew from falling apart until only the worst of the worst is left, and Ryan and Darren are the best people I know.

I pop back to the surface and spit out water. "We need to go back."

She scrunches her brows. "Are you kidding me?"

"I can't just swim here and do nothing."

"You will get killed. There's no way any of those pirates will—"

Sinking under, I release a scream into the water. The ocean swells around us, reacting to me for the first time in hours, and Talia rises a few dozen feet on a wave glittering in the moonlight shining from above.

I dart back up, wrapping my arms around her, and pull her under before it crests to throw her away from me. We break through to the surface, and I hug Talia tighter, watching all the nearby vessels rocking in the water.

"You need to take a breath and calm down," Talia says into my hair. "The tides are unpredictable with you."

"I just need my damn magic!" I yell to the sea, making Talia wince.

She blinks a few times, stunned by the words that even astonish me, and then she releases a laugh. "You're starting to sound like a pirate."

I groan in response. "I need to do more than sound like a pirate."

A light beams across the water, startling me. I drag Talia under in time to avoid a boat speeding over the spot we were treading. It cuts the engine, and I watch the glittering wake behind it disappear. I recognize the bottom of it to belong to The Mermaid, the boat Wren had stolen from the hostages I managed to save but in doing so also managed to ruin my chance to fix things with Wren. All it took was a common enemy to get us to work together.

I ascend to the surface, slowly breaking through to peer at the side of the boat. It's small, just enough to fit four people, but the perfect size for us. A smaller boat means fewer pirates, and I can't tread with Talia forever.

"I think we should board that boat," I whisper.

She eases herself away to peer into my eyes. "And then what exactly?"

"Seize it. It doesn't belong to them anyway," I say. "I want to transform back into a human and think things through better."

"Looks like there are four people on it," she whispers. "And they're armed."

"But we have surprise on our side."

"I guess I get to prove my fighting skills now," she says, her voice not into the idea, which I'm thankful for. "You know, growing up thinking that merpeople were going to drag me out to sea was enough to make me sign up for every self-defense and combat class I could afford."

I pout at her words. I hate that merpeople are the reason she felt she had to, but I'm grateful in a way. If Talia were a mermaid, she'd definitely be a warrior for Pearlestria. I just need to summon her strength into me.

"No time to sulk," she whispers. "Look."

I turn my gaze to the boat, spotting the four men standing on the bow, staring at the Ocean's King. None of them have weapons ready and waiting. They're too interested taking turns looking through binoculars to see what's happening aboard the boat.

Inhaling a deep breath, I steel myself, remembering Ryan's words about fighting. Not only does recalling that memory of us alone on one of his favorite uninhabited islands elicit warmth through me, it also gathers everything good from every second I've spent with Ryan and balls it up to fill my heart.

I can do this. I know I can do this. I'm no longer the naïve princess of Pearlestria, daughter of a shunned king and lost queen. I'm Luna Torres-Lazaro-Reyes, mermaid princess and pirate, and soon to be queen of the Reyes fleet, because there is no other possible outcome. I won't allow it. I won't let my pod or my colonies down anymore. I won't let the ocean down.

"I'm going to swim you to the bathing platform," I whisper to Talia, keeping my voice low enough to be drowned out by the hum of the sea. "As soon as you see my signal, attack from behind. Our goal is to disarm and capture, not to kill."

She nods. "Okay. Let's do this."

I puff air through my lips. "Take a breath."

I swim Talia the short distance and help her onto the boat. She tiptoes her way across the deck, scooping what looks like a rod of some sort into her hands. Swimming along to follow her, I make sure she gets behind the pirates unnoticed.

Diving deeper, I turn away from Talia to put distance between me and the boat. I need as much space as I can to gain the speed I need. I flip underwater and use the moon hanging in the sky behind the boat to focus on while I build speed, swimming as fast as I can. Extending my arms out in front of me, I straighten my body and launch from the water so swiftly that none of the pirates has even a chance to withdraw their weapons.

I fly onto the boat, crashing between two men, and knock them off their feet with my outspread arms. We all land on the deck and slide across it to smash into the wall. The guy on the outside, older with gray hair, slumps forward, knocked unconscious. But the younger guy manages to get to his senses and unsheathes the knife on his belt.

He swings his arm out, stabbing the deck right next to my tail. I spin on my back and fling my fin around knocking one of the guys facing Talia off his feet. He hits the deck with a thud, yelling out, but I continue to spin until I smack the guy who attempted to hit me with my expansive caudal fin.

His knife clatters across the deck, and he scrambles to stand, stepping on my tail in the process. I cry out, drawing Talia's attention to me. A hulking guy slings his arm around her and forces her to the wall, locking his fingers in her hair.

Fear crashes over me in a wave, and the boat rises on a sudden swell, knocking the guy off balance. Talia jerks her leg up and knees him in the groin, sending him to the deck next to me. I grimace at his reddening face, but don't get a chance to watch him long, because Talia reaches down and grabs him by his shirt, dragging him back.

A burly arm latches around me, hooking across my stomach. The old man bares his teeth at me with blood smeared across his face from a head wound. He squeezes me, sliding his arms around my neck, cutting off my airway and sinking his fingers painfully deep into my gills. I thrash my entire body, smacking my tail on the deck.

Tears burn my eyes, and I can't even use my voice to call out for help. He's too strong for me. I lift and drop my tail, attempting to get Talia's attention, but she's busy with the last standing pirate. They circle each other, and she swings the bar she stole from the stern at the man. He ducks out of the way, but she's prepared when he jerks back up and swings again, clocking him in the side of the head so hard he stumbles and falls overboard.

The edges of my vision darken, and I lose consciousness for a moment. One second I'm gaping at Talia and the next she's in front of me, yelling into my face. But it's not me she's yelling at. It's the old man loosening his hold on me.

His hollers pierce my ears, stealing my senses, and Talia drags me away from him. Something red splashes across the deck, and my stomach rolls at the sight of my bloody hand. I touch my neck, feeling around for a wound, relieved at my smooth skin.

And then I realize the blood doesn't belong to me. The old man clutches his leg, pouring blood from where I staked him with my sharp nails. I flip around to scoot my way back to him to help him with his wound. Talia steps between us, yelling my name. A loud pop sounds out, startling me. Blood splashes across Talia's face. She opens her mouth and screams, but I can't hear her voice over the ringing in my ears. She blinks for a second before dropping to her knees.

A shadow falls over us, and I crawl the best I can to my cousin, throwing myself on top of her. Swiveling around, I peer at the young pirate clutching the side of the boat holding a gun he pulled off his unconscious crewmate.

His face contorts, and he aims the gun at me. But I don't flinch or turn away. All I do is raise my hand up and point at the wave swelling behind him. It crashes over him and spills onto the boat. I hold tightly to Talia and the bolted down bench, swaying in the water.

The sea drains away, leaving me and Talia on the deck alone with only the body of the old man crumpled against the wall. Talia heaves a breath, clutching onto me. I push up on my hands and peer down at her, running my fingers over her still bloody T-shirt in search of the injury behind the stain.

"Oh, Ocean," I whisper. "Please, stay with me, Talia."

Talia reaches up and grabs my face. "Luna."

"Don't talk. Save your energy. I'm getting you to a healer." If only I wasn't so heavy outside of the sea I could lift the both of us over to swim.

"Luna," she says again. "I'm okay."

"You're in pain."

"Because you're squishing my legs."

"But the blood," I say, shifting off her.

She bats at my hand before I can tug up the hem of her shirt to inspect her stomach. "Wasn't mine. I'm okay. He missed me."

My eyes widen. Oh, Ocean. If he didn't hit Talia, he must've hit me. The blood is mine.

"He hit that guy," she adds, drawing my attention to the old man. Lifting her hand, she points to the blood staining the back of his shirt where blood seeps from a wound. "Killed him."

My stomach clenches, and I throw up ocean water over the deck. Talia scrambles to her feet and to the old man, digging her arms under his to drag him away from me. I cover my mouth with my hand, my vision darkening.

A light cuts across the deck from another, much larger boat, and I attempt to pull myself from the deck to flip over into the water.

I don't get far. My body gives out on me.

I pass out.

20

LOST

"I'M LOST, MOM. I need you. I don't know what to do," I say, pulling my tail up to rest my chin on the bend.

My mom slides her arm over my back and pulls me into a hug. Her silver tail sparkles like a rainbow in the bright sunshine overhead. The blue ocean, the same aqua as her eyes, stretches out into the distance.

"My daughter, you are not lost. You're exactly where you're supposed to be. Can't you feel it?" she asks, cupping water from a rolling wave into her hand. Droplets float from the pool in her palm and freeze in the air. The sun reflects on the clear orbs, appearing like a dozen tiny light bulbs over her fingers.

"I feel nothing but my failure. The pirates have turned on each other. Ryan, he's—I've failed my mate and his family. I've failed Darren. I don't know how to change things or save anyone. I'm afraid Dad was right."

My mom's face remains expressionless as she stares at her glittering orbs. "The only thing he has been right about is how worthy of the sea you are, Luna."

"But I'm not. I could barely manage to keep the cove you gave your life for safe—and it was at the expense of our pod. I just—I'm lost."

"My daughter, like I said, you're exactly where you're supposed to be. Just close your eyes and call to the sea like it calls to you." She flicks her fingers, shooting the glowing orbs back into the water. Being with my mom now, in a place of my dreams, helps ease the fissure of pain cracking through the wall of steel I imagine around myself.

"It doesn't listen to me anymore." A wave rushes over our tails, and I graze my fingers through the foam as it's dragged back to sea and out of my reach again.

Offering me a loving smile, she brings her hand up and touches my cheek. "It does, my daughter. I'm here, aren't I? Just close your eyes."

I do as she says, shutting my eyes, just listening to the sound of the lapping waves until it fades into the hum of the ocean. My red eyelids turn dark, and I snap my eyes open, startling at the sight of a body floating in the water in front of me. Hands lock onto my shoulders, and I flick my tail, darting a few dozen feet away from the silhouette of a boat.

Anger rushes through me to replace the moment of relief given to me by my mom. She abandoned me once again, leaving me amid turbulent waters I can no longer navigate like I used to. A yell hums through the ocean by my ear. Fingers dig into my shoulders, getting me to slow down. I spin around and face Talia floating in the ocean with me. She swims forward and wraps her arms around me again, and I shoot us both toward the surface.

"Thank God," she says into my hair. "I wasn't sure if you were going to wake up, so I threw you overboard in case. I don't really know how to take care of a mermaid."

I clear my throat, trying to summon my words, but I can't speak. It feels like hours have passed, but it couldn't have been more than a few seconds. Talia kicks her legs, swimming me in the direction of The Mermaid, and I remember what I am and close the distance for the both of us.

Her words resonate with me, about how she doesn't know how to take care of me, but she still tried. It makes all of this less daunting. I'm not alone, fighting against the world. I have Talia with me. Ryan and Darren, too. The ocean—if only I could figure out how to use it without my magic.

Sinking under, I transform into a human. Talia helps me onto the platform of the boat, stronger than she looks. I don't even know how she managed to get me in my mermaid form into the water. Ryan struggles under the weight of my tail.

All these little discoveries about my cousin pull me closer to her, and it makes everything I feel even more catastrophic. I have a lot to fight for but too much to lose.

Talia hands me a towel. "Can you say something?"

"Like what?" I manage to ask.

She exhales a breath and hugs me again without responding.

A few more vessels float nearby, gathering around the Ocean's King. It takes everything in me not to jump back into the water to swim to the pirate ship, but Talia hugs her arms around me, keeping me in place while she adjusts my sarong around me, retying it to wrap around my neck in a halter fashion so it stops sliding down with the water dripping from the colorful fabric.

Her fingers glide across my back to straighten it. She frowns and lifts my bikini strap to pull something free. I stiffen and spin around to face her. Oh, Ocean. I forgot about the map. I carry stuff on my body so often that it slipped my mind when we were forced to jump from the Ocean's King, and now it's ruined. The map falls apart in Talia's fingers before she can unfold it properly—not like it matters. The ink with the coordinates probably washed away the moment we entered the sea.

And now everything is gone forever.

I sink to the deck, washed clean of blood with the help of the ocean, and curl my knees to my chest and rest my chin on them. My mom was wrong about me and the sea. By the time this is all over, I'll be stripped of my mermaid essence and left on land like my dad. Maybe it's a good thing. It's not like Ryan can follow me into the sea. It guarantees our life together. We can grow old and remain on land like the mermaids before me.

Tears prickle my eyes. I should be okay with the thought. I should be happy to build a life on land with Ryan no matter what. But then sadness sinks into me with the thought of abandoning the sea.

"Don't cry, Luna," Talia says. "I have the map memorized, remember? Just find me something to write on, and I'll copy it again. In case..."

I hold my hand up, not wanting to face the idea that she's thinking in case something happens to her. It's more than the map. It's everything. I don't get the chance tell her that, though.

A whistle cuts through the air, drawing our attention from each other and back to the Ocean's King. Talia swipes some discarded binoculars from under the bench seat and gets back to her feet to peer through them.

"Something's up," she says. "I see Titus on the bow wit—" She snaps her mouth closed.

"He caught Wren, didn't he?" I ask, rubbing my hands into my eyes to clear my vision. "We're out of time."

"It's not that, Luna." Talia helps me to my feet and hands me the binoculars. I peer through them at the Ocean's King, slowly trailing my vision across each deck and pathway until I stop on the bow where several figures gather.

In the water below, I spot the tender boat dropping anchor. Someone moves on the boat around the bodies Wren had propped up on the seats. One by one, the man throws the bodies overboard, creating splashes big enough to rock the small vessel.

I adjust the binoculars and peer at the main deck. My heart picks up pace, thrumming against my ribcage, demanding to leave me to drift on the waves toward where Titus shoves Ryan. My mate falls, disappearing from view. I cringe when Titus closes the distance. I don't have to see his whole body to know that he's kicking Ryan.

Darren emerges with another pirate, and Titus swivels away from Ryan and swings his arm out, clocking Darren hard enough in the face that he falls back into the pirate holding him, and they crash into the fiberglass wall of the boat.

Titus waves something in his hand, aiming it from Darren to Ryan. My hands tremble so hard, and I accidentally drop the binoculars, losing them over the side of the boat. Without thinking, I swing my leg over the side of The Mermaid to jump into the water, but Talia locks her fingers on the back of my sarong and pulls me into her arms.

"You can't just jump in and leave me without a plan," she says, surprising me with the strength of her arms. "It'll do neither of us any good. Titus probably knows that you wouldn't be far. He might even think you're still on the boat."

She's right. He probably also knows that Wren is on the boat, too. But he was nowhere in sight that I could see. We were supposed to meet on the sundeck after I found Talia, Ryan, and Darren. That was the plan. The four of us were to be the distraction while Wren took care of Titus. But I'm not there, which means...

"I was supposed to be there, anyway. It was the plan," I say, wiggling to test Talia's hold, but she doesn't relent.

"Now what kind of plan was that?"

"Wren was going to take care of Titus," I say.

She releases a breath near my ear. "That man is so full of himself. It's more than Titus. It's all the crew. Titus promised to divide all of Wren's wealth among them. He promised the crew that they could do what they wanted. There isn't one damn pirate on these waters who doesn't want to do whatever they want without consequence. Wren could kill Titus, but it doesn't change the fact that the power Wren once had is gone. It's dispersed just like the magic of the sea, and everyone's taking what they think is their rightful share."

I stop struggling, and Talia releases me, sensing that I'm no longer going to hop overboard and swim to board the boat to attempt to save Ryan and Darren. Combing my fingers through my hair, I push it out of my face and hang my head, staring into the glittering water.

"Why am I even here?" I whisper to the waves. "Why put me in a position I'm not prepared to handle?"

Talia drapes her arm across my shoulder to stand next to me, staring into the sea by my side. "Did it answer you?"

I lift and drop my shoulders. "No..." My voice trails off, my mom's words suddenly spinning through my mind again. I blink my tears away and straighten my back. "Actually, I think it has. My mom told me I'm exactly where I'm supposed to be."

I thought she had meant that I'm exactly where I'm supposed to be to fight off the pirates and regain order on the surface, but it's not what she meant at all. She wanted me to close my eyes and listen to the sea. I'm in this spot for a reason. I ended up with Titus and back on the Ocean's King for a reason. It wasn't because of the vicious pirates. It's because of my magic. That was where my current was supposed to lead.

"Talia," I say. "The map. Where was the next location?"

She tugs me away from the side of the boat and the commotion still happening on the main deck of the Ocean's King. We climb into the enclosed cockpit, and Talia messes with the navigation system on the boat for a moment, tapping in some of the coordinates she had memorized.

She swivels on her feet to grab my shoulders and gives me a shake. "It's here. I mean, we're a little off, but it's here. Do you think...?"

I nod. "My magic. It's in these waters. It's why I saw my mom again. She told me I'm exactly where I need to be."

Talia's face lights up, her eyes nearly silver in the reflection of the moonlight dancing across the blue color, looking exactly how I see it over the glowing sea. Turning away from me, Talia heads across the deck and starts to reel in the anchor, surprising me.

"What are you doing?" I ask.

"What do you think? We have to go."

I cross my arms over my chest, hugging myself. "I was going to swim."

"Not without me, you aren't. But I'm suiting up. There is diving gear already prepped."

"I can't take you with me. I'm too fast. You'll get decompression sickness."

Talia strolls to me and rests her hands on my shoulders. "I can handle myself. We'll each take a flashlight so I can see you."

"Talia," I say.

She shakes her head. "This is how it's supposed to be. I'll have your back. You'll have mine. Now, stop arguing. We have to go while everyone's distracted."

Talia starts the engine and motions for me to sit down on the seat next to her while she navigates the boat, picking up speed to zoom us away. The vessel bobs a few times and evens out, and I peer around the sea to make sure no one follows us. As far as the other boats know, we're still the crew of four that arrived.

Talia slows in speed, and I realize how close we were to where my mom left her belongings—and hopefully my magic— for us to find. The lights on the boats pepper the dark sea around us like the orbs of water frozen above the surface, glittering in the moonlight. Even though I know they're the lights of the pirates, it still reminds me of my mom's magic. It helps ease the fear and heartache constantly attempting to destroy every ounce of goodness washing through me.

Talia drops the anchor, leaving me in the cockpit, and a strange static noise erupts through the radio on the dash. "The

Mermaid, do you copy?" a masculine voice says through a speaker.

I stiffen and glance around, half expecting another pirate to suddenly show up at the summons of the voice that repeats the words over again. I rush from the cockpit to find Talia already prepping for the dive.

"Someone is calling the boat," I say. "What do I do?"

She presses her lips together in thought. "Ignore it."

"What if they decide to come to us? We're not that far."

She shrugs. "Well, they definitely will if you answer it," she says.

Turning back to her equipment, she readies herself for what might possibly be the most dangerous dive of her life. Fear trickles over me, dripping ice through my veins, and I pace around the boat, walking the short pathway from the bow to stern over and over again until Talia stands in my way, suited up with her tank on.

She holds out a dive light to me. "You can go as fast as you need, just make sure to wave this around every once in a while. I'll follow at my own pace."

I bob my head, taking the light from her to look at it once, sending stars bursting in my vision. Stepping to the bathing platform, I bend over and glance into the water again to assess it the best I can from the surface. I have no idea where my mom would have hidden anything, but I suspect like the times before, she might have built or found an abandoned merpeople house. Because even though we live in colonies, it sometimes takes days to travel and not everyone is fond of sleeping out in the open of the sea.

"I'm going to dive straight down first and see if I can find anything that looks out of the ordinary," I say to Talia.

She grips the railing, standing with her back facing the water. "Just give me the signal if you—"

The sound of a boat hums through the air, and I jerk to spin toward the direction of the Ocean's King. But it's not a boat. It's two men on one of the jet skis heading in our direction. Talia's eyes widen, and she flips her goggles down.

"Time to go," she shouts.

Jumping backward, Talia enters the water first without waiting for me. She clicks her light off as she descends cautiously, waving her hand for me to hurry. A shout echoes through the air, and I dive overboard head first, swimming a few feet under. I transform, leaving the sarong on, and then I dart even deeper and peer up at the jet ski now circling the boat.

It stops, the bubbles clearing from the surface. One of the men bends over to search the water, and he points in my direction. My heart thrashes in my chest, because he shouldn't be able to see me, but then I realize it's not me that has drawn his attention. It's the flashlight I'm holding in my hand.

I immediately click it off and swim away before the men can raise their weapons in an attempt to hurt me or get me to the surface. I spin around in the water, fighting against the nerves bunching in my stomach to look for Talia. She floats in the water barely moving, just hovering and releasing bubbles in the sea.

Without the light of her flashlight, she's amid pure darkness with her human vision apart from the light of the moon rippling across the surface. Flicking my fin, I jet closer to her but slow down so that I don't startle her.

I flash my light on and off, letting her know that I'm coming up on her, and she gives me the signal that she's okay. I flash the light again, and she does the same, and then I dive down and toward the reef below us. Fish dart through the coral, and I catch sight of a Moray eel hanging out of a hole.

I fan my tail, shooing away a few of the larger fish starting to congregate and take a moment to look around. As far as I can see, it looks like an ordinary reef. The water isn't as deep here, and the ocean magic is faint, not stopping Talia from making her way in my direction as I continue to flash on and off my flashlight in quick bursts that hopefully only she can see.

Tilting my head back, I peer at the surface again and watch as the jet ski drives once more around the boat before taking off. I release a bubble through my lips and stare at it floating toward the surface. I'm surprised when no one starts to reel in the anchor to take The Mermaid back to the Ocean's King. By now, the men probably already informed Titus of the strange ghost ship now that neither Talia nor I are on. He probably also discovered the three men the ocean swept away from us clinging to the floatation device Talia said she knew I'd insist they get.

My spark blinks in my chest, slowing down into a steady rhythm as I breathe in and out the sea. The quiet of the ocean calms me. Nothing seems so out of control as I'm floating in a place that feels as good as the waters of Pearlestria.

Talia swims up beside me, turning on her flashlight again and waving it in my face. Her eyes smile at me from behind her mask, though I can't see her mouth with the bubbling mouthpiece. Extending her arm, she peers around the sea life, taking in the vibrant reef and all the creatures suddenly scattering away from me at her presence.

"Amazing, right?" I say out loud into the water.

Talia nods her head and swims a few feet away from me, trailing her flashlight across the coral. I follow behind her, keeping my distance as to not jostle her around in a current of my making. It's strange to swim with her in her full dive gear, and I resist touching her. My mind wanders to Ryan and what it would be like to do the same with him. I prefer he free dive so I can hold onto him, but now that I'm experiencing a different kind of dive with Talia, I would resist my urge with Ryan to keep him in the water as long as a tank could last.

Talia flashes her light in my face again, motioning toward the reef, and I swim next to her and peer at the glimmering white rock. She reaches down and picks it up in her gloved hand and holds it to me.

It's a misplaced rock, brought straight from the castle of Pearlestria and my bedroom. I know it, because I've stared at the blank spot on my wall all my life. I could never find another white rock like it, and it felt wrong to put another color in that particular spot where my mom had arranged the stones to look like the moon rising over a green island. It was always my favorite masterpiece besides the flaw of the missing stone because my mom made it for me.

I blink my burning eyes, though my oncoming tears blend with the sea. Even if this is the only thing I find in this spot, I'll be happy. It's the one piece I need for my wall in Pearlestria, and now my home can be complete again.

I tuck the white stone into the tight bodice of my sarong and smile at Talia, reaching out to carefully touch her shoulder to show my appreciation. We continue to swim along the reef, finding colorful rocks along the way, and I can nearly place their exact spots all over my home mermaid colony.

This hunt for treasure is different than the others. My mom didn't take rocks from the sand channel—ones of reds and blues, of greens, yellows, and oranges—she's taken the ones mermaids favor in the rare colors. The pinks and indigos. The silvers and golds. Even a few that shimmer like the inside of shells.

And then I see it.

The reef grows in size, towering at least two dozen feet to stretch toward the rippling surface above us. It's larger than the rest of the reef, and I spot the pearlescent rock found in Pearlestria that makes up most of the houses.

I motion to Talia with my light, and she swims next to me. I do my best to keep from speeding off and leaving her in my current. She swims above me, slowly going toward the top of the reef while I dart around it and through an open channel guarded by a gray fish that bumps into me when I get too close to his home.

I shoo him away and make my way to the other side of the reef. I glance up to Talia, my heart faltering. She no longer hovers in the water above me. A burst of light engulfs my vision, and I startle, flying back in the water.

A hand pops through a hole in the coral, and I release a relieved laugh catching sight of Talia peeking at me from inside the mermaid house. Darting up, I head to where I last saw her and wave my flashlight down a tunnel the right size for a hulking merman. Talia shines her light up while swimming closer, extending a bag out to me.

I smile and hold onto the reef, letting my tail float toward the surface behind me to quickly dart inside. I remain in the tunnel and tear the bag open with my nail, searching through a bag of glittering stones shaped like different animals from the land and sea. I recognize them from when I was a merbabe, but nothing calls out to me.

I shake my head and dump the bag completely, watching everything scatter around Talia to disappear into the sandy floor. A fishing line catches on the edge of the bag, making me inhale a breath of the sea. My heart flickers to create glowing light around me in the tunnel, lighting Talia's face morphing from excitement to sadness and what looks like fear as I pull out the necklace with nothing on it. No stone or jewel. Not even a piece of sea glass. Just an empty loop where a stone used to be.

My stone isn't here. It's gone.

Talia waves her hand at me, flashing her light in my eyes. She releases a stream of bubbles that tickle my face as they kiss my skin suddenly frantic.

I reach out my hand to her, and she links her fingers with mine, tugging me down. "My magic isn't here—"

Pain bursts through my tail, startling me, and I grip the coral tighter in shock stopping Talia from pulling me into the mermaid house. I swim out of the tunnel and turn to glance behind me and catch sight of a figure in the water, half expecting to find another mermaid.

But it's a diver with a spear gun, and I'm caught on the end of his line.

21

CALL OF THE SEA

I SCREAM IN PAIN, reaching for the spear in my tail, but the diver pulls the line, attempting to reel me in. Talia swims up toward me, but agony forces me to let go of the reef, and I fly through the water a dozen feet. Automatically flicking my tail, I propel forward, dragging the line with me. More pain cuts through me, and I scream again.

Every time I try to stop and cut the line, the diver yanks me toward him. I can't believe this is happening. I can't believe I'm being reeled in.

Anger rushes over me. I refuse to be treated this way. This is my home. My waters. This diver has no right to attempt to hurt me in the place I should feel safest. I have never been so afraid of being who I am until this moment. Dad warned the colonies about the dangerous humans on the surface, but that's where they've always remained. I'm the first mermaid to have ever been caught like a fish, and I'm afraid of what happens next.

I do the only thing I can think of.

Squeezing my eyes shut, I will my transformation to take hold of me. My lungs burn from the sudden shift in my body, my gills no longer letting me breathe. And now, the pain is worse than ever. The spear remains lodged in my leg, and I can see the barb sticking out through the other side of my calf.

But now that I'm human, I can bring my leg up to my chest better than if I had my tail. I kept automatically flicking it, making everything worse as the diver played tug of war with me. Wrapping my hand around the spear, I try to rip it free.

I don't get the chance.

The diver reels the line again with him as he heads back to the surface for a breath of air. I jerk through the sea, the space between me and the diver growing smaller as he heads in my direction.

The edges of my vision shadow with the lack of air, and I thrash a few times, still unable to free myself. Peering around through the blurry water, I try to search for Talia, but the diver tugs me to him completely and squeezes me in his arms, propelling us to the surface.

I expel the sea from my lungs and scream out, my voice

ripping through the air loud enough that the man shoves me back underwater, making me inhale a breath of the sea. I wiggle and fight, kicking my injured leg, attempting to put space between us.

A light flashes in the water, drawing my attention away from the pirate digging his hands into one of my shoulders while holding me by the waist, and I spot Talia heading in my direction.

The man tugs my head back out of the water, and I cough and spit, thrashing to break free from his hold. Another light shines in my eyes, blinding me, and I freeze, my senses overwhelming me.

"Luna," a deep, soft voice whispers. "Stop fighting."

I blink the haze from my eyes and peer in the direction I heard the voice. Darren stands aboard The Mermaid with an unfamiliar pirate holding a knife to his neck. All the snarling man would have to do was flick his hand, and Darren would be dead.

So I stop struggling. I go limp in the diver's arms.

The man shoves me toward the boat, knocking the breath out of me. I heave, dipping under the water again. Pain pours through me, and I fall face first onto the platform, just lying on the rough surface without moving. I don't think I could if I wanted to.

"Please, don't hurt him," I manage to whisper, my throat croaking as the words come out.

"You killed Favi," the man holding Darren accuses. "A life

for a life is fair."

Shaking my head, I raise my hand toward Darren. "I didn't. I don't even know how to shoot a gun. It was one of his crewmates. Please."

The man shakes his head, spins Darren around, and shoves his knife into his shoulder. Punching him in the face, he knocks Darren overboard and into the water. I scream out, dragging myself toward the edge of the platform to dive in, but the diver slams his hand on my leg, shooting searing pain through my body. In a quick motion, he rips out the spear, and I fall forward, hitting my cheek on the deck. The pain overwhelms me, stealing my breath along with my will to fight. I can't protect myself from these pirates. I can't even get to my knees.

The boat rocks on the water, and I press my lips together to stop from crying.

"Ocean, please," I whisper. "Please."

A laugh sounds from my right, and the diver rolls me over onto my back. The glittering sky sparkles above him as he looks into my eyes and pushes my hair from my face. Moonlight halos around his head, reminding me of all the moons that have called me to the sea, and how the sea still calls to me.

So I call back.

Closing my eyes, I whisper for help again.

And then I listen.

The engine of the boat hums through the air, louder than the water, and the world blurs around me as the pirates navigate to the Ocean's King, leaving behind Darren and Talia. I pray for their safety. I pray that the ocean shows them mercy. And I pray for me.

A whistle sounds through the air, and the diver shoves his hands under me and lifts me into his arms. He jostles me as he crosses the deck of the boat, and I keep my eyes trained on the moon, ignoring the laughter and shouts of the men who torment me from the diver's arms.

He tosses me away from him and onto the coarse deck, and I can't stop another scream from escaping, making the pirates laugh even more.

"Luna," a deep, familiar voice whispers so softly I think I might have imagined it. "Oh, Ocean."

I blink a few times, hearing the whispered prayer from my mate in words I've never heard him say. Something slams into my back, knocking me over, and I curl my legs up, catching sight of Ryan standing at the bow of the boat with his hands bound, his face bruised and bleeding.

But he doesn't frown.

He smiles in relief, with love, with everything amazing that comes with our bond. He might not look much better than me, but he's alive and that's all that matters. His whisper of my name gives me exactly what I need in this moment. He gives me hope and strength, courage to get back to my feet, and the best thing in the whole universe: Love. So much incredible, unwavering, unending love that flows over me and lifts me up without having to think about it.

His love ignites my spark, now blazing brighter than the

waning moon in the sky. The commotion settles, and all I can hear is the sound of Ryan breathing in a small breath of air, catching sight of my mermaid essence that begs the ocean to listen to me.

And then I hear it. The call of the sea.

It hums through my being, steadying me on my feet despite not having my tail. The sea reacts to me, rising a swell that lifts the Ocean's King on the water before dropping it. I'm so focused on Ryan and the sea that I notice the shadow creeping up on me too late. Ryan's face morphs, his brows puckering, his mouth opening to yell.

Pain burns my back, and a hand tangles in my hair, yanking me up and onto my tiptoes. Warmth trickles down my spine, and I realize that the sensation comes from the heat of my blood dripping over my skin.

"Calm the seas or I'll cut your heart out and give it to your boyfriend," Titus says, growling into my ear.

"I can't control it," I say without taking my eyes off Ryan's. The weight of a hundred gazes, possibly more, bores into me as the fleet of pirates from everywhere takes in the sight of me, weak and unable to defend myself in Titus's arms.

"I said calm the damn water, Luna." He puts more pressure on my back, the blade of his knife sinking deeper. A sob heaves my chest, making it burn worse, and the water rises even higher. Panic squeezes my lungs, stealing my breath away.

"I—I can't with the knife in my back," I manage to spit out. "Please, you have to stop."

Ryan holds my gaze, his green eyes reminding me of the beauty the ocean carries under the toxic surface created by humans and pirates. The sea glass I love so much wasn't born from the sea, but was created by it. The once sharp edges, deadly and dangerous, were smoothed out by the constant roll of the tides, leaving behind pieces as pretty as the sparkle of sunlight across the open water. It reminds me that even something that could cause so much pain left unattended and in the wrong hands cannot withstand the power of the sea for long. Because the ocean, great and so full of life, is also treacherous if not navigated with care. And Titus will find out. He might hold my life in his hands, but the ocean holds his, and like him, it won't grant him mercy.

"Last warning, princess," Titus says into my ear, his hot breath making me shiver.

But I can't back down. I can't allow him to continue stealing what he wants, destroying everything in his wake he finds worthless. Even if it means I fulfill the sea's purpose by standing on my two feet, holding onto the courage Ryan sends to me in wave after wave as strong as the swelling ocean around us.

"No," I whisper. "If you kill me, you'll take your whole crew with you."

Titus releases a whistle, stinging my ear with the sudden noise, and a huge, muscular man stomps toward Ryan, towering over him by a few inches. Ryan jerks his bound arms together, swinging them at the man, but he only missteps, ramming his hands into Ryan to support himself.

"Don't," I say, my steely resolve cracking as the man yanks a short sword from his belt and aims it at Ryan.

My mate straightens his shoulders, flaring his nostrils, without giving away anything else except for the same bravery still coursing through me.

"Cut his heart out," Titus says, nodding to the man.

I scream out, thrashing so hard that Titus loses his grip on me. Ryan closes his eyes as the pirate pulls back his arm, and a wave crests over the side of the boat, spilling water across the deck.

"No!" I scream, stumbling forward without making it far. Titus grabs the back of my sarong and pulls me into him.

He releases another whistle, and the pirate stops short, tearing the front of Ryan's shirt open, only nicking the skin over his chest. I bend forward, clutching my knees, barely able to stand with the thought that all it would take is a blade to end Ryan's life right before me, severing my life with him, stealing our bond before we even have a chance to make it official. Our eternity could very well end here.

The boat rises and falls on another wave, reacting to the turmoil raging in my heart. Ryan closes his eyes for a moment, swallowing the ounce of fear that shines on his face. The realization hit him as hard as it did me.

"Calm the damn o—"

A strange shadow crosses the deck between me and Ryan. I fall forward and away from Titus. He yells out, and a thud radiates from the deck. Wren flips Titus on his back, punching him in the face. Titus spits, sending blood across the deck. Chaos breaks out, more men jumping from the sundeck, and fists and arms fly. Blades sparkle in the light of the moon and loud pops ring in my ears as a war between pirates rages on despite the choppy waves surrounding us, threatening to sink all the ships.

"Luna, watch out!" Ryan yells in time for me to catch sight of a woman with a long braid rushing from the fray in my direction.

The woman swings her arm at me, but I duck and jab my fist into her stomach like Ryan taught me. She stumbles back, and a man charges from the pathway and pulls her up. I brace myself, expecting them to team up to take me down, but the man hooks his arm over the woman and tosses her right over the side of the boat.

He turns, and I gape at Ali, obscured by a baseball cap I've never seen him wear. He motions me forward, and I hobble to him, closing the space between me and Ryan in the process. Ali swipes his knife from his belt to cut the zip ties from Ryan's wrists, but I cut him off and use my nails, throwing myself into my mate for a hug I desperately needed. He releases me as quickly, spinning me around so my back isn't facing the pirates.

His fingers brush the tender skin on my back and then he shifts down to glance at the wound on my leg. The longer I stay still, the more pain radiates from my body as my adrenaline slides away with another curling wave, knocking a few more pirates off their feet.

Yanking the shirt over his head, Ryan ties it around my

wound tight enough to stop the bleeding so I can heal faster. Ali peers around the deck, blocking me from the front while Ryan holds onto me from behind, and together we step along the outskirts of the massive fight.

"There he is," Ali says, pointing to Wren as he throws another punch at Titus, now lying on his back.

"Captain, come on," Ali yells. "Time to go."

"I ain't leaving my ship," Wren yells, turning his attention to another man who approaches him with a knife. "Get my kids out of here, all right? I'll handle this."

Ali turns to glance at me and Ryan from over his shoulder, and I yell out as a woman with short hair aims a gun and pulls the trigger. It happens so quickly that I can't even move. Ali thrusts back into me, knocking both me and Ryan to the deck, saving all of us.

The woman raises the gun again, and Ryan locks his fingers to my sides and flips me over his head to land on my knees above him. I scream out at the same time the woman swears as nothing happens with her weapon. A wave rises again, crashing over the side of the boat, knocking the three of us away from each other.

I roll a dozen times until I thud into the wall of the boat, my body clenching in pain. My arms shake and it takes me a few tries to push onto my hands and knees to get to my feet. I search the deck for Ryan, catching sight of him on the other side. A man grabs onto his ankles, dragging him back a few feet before Wren charges in their direction and shoves the guy back into the railing where he flips over backward, knocking his head on the edge of the deck before disappearing into the sea.

I crawl forward, trying to get to Ryan and Wren, the ocean out of control and angry, crashing wave after wave over the deck any time a pirate gets to their feet. I'm terrified they'll get swept away at any second.

"Hold on to something!" I yell out, the Ocean's King rising on another swell a few dozen feet into the air.

Wren grips the railing with one hand and then onto Ryan, grabbing his arm to stop him from stumbling forward. The remaining pirates all brace themselves through the descent down on the massive wave comparable to the many my dad made to sink ships.

I scramble to hold onto the deck, digging my nails into the rough surface. The motion of the next wave sends me sliding right into a body against the wall. Titus hollers and jerks his hand out, wrapping his fingers through my hair. He tosses me off him and pins me down, spitting at me as he yells into my face.

"All you had to do was calm the water!" he hollers, shoving his hand against my neck.

I can't respond, the pressure of his hand too much to allow me to form words. His whole face distorts, and he aims his knife over my spark. Light glimmers off the shiny metal, sending beams of light through the dark to illuminate the deck with a bunch of starbursts of light.

And then I feel it. A wave of magic burning in my chest

floods over me from the stone I found lost in the sea. The stone that reminded me of my room in Pearlestria. Of my mom. The stone that reminded me of me.

"Let her go!" Ryan yells, breaking free of Wren to rush across the deck with another swell.

I close my eyes, whispering a prayer to the sea to accept me into its depths, to pull my essence from me to mingle with the magic begging to be free to save the seas from this murderous man. Tingles rush through my body, sending a wave of heat and muscle spasms through me as my transformation takes hold.

A loud pop sounds through the air, startling me, and I open my eyes to meet Ryan's as he stands a few feet away, clutching his chest. Blood pours from his hands, staining his skin in a river of red that makes my whole soul scream. He drops to his knees and sprawls forward, his arms reaching out for me.

Titus squeezes my cheeks, forcing my gaze away from Ryan to look at him. His eyes, ones so full of hate and anger, darker than the trenches of the ocean, bore into me. He raises his blade and jerks his hand down toward my chest.

I brace for the ocean to swallow us whole.

I brace for the sound of Ryan's last breath.

I brace for my death.

22

LAST BREATH

PAIN BURSTS THROUGH MY body, starting in my chest and pouring through the rest of me. Titus shields his eyes from the bright flash that lights everything around us, turning night to day before leaving the world in pitch black.

I cup my hands to my chest, slicing my skin on Titus's blade that pierces through the sparkling, white stone and into the skin of my chest. A comforting, familiar burst of energy explodes through me. The stone cracks and shatters, crumbling in my fingers, releasing my magic to pour through me, filling up my insides to give me the strength to fight. The knife clatters to the deck next to me, and Titus swipes it away to stab me again.

"No!" I say, swinging my arm out to knock him away. I summon a tidal wave that crashes over us, sweeping Titus across the deck and into the side railing. His body bends backward with the weight of the sea crushing him until his yells stop and he flips off the boat. The ocean swallows him, dragging him into its dark depths, showing him no mercy like he showed me.

My chest heaves with burning air I can't breathe. Scales sprout on my legs as I transform, my spark flashing in quick successions, illuminating the suddenly dark boat unlit by electricity. I flop forward, dragging my body toward Ryan instead of the sea to take a breath of the ocean. My skin tingles with pain and something else, something hot that flows through my veins from my heart. It washes over me, and I pray to be consumed by the sensation. Because I can't stand to feel anymore. I can't stand seeing Ryan's look of terror, of hopelessness branded into my mind.

"I got ya, Luna," Wren says, thudding across the deck. He scoops me into his arms, lifting me from the floor. "You ain't gonna die on me, too."

Too. My eyes swell with tears, hearing the hitch in his voice. Agony pours through me worse than the heat that leaves me breathless. I gasp again, unable to suck in air. Thrashing in Wren's arms, I force him to drop me. I land on the deck and roll right into Ryan's arms.

"L-Luna," Ryan whispers, curling his fingers around my arms but unable to pull me to him. I can feel his life slipping from mine as the seconds tick by, the wound worse than anything I've seen. "I-I love y-you."

Grief and heartache steal away the words I try so hard to say to him. I shift, dragging my tail with me, scraping off my scales on the deck. Pressing my hands to the wound in his chest, bleeding his life all over the ship just to be washed out to sea like it was never here, I attempt to staunch the wound the best I can to give a healer a chance to save him.

But there's no one around and no magic in the world that could save him.

I frame his face with my arms, running my fingers through his hair, peering into his green eyes blinking to stay open. My hair veils us from the world, shutting out a reality I refuse to face. I can't do this. I can't face the land or the sea without my mate. I can't bear to think that he's going to give his last breath to me, but I have nothing to give him. Not the sea, not the land. I failed him as my mate. I failed to protect him. But he kept his promise to protect me with his last breath.

"Ryan, please," I whisper, pressing my body into his. His hand runs down my back and over my scales before dropping to land at his side.

I kiss him, sending him every moment we shared together—every kiss, every touch, every gasp of breath. I imagine how our life together was supposed to be, me and him and the sea. I send him everything I love about him, from the way his eyes crinkle when he laughs and how blush sweeps across his face in moments of desire. I give him our life together, summed up in a kiss I refuse to let end, a kiss that should've been the one to save

Ryan as he gives his life to me. A kiss that kills me at the same time it helps me breathe.

"Luna, please," Wren says from beside me. "I can't lose you, too. Ryan wouldn't want this. You have to let him go."

I cry against Ryan's lips, my tears spilling across his face. "I'm not leaving him. Don't m-make me. This is h-how it's supposed t-to be. He's my m-mate. I'm ch-choosing th-the l-land."

"Damn it, no," he says, swearing a few curse words to the sea.

Wren grabs me by my waist, yanking me up, but I refuse to let go of Ryan. I grip him as hard as I can. I will not let this fallen pirate king pull me from Ryan. I'm never letting him go. I don't care what it means for me or the sea.

"Stop!" I yell, flicking my tail, trying to knock Wren away.

But he doesn't. He yanks me to the side of the boat and drops me back down to the deck to prepare himself to hoist me over the side. I sob, clutching onto Ryan, willing the world to stop for another moment. Wren's about to throw me over without giving me a choice.

"Luna, live," Ryan whispers.

And then I hear it.

An intake of breath.

Smashing my mouth to his, I kiss him once more, inhaling against his lips to steal his last breath. The world shifts around me, and I fall overboard, still clutching Ryan in my arms. We sink under together, the ocean filling my lungs, giving me what

I need to live as a mermaid.

"How could you!" I scream out telepathically through the water. "How could you do this to me? You can't have him!"

The water lights with the blink of my spark, turning the glowing night ocean as clear as the water in the day. I cup Ryan's face and stare into his open eyes, empty from the life I had planned to live with him.

"Don't leave me," I think to him, opening my thoughts up like he could hear me. "Please, you can't leave me."

I hug Ryan against me, combing my fingers through his hair, and I kiss him again. My lips tingle with warmth, the current shifting around me, but it's not reacting to me. I'm controlling it. I can feel every molecule, every bubble, every spark of life humming in the ocean, buzzing over me in the magic waters glittering around us. Magic flows from my chest and up my throat to my lips, and Ryan jerks in my arms, inhaling a deep breath of the sea.

I swim back, holding his hands. Confusion washes over me as I see my mermaid essence light up his lips and flow through his veins until his heart beats wildly in his chest, syncing up with my own.

A hot current crashes over us, yanking us through the sea. I clutch Ryan against me, feeling his lips brush my neck, how his fingers slide over my back and up to my hair. His green eyes shine like jewels in the sea, more like emeralds than the sea glass I love, and I lean in and kiss him again, our sparks shining so brightly, I can't see anything except Ryan and how he breathes in the water.

And then I see nothing but his spark, his beautiful, magical spark, beating exactly how I imagined. Beating solely and completely for me.

"My son. My handsome, fierce son. The ocean is lucky to have you."

My mom's voice trickles through the air, and I sit up on the sandy beach of her beautiful paradise. The bright sun reflects off the crystalline water, and puffs of white clouds leave spots of shadows across the surface.

"Am I dead?" Ryan asks, speaking the same question on my mind.

"I'm not," I whisper. "I know I'm not." Because I can feel the hum of the magic in the air, the water flowing through my very essence to beat in my heart.

"Neither are you, my son," Mom says, shifting on the sand, her long, tan legs outstretched to run her feet into the water. It's the first time I've seen her without her tail in this paradise her essence lives in. A paradise I somehow can access through the magic of the sea as it engulfs me. And now Ryan's here too, just like the last time.

"But how?" he asks, absently reaching his hand out to lace with mine.

"I took your last breath and returned it with mine," I say, bringing his fingers up to my cheek to feel the weight of his hand against me to make sure he isn't a figment of my imagination or a phantom that'll disappear at any second. But he's completely and utterly real, his soul touching mine, so alive. I feel everything coursing through him more powerful than before.

He leans into me, resting his head to my shoulder, trying to process everything that even I can't explain. All I knew was that I wasn't ever letting him go. Neither the land nor sea was taking him from me. "You used your one chance to change someone on Giselle."

"Luna carries the magic of the sea, born from me. And I'm giving her the chance I never got to use to give her the power to grow her pod in the way she needs," Mom says, reaching out to touch his knee. "The ocean knows Luna needs both an ally on land in Giselle, a young woman so worthy to be her warrior, and with you, a young man with the sea in his blood to take care of the surface. You must never doubt the power of the ocean, my son."

"I just—thank you." Ryan's words drift through the air as he thanks more than my mom and me, sending his appreciation out to the waves.

"A princess needs her pirate prince who can follow her anywhere," Mom adds, hugging her arms around the both of us. "Land and sea, taking care of both from the surface." I can't help the happiness blossoming through me at her words. Giselle as my warrior. Ryan as my prince. Both connected to me to give me the support I need to unite my magic with Ava's to grow our colonies in a way my dad never allowed.

My mom gets to her feet and peers around the glittering beach. Her long, black hair waves down her back to sweep back and forth with her movements as she heads into the sea. A small wave washes around her, swaying her on her feet, and she reaches down to cup the water. I expect her to create a dozen shimmering orbs in her hand, but the water drips through her fingers, and she turns to smile at me.

"Take care of each other and the colonies," she says, walking deeper into the surf. "The surface, too."

I blink a few times, tears welling in my eyes. "Where are you going? Please, don't leave. What do I do now? What happens next?"

Mom smiles, her whole face lighting up as bright as the sun behind her, haloing her in pale light. "That's up to you, my daughter. Listen to the call of the ocean, and it'll always guide you."

"But—"

Before I can argue, my mom dives into the crystalline water and disappears, leaving me alone with Ryan. I fling my arms around him, knocking him into the sand to shower him with a dozen kisses, making him laugh, and then he showers me with a dozen kisses more.

"I love you," he whispers.

"And I love you more than anything—the land and sea and the surface. I love you more than the magic in the water and the stars in the sky."

Sliding his arms around me, he hugs me tighter. "My beautiful, perfect, warrior princess," he whispers. "Thank you for keeping your promise about not letting me get away so easily."

"Never, ever. I mean it."

"I promise the same."

I close my eyes, breathing in the scent of the sea, tasting the salt of Ryan's skin as I kiss the crook of his neck. His heartbeat thrums as loudly as mine, in perfect sync, and I shift in the sand to peer down at him once more.

I startle, splashing my tail on the surface of the ocean with no land in sight. Ryan rests his arms across my body, treading beside me as I face the lightening sky of early dawn. A blip of grief rushes through me at the sudden disappearance of the vision the ocean had given me of my mom, but Ryan shifts, splashing me, and I turn to meet his smiling face.

"Hey," he whispers, his throat croaking the words.

Bruises still mar his face, and dark circles shadow under his eyes, but he's still as handsome as ever. Running his finger across my cheek, he brushes my wet hair away and kisses me on the lips again like it's the only thing he wants to do for the rest of our lives, and I'll gladly fulfill his need.

"You're alive." I don't know why, but I need to say the words out loud. I need the whole universe to hear them and confirm that none of this is in my head and that I saved my mate by giving him my mermaid essence, flowing with the magic my mom gave up to allow me to do so.

"And your tail is silver," he says, running his hand across my fin. "And as sparkly as a rainbow. I love it. You look like—"

"My mom," I say, peering down at my tail. My expansive caudal fin slaps the surface, and the tiny orbs of water freeze mid-air, glittering in the pale rays of dawn breaking on the horizon. I almost can't believe it. It's like part of me has shifted, and I no longer feel like I'm drowning in the sea which gives me life. "It's my magic. I found my stone. I didn't even know. I thought it was just a rock from my bedroom wall in Pearlestria."

A whistle sounds through the air, and the hum of an engine draws our attention away from each other. I tense, fear rushing over me. Ryan gulps in a deep breath at the same time I dive us both under, swimming us a dozen feet down and away from the vessel cutting across the surface. I have no idea what I left behind in the churning sea or the wreckage I'll find littering the bottom of the ocean from Wren's fleet of pirates.

The boat slows and the glittering wake dissipates as someone cuts off the engine. Ryan clings to me, digging his fingers into my shoulders in need of a breath of air. My spark might glitter in his chest, but he still needs the light of the full moon to complete his transformation. Until then, he's still partly human until he takes a breath of the sea on the most magical night of the month.

I flick my tail, swimming us far enough away from the boat to give us a chance to dive again if we need to. We're not far from where Wren forced me to abandon the Ocean's King, and I wouldn't put it past a pirate to continue to search the water.

Breaking through the surface, I expel the sea from my lungs

and give Ryan a second to gasp for another breath, preparing to dive back under.

"Luna!" a familiar voice calls. "Please, don't go. Come back to me."

The familiar voice makes me freeze in my place. I shift in the water, turning Ryan without letting him go, and catch sight of Talia standing at the bow of a tender boat. She waves her arms over her head, begging me to swim closer.

Instead of diving under, I swim on the surface, hugging Ryan to me. He breathes in my hair, and I can't stop thinking about what an amazing sound it is, one I'll never take for granted.

"She has someone," Talia says to someone on the boat. "I think it's Ryan."

Wren appears next to Talia, lacing his fingers on the back of his head. He looks worse off than the last time I saw him, his eyes red and puffy, his usual scowl twisted into a frown. Glancing once at Talia, Wren hooks his fingers to his shirt and pulls it over his head before jumping off the side of the boat to swim the rest of the way to me.

"Luna, please," he says. "I know this is hard—"

"You better not suggest she leave me again," Ryan says, nearly snapping at his dad.

Wren's grieving face morphs into surprise before a smile cuts across his cheeks, his dark eyes widening. He shocks us with a hug, sinking us both under for a moment. I shoot us back to the surface, and Talia jumps into the water next, throwing her arms around me while Wren hugs Ryan, still cursing the world but with words of thanks.

Talia pulls away from me to stare into my face. "Whoa, your eyes. Crap. What the—now we really look the same. I'm so confused. I thought for sure I was never going to get you back after—"

I cut off her words with a hug, burying my face in the crook of her neck. "I'm just so happy you're alive. Darren, is he..." I can't even think the words. "Oh, Ocean. I should've—"

She embraces me. "He's alive and okay, Luna. You don't think that a man worthy of Celestiana would go down so easily, do you? He's on the Ocean's King now. You should see him with the crew. He's got everything under control."

My brows crinkle.

"It helps that whatever happened with you has caused the ocean to react."

"What do you mean?"

"Come on, princess," Wren says from behind me. "Transform and get on the boat. It's best you see for yourself."

23

DREAM LIFE

"OH, OCEAN."

"No, kidding," Ryan says, sliding his hand around my waist. "Now this is one way to control the surface."

Dozens of boats rest on top of frozen swells, held in place by ocean magic. Not a single ship that I can see even manages to go anywhere. People yell out from their vessels, and the few pirates who've attempted to abandon ship float in their own swells with only their heads out of the water.

I've never seen anything like it. But it's better than what I had imagined. I was afraid I'd return to a surface clear of pirates with no evidence of their existence apart from the sunken ships left behind.

"Help!" a man calls out. "Please!"

I turn to look at Ryan. He meets my gaze with raised eyebrows, unsure of what to do. I draw my gaze back to the boats of all sizes with pirates still calling out for help from their captain. But Wren doesn't respond either. He stands quietly beside me with Talia on his other side.

"What would you like me to do?" I finally ask Wren, turning my gaze to the old pirate king. "This is your crew."

Ryan clears his throat. "No. Not happening. We did not go through all this to hand things back over to my dad. He doesn't deserve any of this."

I expect Wren to yell out, to backhand Ryan for talking like this, but all he does is nod his head in agreement. The old pirate king looks more tired than anything.

"He's right, kid. I made a deal with the ocean, and it kept its word," Wren says. "I ain't messing with this shit. It ain't worth it to me anymore."

"You're giving up your crew?"

He shakes his head. "Not giving it up. Giving it to you and Ryan. You want to better the sea, these people will work hard to do so. They all want what you do. A good life on the place they love. Hell, maybe you'll show a man some mercy and let me stay. I'll be—"

"A great member of my pod," I say. "But things are really going to be different. Understand? We're following the mermaid way. If you can't accept that—"

"I got it. To hell with island living, give me a boat on the water any day, especially with my fam—pod? Hell, that shit's too weird for me to say."

I release a small laugh and hug him. Ryan sandwiches me between them, kissing my hair, and then finally pulls me away to spin me in his arms to meet me with a kiss to my lips. My heart races, matching his, and he hooks me around the waist, diving us both into the water. I transform into a mermaid, still surprised about the new color of my tail, sparkling like a diamond in the morning sunlight.

I swim a few quick circles around Ryan, spinning him in my current, and then I dive under him to come up in front of him, motioning for him to hold onto my back. I flick us to the surface and take a breath of the sea air.

Raising my arms up, I slowly lower the tide like all the times I've seen Ava do so, setting all the ships on a calm surface. The crew helps those floating in the water back onto the boats, and I swim around to make sure everyone is safe.

Darren sits on a bench on the stern of the Ocean's King, his shoulder stitched up and covered with a bandage. Ryan helps me onto the swimming platform, and we wait for Wren and Talia to navigate the tender boat into the side garage.

For the first time ever, I enter the cockpit of the yacht, and Wren motions for me to take a seat behind the wheel. He messes with a radio, sending static through the air, and then he hands it over to me.

"This is Princess Luna speaking, do you all copy?" I ask,

trying to remember the few times I've heard people talk over the radio.

"Hurricane copies," a woman says, the voice cutting through the air.

"Sea Monster copies," a masculine voice adds.

Dozens of voices come through the radio, all confirming that they've heard my call, the same call I hear resonating through the ocean as it listens to me, humming with the ocean magic that completes me as much as Ryan does.

I clear my throat and press the radio button again. "Listen up, crew. I am your new captain speaking, and there's a mandatory meeting taking place at first light tomorrow. There are new laws of the sea now in effect. If you do not agree to my terms, I will provide permanent residency on the land. Now, I'm handing you over to—" I glance at Wren, not sure of what to call him.

"There's a position for chief mate open," he says to me.

I crinkle my nose at the thought, about Titus and how unworthy of the sea he became. I wanted so badly to see to it that he could at least have a life on land for Nalani's sake, but the ocean wouldn't even grant him that—not that I can blame it.

I click the button again. "I'm handing you over to Chief Mate Reyes. He'll lead you all where you'll be going."

Leaving Wren speaking into the radio, I guide Ryan with me back onto the main deck to peer at the ocean once more. For the first time in weeks, it no longer feels as if I'm being split between the land and sea. I've finally come together as myself, no longer daughter of a shunned king or a lost queen. I'm just a daughter of the magnificent sea.

"Want to swim?" Ryan asks, leaning on the railing to peer into the water. "Or should we take a boat?"

"I must swim. Are you sure you can handle the trip?" I ask, meeting my mate's sparkling eyes. "I can go alone and meet you at Celestiana Cove."

He hugs me, laughing. "Oh, I can handle the trip. I can handle anything with you."

"I promise to keep you safe," I whisper.

"And feed me?" he asks, chuckling.

"Mermaid style."

Moaning into my neck, he brushes his lips across my skin, working his way back to my lips. I hop up into his arms, wrapping my legs around him, and we plunge from the swim platform and into the sea.

I sink us under and transform into a mermaid, not even getting to take a breath before Ryan kisses me again.

"Ready?" I ask, cupping his face.

He nods. "Always. You, me, swimming. Adventure. This is my dream life, Luna. I'm the luckiest guy on land."

"Soon to be the luckiest merman."

He nuzzles his nose to mine. "God, I can't wait for the full moon. You are really my perfect mate."

"I'm so sorry I couldn't be here for you sooner. Your magic did a number on the currents, and even the best trackers in

Pearlestria couldn't find you. It drove me crazy." Ava hugs me to her. "But it's also so incredibly amazing. I always knew the sea would see to it you got the life of your dreams."

I blink the happy tears from my eyes that seem to never end. So many emotions wash through me, coming from my spark, from Ryan, from Giselle, too. "Even after I gave my mermaid essence to Giselle?"

She nods. "Because you gave your mermaid essence to her. You put everyone before yourself even though you knew the outcome. If the ocean didn't come through for you, I'd have—" Snapping her mouth shut, Ava swallows and hugs me for the millionth time. "I just knew it would. I could never do any of this without you. You're important to me and the ocean."

"To all the colonies," Carter adds, hugging me next.

Ryan slides his arms around me from behind. "And now to the surface."

"You forgot the universe!" Giselle kicks through the surf toward us with Sun jogging to keep up. "My soul sister is awesome. And you have no idea how glad I am that you managed to score yourself a little of her essence for your damn tail, Ryan," she says, looking at my mate. "Because I was freaking out about how this was all going to work. I do not need a mer-mom. I'm an—"

"Independent mermaid princess, who'll surely create her own waves come the light of the full moon." Sun smiles as he says it and lifts her off her feet, plopping her on his shoulder, spinning her to get her to stop talking.

Neither of us wants to think about a future that won't happen. There's no point. Our currents shifted to take us where we need to go, and it's not separating anyone any time soon. I'll never have to be apart from Ryan. He'll join me in the sea on the full moon with Giselle. I'll be there for the both of them through their transformations. And Sun will do the same. He's already stepped up to teach Ryan the merman ways in full force, even more so than when he discovered we were courting. But I already know Ryan will be the perfect merman mate to me. And I'll be his pirate princess.

I giggle to myself at the thought.

"We've lost her, Aves," Giselle says, her face turning red from being upside down on Sun's shoulder. "Her love is—"

"Grossly romantic?" I ask, cutting her off.

Giselle shakes her head. "Indescribable. I freaking love you even as I feel you drifting to sea."

"It's a good thing we're all already there," Ava responds.

I smile. "I'm just—"

I release a small breath of air through my lips, staring into the distance at the pirate fleet now here to protect the surface the right way. My mom's desire to see to it that the ocean and land be united will finally stick without having to worry about the dangerous surface.

Her sacrifice gave me not only the sea and the land, but it also gave me everything I could have ever asked for—the love of my life, a pod that'll have my back through all of life's currents, and the magic I never knew possible. The magic that now sings to my soul in every curling wave, in every bubble glittering on the surface, in every merperson in the ocean.

"I'm just so happy," I manage to say, my voice a whisper.

"The happiest mermaid in all the sea," Ryan whispers. "I can feel it. It's incredible. You're incredible."

"The best," Giselle adds.

I trail my foot over the magical water, feeling closer to my mom and the sea more than ever. An engine hums in the distance, and Wren, Talia, and Darren glide the inflatable motorboat onto the shore of Celestiana Cove.

"The ship's all set to sail, Captain," Wren says, wagging his brows at me. "Whenever you're ready."

I see a head pop up from the water, and Nalani and her mate, Sandy, emerge from the calm bay to kick through the water. She touches Wren's shoulder in passing, and he offers her a smile I thought I'd never see happen between the two of them. She crosses the beach to us and throws her arms around me and Ryan at once.

"Princess Luna, we'd like permission to join you aboard the Ocean's King," she says, easing back to look into my eyes.

I turn my gaze to Ryan, who looks at his dad. They both shrug at each other, and I slowly nod my head. "Of course. I'd love that."

She embraces me again and pulls Ryan from me, and I give her a moment with her son. Kicking through the sand, I close the distance to Darren and Talia, letting them hug me together. I still can't believe how every droplet of my life finally pools together for me. I never thought much of a future outside of a simple life in the sea with my perfect mate, but now I see the vast possibilities stretching out as far and wide as the horizon before me. And I can't wait to see where the current takes me—somewhere amazing, magical, an adventure I can't wait to be on with those I love.

"I know this is your home, Darren, but I was hoping you'd join us on the sea, at least for a bit," I say. "We still have a bunch of treasure to find from my mom along the way."

Talia slides her arm over my shoulders. "You should join us, Uncle Darren. Sandra said she'd be just fine with the merpeople here and that you could use a vacation from the cove."

"I wouldn't have it any other way," he muses.

"And speaking of treasure." Sliding a bag from her arm, she hands it to me. "I found these last night in the bag."

"In the mermaid house?" I ask, knowing it's true. I was so disappointed, thinking my magic was lost, that I didn't do more than let things scatter.

She nods. "I thought you might want these two things." Digging into her bag, she pulls out a small pouch, opening it up. Darren peers at the contents with me, and reaches in to scoop out something before I can see it.

"What was—" I close my mouth, noticing a key. "What do you think this unlocks?"

She grins. "A house. There was a deed in the paperwork Wren had. I'm pretty sure it's for our home on land."

"But what did Darren take?" I ask.

Talia's eyes light up with a huge smile, and she motions for me to turn around. I bring my hand to my chest, my spark flickering through my fingers, catching sight of Ryan kneeling in the sand, holding out a ring with the prettiest aquamarine stone in the shape of a heart surrounded by diamonds.

"What are you doing? You've already asked me to marry you," I say, closing the distance between us.

"Just making it official with a gift from Darren," he says, grinning. "It was the ring he gave your mom when he promised her forever. And now I promise that to you. Forever. You, me, and the world. Always."

I extend my hand out, and he slides the ring above my sea stone on my finger. Dropping to my knees, I join him in the sand and kiss him so desperately that we fall over together with me on top of him.

A few whistles sound through the air, making me laugh, and I break away from Ryan to smile at our pod, bigger and better than I could have ever hoped for. Wren helps Darren pull the boat back into the waves, and Talia joins them.

"All right, Captain," Wren says. "All we have to do is pick up Dara—"

"Actually, Wren," I say, turning to my chief mate and soon-to-be dad. "Dara plans to stay here with my dad."

He frowns.

Ryan laughs. "Apparently Grandma appreciates a man who can fish with his bare hands and shares his food."

Wren shakes his head, barking a laugh. "I guess we'll set sail without her. Midday sound good?"

I nod. "Soun—"

Ryan pulls me from the sand and dusts me off. "Actually, we'll catch up with you all."

"We will?" I ask.

He leans in and whispers, "You promised me an island getaway and a hot shower."

Warmth blossoms across my chest, and I turn my attention to Wren. "Yeah, we'll catch up in a few days. Don't worry. We'll find you."

After what feels like a billion hugs, Ryan and I watch the others disappear into the sea, some by boat and some by current. I wave from the sand, snuggling against Ryan, and we remain on the beach to watch the sunset on the water.

"So, are you sure you're going to want to leave?" Ryan asks, kissing my neck. "Just letting you know. I can stay here with you forever."

I nod. "At least for a few days."

"And maybe a few more."

"Then what?" I ask, sinking into him.

"I guess we'll have to see where the ocean takes us."

I rest my head on him. "Somewhere magical."

"Everywhere magical." He laces his fingers through mine and smiles. "Now come on. Our adventure awaits."

EPILOGUE

FOREVER

"RYAN, IN FRONT OF the witnesses of the colonies and under the glow of the full moon, I hereby promise to share the very essence of my being with you, the merman who completes me." I smile at Ryan, treading in the open water outside of Celestiana Cove. He leans in to kiss me before I can finish my words, making me laugh. I pull away slightly and continue. "I vow always to protect you. To love you and treat you as the brave, handsome, incredible merman I'm so thankful to share my life's essence with. I promise to calm the waters when the tides are rough. I promise to teach you to swim in even the most unrelenting waves. I vow always to make our life together an adventure and to greet you every sunrise with a kiss and to love you as deeply as the ocean's trenches because my love for you far exceeds the ocean and land. It's greater than anything in this life, and I vow my soul to you forever."

Cheers echo through the air, making me smile so much

that my cheeks will surely never recover. All of the merpeople in the colonies have arrived to watch the coupling of me and Ryan along with all of my human ties to the land. The sea even allowed my dad to bear witness with the new companion he found in Dara from a small boat on the water.

Being here with Ryan, under the light of the full moon, seeing his skin shimmer with a pearlescent glow is better than I could have ever imagined our union as mates to be.

Ryan waves his hand, getting the voices to settle, and then he tucks strands of my midnight hair behind my ear. "Luna, in front of the witnesses of our crew and under the glow of the full moon, I hereby promise to share the very essence of my being with you, the mermaid who completes me. I vow always to protect you. To love you and treat you like the beautiful, powerful, kind, and most amazing mermaid in all the seas. I promise to stand beside you and lift you on rising tides and to catch you as they fall. I swear always to make sure you're safe in any current, in any situation, and every moment of every day by teaching you all that I know."

Ryan's love pours over me in indescribable waves that leave me as breathless as the call of the sea. He kisses me again, unable to control himself. Our sparks blink in perfect rhythm, reflecting off the orbs of water hovering in the air like stars come to earth.

Inhaling another breath, he says, "I vow my life and love to you to assure the world grows into a better place. I vow with my first breath as a merman that my love will remain unconditional, unending, and as madly and deeply and as perfect as the love you share with me. Forever. My heart and soul and being is yours. Always."

With a kiss, I sink underwater with Ryan, embracing the call of the sea as it transforms me into a mermaid. Ryan holds my gaze in the water, his skin shimmering, his emerald eyes shining with the promise of our forever and always.

I open my mind to his, flooding him with every moment of our lives together on land and a dozen more of how I imagine our future in the sea. Ryan gasps, sucking in a breath of the ocean, and I hold his hands to keep us together as onyx scales sprout from his legs, glittering with flecks of emerald green like his eyes. He arches his back through muscle spasms, and the moment his transformation completes, I close the space between us, not allowing any water to separate us.

Kissing him, I show him how I see him as a merman in my eyes—fierce and protective with a smile that lights his face like the spark in his chest, both just for me. The ocean erupts in cheers, and I spin around with Ryan to greet the colonies before jetting to the surface to breach with my mate for all those on the boats to see.

A high-pitched squeal erupts in my mind, and I spot Ava pulling Giselle along through the water with their mates behind them.

"Congrats!" Ava and Giselle say in unison.

I suck in a breath of the ocean. "Gi! Your tail!"

She claps her hands. "Isn't it amazing? I just knew it would be this color."

Sun swims up behind her, running his fingers along the curves of her deep red tail. "And as beautiful as a ruby sky at sunset."

She giggles, burying her face against Sun's chest. "If only I didn't swim like a drunk fish."

"You'll get it in no time," I say, circling around her. "But not like you'll need it with that handsome merman dying for your official coupling."

She points her finger at me. "Don't even start. This is your day and the start of your happily ever after. All we're missing is that damn rainbow."

Ava whirls her hand, gathering bubbles in the sea to capture the moonlight just right to reflect rainbow beams off my silver tail. Giselle tips her head back and somersaults in the water with Sun following her down.

Warm arms wrap around me from behind to hug me. "My beautiful daughter and handsome son. I've dreamed of this moment forever. Your union makes me exceptionally happy."

Ryan hugs me with his mom before another couple spins us away to congratulate us. By the time all the colonies greet us, I'm antsy to swim, and I take Ryan's hand and lead the way. The moonlight shines above us, glittering a trail on the surface that I follow through the vast ocean.

Ryan swims faster than me, pulling me along with him toward the surface. We break through and peer up at the full moon hanging in the sky. Leaning in, he kisses me once more, and we listen to the sound of our hearts beating loud against the silence of the sea.

"Can you hear it?" Ryan asks, pulling away from me.

I tilt my head to the side. "Hear what?"

"The call of the ocean. It's sending me a message."

"And what is it saying?"

"Apparently something about helping the seas flourish with you."

I laugh, splashing water between us. "Don't tease me."

Ryan brushes his tail to mine, his laughter fading, and his expression turning serious. "I'm not teasing you. I love you. Always. I'm a better person because of you, and I know we'll make the world better together."

"Land and sea."

He nods. "And everything in between."

~The End~

Thank you so much for reading the *Call of the Ocean* series! If you have a spare moment, I'd appreciate it from the bottom of my inner mermaid spark if you could please leave an honest review.

Also, to stay up-to-date on future Luna and Ryan releases (Yes, there will be more!) along with other Ginna Moran books, sign up for her newsletter or join her Facebook group today. You'll also get exclusive access to special content on her website.

OTHER YOUNG ADULT SERIES BY GINNA MORAN

PARANORMAL
Destined for Dreams Series
Demon Within Series
Finding Nate Series
Going Ghostly Series
Spark of Life Series
When Souls Collide Series
Demon Watcher Series
Call of the Ocean Series

REVERSE HAREM
The Divine Vampire Heirs

CONTEMPORARY
Falling into Fame Series
Life After Lila

ACKNOWLEDGMENTS

THIS SERIES WOULDN'T HAVE come to fruition if it wasn't for my amazing team—Sarah and Katie—because they both asked for me to continue diving into my magical world of *Mermaid Mates* with Luna's story. Because of their enthusiasm and encouragement, I have a plethora of ideas to share with the world. So thanks to you both! You all rock my water, raise my swells, and curl my waves. XOXO!

ABOUT GINNA MORAN

GINNA MORAN IS a writer from sunny Southern California. She started writing poetry as a teenager in a spiral notebook that she still has tucked away on her desk today. Her love of writing grew after she graduated high school, and she completed her first unpublished manuscript at age eighteen.

When she realized her love of writing was her life's passion, she studied literature at Mira Costa College in Northern San Diego. Besides writing novels, she was senior editor, content manager, and image coordinator for Crescent House Publishing Inc. for four years.

Aside from Ginna's professional life, she enjoys binge watching television shows, playing pretend with her daughter, and cuddling with her dogs. Some of her favorite things include chocolate, anything that glitters, cheesy jokes, and organizing her bookshelf.

Ginna Moran loves to hear from her readers so visit her online at www.GinnaMoran.com. You can also find her on Facebook, Twitter, Instagram, and Snapchat. To stay up-to-date on new releases, sign up to her newsletter. You'll not only get exclusive access to extra stories, but you'll be able to participate in monthly giveaways!

Ginna Moran is currently hard at work on her next novel.

www.ingramcontent.com/pod-product-compliance
Lightning Source LLC
Chambersburg PA
CBHW051645180726
48284CB00006B/1872